THE RANCHER AND THE HELLION

"You need a good spanking," he told her.

"You wouldn't dare." She faced him, hands on hips, head tilted up, a challenge in her green eyes.

He stepped quickly to one side, grasped her about the waist and pulled her down across his upraised knees. He raised his hand, but before he could bring it down, she twisted free. Caught unaware, Jason tumbled backward and Tamar sprang at him, her fingernails clawing. He grasped her wrists, wrestling her away. Then Tamar reached forward, kissing him, holding him. He could hear her rapid breathing as she drew back, scrambled to her feet and began brushing herself off. Still lying on his side, Jason rested his head on one hand and watched her.

"Well," she asked. "Are you just going to lie there for the rest of the day?"

The Making of America Series

THE TEXANS

Lee Davis Willoughby

A DELL/BRYANS BOOK

Published by
Dell Publishing Co., Inc.
1 Dag Hammarskjold Plaza
New York, New York 10017

Dell ® TM 681510, Dell Publishing Co., Inc.

ISBN: 0-440-08665-5

Printed in the United States of America

First printing—October 1980

1

JASON BRISCOE slowly circled his two-thousand head of beeves. The night was dark except for distant heat lightning flickering along the horizon, momentarily lighting the men, the longhorns, and on all sides of the herd, the empty stretches of the Kansas prairie.

The riders talked or sang to the cows to soothe them. They'd had a good drive north from Texas; after fifty days on the trail they were now only two days out of Abilene. The cattle had fed well on the spring grass, fattening as they trailed north. Jason smiled to himself—men passing them, heading south on the Chisholm Trail, told of high beef prices in the Abilene yards, up to twenty-five dollars for prime stock. Twenty-five times two thousand equaled fifty thousand American dollars.

Jason crooned to the cows. Despite the lightning they were quiet; this had been a good, tractable herd. Luck had followed the drovers north starting at the Red River where they'd found the water low and had been able to ford without losing a head. They'd crossed the Washita, the Canadian, and the Cimarron, traversed the Indian Territory where the government had herded the Cherokees, Creeks, Seminoles, Choctaws, and Chickasaws, having to pay only an occasional cow to the Indians as toll. All along the Chisholm they'd found good grass and good weather.

Jason always looked forward to trailing, the long hard days followed by the quiet nights under the brilliant stars, the adventuring into the unknown of a new and virgin country.

All at once he tensed. He looked around him, listening. Everything seemed as before, quiet, the darkness broken by an occasional flicker of lightning. A tremor ran through his horse and in an electric instant the herd was on its feet. With an unearthly roar the ground shook beneath the beat of thousands of hooves.

Stampede!

Jason's horse whirled and charged into the night alongside the herd in a wild race to God-knew-where. The cattle uttered no sound at all; as they ran heat welled up from their bodies and beat against Jason's face.

He spurred his horse, trying to overtake the lead steers, unable to see in the dark, all the while forcing visions of prairie dog holes and gullies from his mind, depending on his night horse, trusting him with his life, hoping not to trade this hell on earth for the other. He reached the front of the herd and, with the stampeding cattle a thundering mass beside him, bore to the right.

The lead steers refused to turn. Jason raced on, still bearing right and this time the steers gave way. They turned, maybe only a hair, but they turned. Behind him, Jason knew, the other trail riders were also working the cattle to the right. He reined his horse more and more in that direction and now the cows began arcing that way. Jason heard a shout behind him, "Whooo-eee," the cry of one of the other riders and he sensed that the arc of racing cattle had tightened and their pace had slowed. Ahead he heard the rumble of the drags and knew they had closed the circle, the lead steers coming up on the tail of the herd.

After a few minutes the cattle went into a mill, thundering around and around, still running, the horses forcing them in from all sides, tightening the mill until the cattle slowed and stopped.

The stampede was over.

Three days later, his cattle sold—not for fifty thousand but enough to make the long drive worth while—his men paid off, Jason walked down the dusty main street of Abilene. He'd been to the barber and now he ambled into the Alamo Saloon, lifted a glass or two to wash the trail dust out of his throat, watched the gambling, eyed the girls with their fancy dresses and the lone stars emblazoned on their boots, left and walked down to the Brave Bull, feeling good, heady from the liquor, had another shot or two, more than he'd intended, left, admiring the painting of the black bull on the wood side of the saloon, its genitals half-hidden by splashes of whitewash brushed on by do-gooders, pushed his way into the Longbranch where he had another drink and stood at the bar surveying the smoke-filled room, the glittering chandeliers, the mirrors, the inviting array of decanters, the carved wood, and the painting of Cleopatra's court.

He was entitled to a few drinks and a flutter at cards. He'd gathered the herd, his herd, trail-branded them, led his crew north, turned the stampede without losing more than ten head and without the cows running off more than a few pounds of flesh, and he'd gotten top dollar for the beef, settled his accounts and was sitting with enough money to go back to Texas, buy more longhorns, buy more land and drive north again next year. By God, he'd have the biggest damn herd in the State before he was through.

But, first things first. He had enough money now to head East and find himself a wife. By the time he was twenty-six a man should have a wife. Even a man used to the frontier got lonely, needed a woman. He grimaced at the whores in black lace plying their trade at the gambling tables. He'd never paid for a woman in his life and he never would.

No harm, though, in risking a few dollars at the poker table. He left the bar, his head a-spin, the lights brighter than they'd seemed before. As if by magic, an empty chair appeared beside him and Jason found himself sitting in on a game of shotgun. He won a few hands and then luck turned her back and Jason saw his pile of chips dwindle like a snowball in hell.

He bought in again and once more won a few hands only to see luck turn and his pile melt. Alert now, he watched the man opposite him, the big winner, a fancy-dressed gambler smoking a cheroot, a man the others called Morgan.

After Morgan shuffled and took the cut cards in his hand, Jason heard the tell-tale click of a second card being dealt. He glanced from the stack of Morgan's chips to those in front of the other men around the table. As far as he could tell they were all about even while he, Jason, was the big loser. Again he heard the tick of a second-card deal. None of the others seemed to notice anything unusual. Jason folded and Morgan laid down three aces, raking in the pot.

Jason pushed his chair back from the table and stood up with his hands loose at his sides.

"You're dealing from the bottom," he said.

Morgan rose slowly to his feet, stubbing his cheroot in a tray on the table and smiling across at Jason. "Are you calling me a cheat?" he asked.

"I am."

Morgan nodded and Jason felt his arms pinned by the men who had been playing on either side of him. The cowhands at the bar scrambled for cover while the others at the table grabbed their chips and backed away, watching warily. Morgan reached inside his red vest and brought out a derringer. Nonchalantly he pointed the small gun at Jason's groin.

"Perhaps I heard you wrong," he said. "I've known big losers to misspeak themselves before. I'll ask you one more time. Are you calling me a cheat?"

Jason's head had become remarkably clear. He saw the derringer aimed at his groin, heard the hush of expectancy settle on the room, smelled the heavy odor of smoke, whiskey and sweat, felt the two pairs of hands gripping his arms. He knew he couldn't free himself in time to draw before Morgan fired. Reason told him to back off, to live and fight another day.

He drew in his breath, smiling. "Morgan," he said, "you're a goddamn cheat."

Jason saw the gambler stiffen in surprise, his dark eyes glittering in the lamplight. Morgan's finger tightened on the trigger of the derringer.

"Morgan!" The warning came from somewhere

behind Jason and the gambler looked past him toward the saloon's entrance. Jason resisted the impulse to turn his head.

"He threw cheat in my face," Morgan said.

"Holster your toy," the man behind Jason ordered. Morgan shrugged and slipped the derringer inside his vest.

"I deal a clean game," the gambler said, holding out his hands, palms up.

"Be that as it may, we need Briscoe alive and well, not six feet under. He's coming with us."

Jason felt the grip on his arms relax. He shrugged off the hands holding him, turned and saw two Union soldiers, their Colts drawn, standing behind him. He'd never thought he'd be glad to see a brace of bluebellies but he downright welcomed these two.

One of the soldiers gestured with his head from Jason to the door. Jason cashed in his chips and dropped the silver in his pocket before he preceded them from the saloon onto the dusty Abilene street. Once they were outside, the soldiers holstered their guns and marched, one on each side of him, the hundred feet to the Plainsman Hotel.

"What the hell's going on?" Jason asked. "Not that I don't appreciate the favor, even from Yankees."

"Captain Carleton wants you," the man on his right said. "When you hear what he's got on his mind you might wish you'd never seen us."

2

CAPTAIN CARLETON tilted back his chair. He was a short stocky man with the edges of his full grey moustache stained yellow by tobacco juice.

"You're a bigger man than I expected," he said to Jason. "And younger. You *are* the Briscoe who scouted for the Rangers during the war, aren't you?"

"Under Colonel Obenchain."

"Obenchain? Killed by one of his own men, wasn't he?"

"Some say so. It was never proved."

"A pompous ass, Obenchain, or so I'm given to believe. Something of a fool." He studied Jason, his gaze going from the rancher's black hair to his rugged clean-shaven face down to his scuffed boots. "You don't look it," the Captain said, "but you're something of a fool yourself."

Jason stiffened and then deliberately relaxed, half-smiling. "Every so often a man's entitled to make a fool of himself," he said.

"Not in my business. A soldier's too apt to wind up with an arrow through his gut. Which brings me to why I'm here, Briscoe. General Custer has the idea you're the scout he needs to ride with a raiding party against the Comanches. I hope you're a better scout than you are a gambler."

"The last I heard of Custer," Jason said, "he'd been cashiered out of the Army. Court-martialed for leaving his men while he went traipsing off to visit his wife."

"General Custer's back in uniform. Phil Sheridan needed him and when Sheridan needs a man he gets him. And when General Custer needs a man, like he thinks he needs you, *he* gets him."

"This is mighty late in the summer to think about a campaign against the Comanches."

"Maybe yes, maybe no. I'll tell you the details once we're on the train to Fort Hays."

Jason shook his head. "Do you really expect a man who just sold two thousand head of cattle to go hunting Indians for forty dollars a month?"

"I heard about your forty thousand dollars. Or was it forty-five? I'll see the money gets into the Farmers and Merchants Bank in Kansas City in your name."

"I need to get back to Texas to my ranch."

"If we don't stop the Comanches, you'll have no ranch and no cows either and you know it."

"I don't rightly cotton to working for a man who thinks I'm a fool."

"Not even to prove him wrong?" Carleton squirted tobacco juice into a spittoon beside his desk. "Next time," he said, "remind me not to bother to save your life."

"You've got all the answers, don't you, Captain? I sure enough owe you a favor and I *was*

getting a mite tired of this city life." Jason sighed.
"When does your god-damned train leave?"

"The engine's sitting at the depot with her
steam up. She leaves just as soon as we get there.
And you were wrong about the pay. It's thirty-
five dollars."

Jason sat on the curved wooden seat cursing
himself as the coach rattled and swayed westward
across the prairie on the arrow-straight Kansas
Pacific. He eyed Carleton narrowly—the captain
probably thought him even more of a fool for
letting himself be goaded into this.

"So Custer's planning a fall campaign in Comanche country," Jason said.

"Wrong. He's planning a winter campaign
against the Cheyenne and Arapaho to the west
of the reservation."

"Then he's plumb lost his mind. There's never
been a winter campaign on the plains. I always
thought your man Custer was foolhardy; now I'm
sure of it."

"Know something? That's what Jim Bridger
said, almost word for word. The idea's not all
Custer's, though he's for it a hundred percent.
It's his and Sheridan's. General Custer'll tell you
their scheme when you see him tonight."

"A winter campaign? All he'll do is freeze his
privates off."

Jason was still shaking his head when he entered the General's office in the Fort Hays stock-
ade. There was a large American flag on a pole
behind Custer and a map of the Great Plains on
the wall; otherwise the room was bare.

Custer, his quill pen racing across a paper on
his desk, ignored Jason. The general was dressed
like no other officer Jason had ever seen—he wore

a sailor's wide-collared shirt, a red cravat, and a jacket with an intricate design of interlacing gold braid on the sleeves. His golden hair was long and lay in ringlets on his shoulders.

At last he lay down his pen, shook sand on the ink and folded the letter. Custer's piercing blue eyes looked Jason up and down.

"You're a big son of a bitch," he said, "but can you scout? Do you have the nerve, sir, to face the Comanches?"

"With them curls," Jason said, "you're a right pretty bastard. But can you fight?"

Custer stared at him, reddened, then threw back his head and laughed. He came around the desk and clapped Jason on the shoulder.

"They were right about you," he said. "You do have the nerve. I'll have to tell my wife what you said." He nodded at the letter on his desk. "She'll enjoy it. And yes, sir, I can fight, as you Rebs found out not too long ago. And I have something more going for me. Luck. Custer's luck, my men call it, and it's never failed me yet." He frowned. "Hardly ever," he amended, walking back to the chair behind his desk.

"Sit down, Briscoe," he told Jason. Jason pulled up a chair and sat facing the General. "Smoke?" Custer asked, offering a cigar. Jason shook his head.

"Here's Sheridan's plan," Custer went on. "As you know, the Indians go into permanent camp in the winter. It's a time when they can't ride far and can't hit and run, not without feed for their ponies. We aim to destroy their villages, beat the warriors into the ground, starve the hold-outs into submission. Just like Sheridan did in '64 when he turned the Shenandoah into a burned-out desert."

"I heard what Grant said about the Shenandoah." Jason's tone was bitter. "That any crows flying over the Valley would have to carry their own food with them."

"Exactly. In this Indian campaign Sheridan'll send out three main columns, one from Fort Bascom, one from Fort Lyon, and one operating from Indian Territory. You, Briscoe, you'll head even farther south." He swung around and pointed at the map behind him. "Here, on the flank of the Bascom column. You'll scout for Captain Carleton. His assignment is to worry the Comanche, keep them off our rear. You'll be one of three scouts."

"Yes, sir," Jason said.

"Now pay me close heed. We have our orders from General Sheridan—any warriors not killed in battle are to be hanged, all women and children are to be taken prisoner, all Indian ponies are to be killed, and all villages are to be destroyed. Any questions, Briscoe?"

"No, sir."

Custer nodded, picked up his quill, dipped the point in an inkwell and began to write. Jason pivoted and left the room. Once outside he shook his head. Damn Custer, he thought, damn the man. He'd had him acting like a soldier. "Yes, sir," and "No, sir." A few more minutes and he'd have been ready to sign up.

Three months later, on the Staked Plain of North Texas, Jason woke in the milky-white light of early dawn.

"Carleton," he hissed.

The captain, sleeping on the open ground six feet away, stirred.

"Carlton," Jason said again.

The captain sat bolt upright.

"Move careful," Jason told him. "I got a favor to ask. This bugger next to me has me concerned."

Carleton stared at the rattler coiled next to Jason's face. He removed his Walker Colt .44 from his bedding, aimed and fired. The rattler's head, partially severed, flopped to one side and the snake thrashed about in its death throes.

"That's two I owe you," Jason said, rolling away from the dying rattlesnake.

"My God, man, how could you be so calm?"

"Easy. I was scared stiff as a board."

After that, Carleton thawed, and when Jason and the captain were riding a short way ahead of the troop, Jason asked him about Custer. The captain spat and shrugged.

"Some say he's a hero," Carleton said, "and some say he's a madman. I can tell you he's brave; I've never seen a braver man. In a cavalry charge, I'd follow him to hell and back. In a campaign against well-armed, well-led Indians where a tactician's needed . . ." He paused. "That'd be another story."

Carleton wheeled his horse and returned to his men. Jason and the other two scouts were leading the way, behind them came Carleton's sixty troopers, and behind the troopers were the pack-mules. December had brought bitter cold to the Plain and the horsemen rode wrapped in blankets and buffalo robes by day and shivered around frugal buffalo chip fires by night. The chips were plentiful. They sighted herd after herd of buffalo; thousands upon thousands of the animals were wintering on the southern plains.

On the evening of the fifteenth, Jason cut the sign of Indians for the first time.

"Comanches," he told Carleton. "A raiding party more than likely."

"We'll camp yonder," Carleton said, "on the north bank of the Prairie Dog Fork and set out after them at dawn."

The next morning they followed the Indian track for ten miles before Jason, scouting well in front of the troop, dismounted and knelt. His eyes hadn't deceived him, he *had* seen a book on the ground.

He picked up the book, a Bible, and examined it. The lids had been snapped closed and the pages were undamaged despite the rains of the last two weeks. Opening the Bible, he saw the name "Caroline Ross" written inside the cover.

"The Comanches took it along to pack their shields, more than like," Carleton said, riding up beside Jason.

Jason nodded as he remounted. "Reminds me of the time I read the history of Rome," he said. "We were . . ." All at once he noticed some trees in the low hills south of the river. "Chittam trees," he told Carleton. "Indians fancy the berries. I'll ride over and see what I can find."

Ten minutes later he rejoined the captain.

"They've been and gone. Can't be more than thirty minutes ahead of us, no more than just out of sight over the hills. Their trail leads west."

Carleton signaled the troop forward and they rode west at a trot.

"The Fork's gyppy along here," Jason told him, "too salty to drink. Just ahead maybe two or three miles a creek comes in from the south, a fresh-water creek. If I know Comanches, they'll be camped there."

He left the column and rode to the south into the hills, keeping Carleton's command in sight. From the top of a rise he saw brush marking the path of the winding creek and he spied the tell-tale wisp of smoke coming from another grove of chittams.

Signaling Carleton with his hat, Jason waited until the Captain and his troop joined him before he led them on up the river, galloping the mile and a fraction to where the creek entered the Prairie Dog Fork. A short distance from the river a row of barren hills intersected the course of the creek. As the troop topped the first of the hills they saw the Indians not more than a hundred yards away. The Comanches had packed their belongings on their ponies and were ready to move out.

Carleton, after sending a sergeant and ten men to the right to cut the Comanches off from the hills, signaled a charge. The Indians, seeing the troopers so close, panicked and instead of heading for the cover of the hills, they crossed the creek where it made a series of short twists and struck straight west for the foothills of the mountains, the braves on ponies, the squaws on foot leading the pack horses.

The troopers galloped past the squaws, shooting the warriors as they overtook them. The Indian horsemen scattered. One, a feathered chief, shot an arrow at Jason and the shaft embedded itself in the horse's flank. The animal reared, Jason holding the mane to keep from being thrown. When the horse fell to the ground, Jason leaped free.

He swung around to see Carleton on the ground with the Comanche chief, knife in hand, grappling with him. Jason fired and the Comanche spun away to one side. Carleton scrambled to his feet and ran to the Indian as the chief was trying to rise to his knees, and put a bullet in his head.

Hearing a scream behind him, Jason whirled to

see the squaws yanking at the rope bridles as they
tried to lead their horses up the bank from the
creek but the animals were so heavily loaded with
buffalo meat, tent poles and hides they were unable to run. The sergeant and his men, when they
realized the Indians were heading along the creek
and not into the hills, had circled back and now
began riding to and fro among the squaws, firing
down at them.

One of the Indian women raised a bow, shooting an arrow and then another and another. A
trooper lurched from his horse, an arrow shaft
protruding from his side. The sergeant rode at
the squaw, veering his horse at the last minute.
He fired and the woman crumpled, blood oozing
from her forehead.

Jason ran back across the creek to where the
squaws were abandoning their pack ponies and
running toward the hills.

"Stop," he shouted at the soldiers.

They ignored him, still firing. Just ahead of
Jason one of the squaws raised her bow, shot, and
the arrow hummed past his cheek. Jason struck the
bow from her hand and the squaw fell backward
onto the ground. A trooper rode down on her,
pistol aimed, but Jason flung himself on top of
the squaw and the trooper galloped by without
firing.

The shooting died down, then stopped altogether. Jason stood up, looking around him.
Indian ponies writhed on the ground and a trooper
began walking among them, killing them. The
bodies of the braves were scattered where they had
fallen in the creek and along the banks; the bodies
of the squaws lay clustered nearer the camp.

Jason pulled the squaw to her feet. She stood
staring sullenly at the ground as Captain Carleton

rode up on a dead trooper's horse. He glanced at the dead squaws, shaking his head.

"Sergeant," the captain called.

The sergeant brought his horse to a halt in front of the troop commander and saluted.

"Your orders were to take the women alive," Carleton said.

"Yes, sir," the sergeant said. "I didn't know they were squaws, Captain, what with the way they were dressed, and then once I saw they were women they began shooting at us. I had two casualties, sir, neither fatal. I didn't have no choice but to fire back. Sir."

Carleton frowned. "Carry on, Sergeant," he said and the man saluted and wheeled his horse away to take charge of the slaughtering of the Indians' pack animals.

"We killed all the bucks," Carleton told Jason as they made for a cottonwood grove along the river. "Three squaws were taken prisoner along with two children. The ponies are either all dead or scattered over the plains."

Jason nodded. He noticed some of the troopers riding over the bodies of the dead squaws as the men galloped up to join their companions heading for the cottonwoods. He grimaced in distaste.

When they reached the trees, the men dismounted to make camp. The squaw Jason had saved sat on the ground wailing, first beating her breasts with her fists, then clawing at her cheeks with her nails so that blood ran down over her dark skin. Jason walked to her and raised his hands with his palms toward her.

"We mean you no harm," he said, speaking softly, trying to soothe her.

The squaw covered her face with her hands, her

voice rising and falling in a keening wail. Her hands, Jason saw, were filthy from handling the buffalo meat. Her hair had been cut short and she wore a brave's tunic and leggings made of what appeared to be antelope hides.

Jason knelt on the ground beside the squaw, touching her shoulder gently. Slowly she lowered her hands from her eyes and looked at him. He gasped. Her eyes were blue.

"You're not an Indian," he said in amazement.

She stared at him with her blue eyes. Her wailing had stopped but she said nothing.

Jason strode across the campground to Captain Carleton who was sitting cross-legged writing his report. "We've captured a white woman," Jason told him.

"No. You've lost your senses."

"Go see for yourself."

Carleton put his log book aside, scrambled to his feet and walked to the woman, kneeling in front of her and staring at her face. When he stood up he nodded to Jason. "My apologies, Briscoe," he said, "she is a white woman."

The captain turned to a group of troopers who were smoking and talking nearby. "Send Ben Higgins to me," he ordered. Higgins, who as a boy had been captured by the Comanches and later ransomed by Texans, marched up to the captain and saluted smartly.

"One of the squaws is a white woman," Carleton told him. "See if you can get her to tell you her story."

Higgins nodded and walked to where the woman sat. When the captain and Jason followed, Higgins shook his head, motioning them away. He sat cross-legged in front of the woman, gesturing and talking. At first she said nothing, listening but remaining impassive. At last, she nodded, spoke, and the two talked for many minutes.

"She says she regrets it now," Higgins said when he returned to join Carleton and Jason, "but admits it's a fact she had a paleface pa and ma. They had a name for her, she says, and that name was Cincee Ann."

"Cincee Ann," Jason repeated. "Maybe she means Cynthia Ann."

"Whatever." Higgins shrugged. "She says that she has a Commanche pa and ma and they have a name for her and the name is Palux. She says she has three sons, all warriors who ride with the Comanches in the great land to the west. She says she wants to go home to the mountains and to her people."

Carleton led Higgins and Jason back to the woman who was still sitting on the ground staring straight ahead. She gave no sign that she noticed the three men.

"Tell her," Carleton said to Higgins, "that her people are our people, white people. Tell her we won't hurt her. Tell her we'll take her with us and return her to her people. To civilization."

Higgins spoke and the woman answered. Higgins asked questions; again the woman answered.

"She says her people live in the land of the setting sun. She says she has seen the white men, the Texans, and she knows they hunt and kill her people. She says she wants only to return to her sons and to the campfires of her people."

Carleton shook his head. "She'll soon get over that nonsense once she's back in civilization. For now, keep her with the other women. We'll take them with us and leave them at the first fort we come to."

Higgins repeated the captain's words to the woman. She silently buried her face in her hands and would speak no more.

That night, Jason's sleep was troubled. He woke several times thinking he heard hoofbeats and sat up but saw nothing. Once he left his bedroll and walked around the camp. A sentry nodded to him, a horse nickered in the cavvy; he heard nothing else. Shaking his head, still not satisfied, he returned to his pallet where he lay staring up at the brilliant stars in the cold sky.

The next morning they discovered that the squaw with the blue eyes was gone. Though Jason and Higgins cut for sign, they found nothing. The woman had vanished into the limitless plains.

"Let her go," Carleton said. "She's become more Indian than white. I was willing to help her if she'd have let me but I'll be damned if I'll waste time looking for a will-o-the-wisp. She probably caught one of their loose ponies and made for the foothills."

"Seems a shame," Jason said.

"Letting the woman go?"

"No, not that so much. All of it, killing the squaws, killing the horses. I know the Comanches are savages and yet . . ."

"We're going to civilize them if we have to kill every Indian to do it. We have to make the country safe for white men. Indians are as cruel or crueler to their own kind, you know that as well as I do."

Jason looked west across the plains toward the distant mountains. There must be another way, he told himself.

That day he rode far ahead of the troop until he was out of sight of the pony soldiers. The weather had changed so he no longer faced the cold wind sweeping down from the north but instead felt a mild breeze blowing from behind him, from the south. The sun had risen large and red and mounted the sky in a blaze of heat. Strange weather, Jason thought; he didn't recall ever seeing its like this time of year on the Staked Plain.

The sun rose until it was high above him, then settled toward the west, and still Jason had found no sign of Comanches. He reined in on the top of a low hill, squinting as he looked to the west, and there he saw, through the shimmering waves of heat, a great herd of buffalo, thousands upon thousands of the shaggy beasts. The buffalo seemed to blur before his eyes and in a few minutes they were gone. A mirage, he told himself.

Jason rode on feeling strangely lightheaded, wondering if he had a sickness coming on. He prided himself on never being sick. The sky darkened and when he glanced overhead he saw that a single cloud had blotted out the sun. The cloud drifted on to the north and the sun shone again.

Ahead of him, on a rise, he saw a lone horseman. He stopped, knowing instinctively it was a Comanche, and waited for the rider to signal others to attack. Jason debated whether to warn Carleton's troopers with a rifle shot or to gallop back to the cavalry column. He decided to do neither. He waited. The Indian seemed to be waiting as well and Jason rode forward until he was close enough to see that the rider wasn't an Indian brave after all. It was the squaw with the blue eyes.

When Jason came to within a hundred feet of her she turned her horse and rode north, looking behind her and motioning him to follow. He hesitated, then urged his horse after hers, keeping the same hundred feet between them.

They rode for an hour, until the sun was low over the plains, before she stopped and waited for him. When he came up beside her she pointed ahead and downward with her open palm. Jason drew in his breath in surprise.

They were on the cap rock of the largest and most beautiful canyon he had ever seen. A creek rushed down the slope at their feet to cascade over a falls into the valley. In the distance, on the canyon floor, the stream curled away like a ribbon. Directly below them the gorge was narrow, no more than a hundred yards across, but he saw that farther to the east it broadened and the canyon floor leveled into rich green pasture land.

Buffalo grazed along the distant creek and Jason had the notion they had lived there forever, undisturbed by prowling wolves, Indians, or hide-hunting white men. In his mind's eye he saw cattle grazing in the canyon, longhorns fattening as they were readied for the drive north to market, saw, on the canyon's south slope, a ranch house with many outbuildings and a corral where horses ran.

He turned to the woman, to Cynthia Ann. If that were truly her name. "It's beautiful," he said and he thought she understood, if not his words then the thought behind him.

She turned her horse away and he rode beside her through the gathering dusk. Night came and they stopped and made camp. He ate beef jerky, offering her some, but she shook her head, watching him as he ate but eating and drinking nothing herself.

Jason lay on his bedroll under the stars. His last thought before he fell asleep was that he should be afraid but, strangely, he was not. He woke to see the moon rising over the low hills along the canyon's rim.

A voice near him murmured words he couldn't understand.

The woman came to lay beside him and he felt her hand pass lightly over his body. He loosened his clothes, turning over to find her lying naked beside him. This was meant to be, he thought, not surprised at her nakedness. When he knelt above her she drew his body down and accepted him into her. They joined, one to the other, in a tide of passion that rose and fell, rose and fell. Afterwards, they lay in one another's arms with the moon high above them.

Again Jason slept. When he awoke, the moon was a ghost in the west and the sun was already paling the eastern horizon. The woman was gone, her pony nowhere to be seen. Though he searched around the campsite he found no sign of her or her horse. Making his way back to where he had seen the canyon, Jason half expected to find only the empty plain, to discover that the canyon had been as much of a mirage as the buffalo, a vision, a feverish imagining.

He stood on the cap rock and stared down at the creek flowing through the lush green meadows far below him. The buffalo still grazed in the distance. The canyon was real.

He returned to break camp, saddling his horse for the ride back to Carleton's troop. Again the weather had changed, the wind coming from the north, bringing the Arctic cold down across Canada and the plains of the northern territories.

For a moment he looked west to the foothills and the mountain fastnesses of the Comanches. Somewhere on the Staked Plain the woman whose name was now Palux rode to return to her people and to her children. He knew he would never see her again.

Jason felt an ache, a sadness, a sense of great loss. With an oath he mounted, spurring his horse and riding south to find the troop.

3

Two of the three men sitting in front of the Georgian Hotel peered intently down Peachtree Street. The brown-haired man in the middle stared straight ahead, his small brown eyes focused inward as though looking at something only he could see.

"Here they come, Colonel." The man who spoke was the youngest, fresh-faced and cleanshaven.

Print Varner turned his head slowly to glance down Peachtree, lifting a hand to smooth his trim moustache. "Look at them, Ed," he said. "You'd think they were marching in some damn parade."

The young man grunted in agreement. Josh, on the other side of Print, said nothing as they watched the four men approach, three in the blue uniform of Federal troops, the other in civilian clothes. One of the soldiers led the way, the second walked beside the civilian, while the third soldier brought up the rear. And they did march rather than walk. Self-conscious, aware of the hostile stares of the Atlantans who grudgingly made way for them, they looked neither right nor left.

Ed spat across the wooden sidewalk into the street. "Damned bluebellies," he said.

After his first glance at the soldiers, Print Varner ignored them, studying instead the man they escorted. Short and fair, the civilian wore a broad-brimmed gray hat and a gray frock coat unbuttoned to reveal a gold watch chain looped on his vest across his paunch.

"Bastard," Print muttered. He pushed his hat forward, putting his face in shadow.

Ed looked quickly at the Colonel, surprised at the venom in his voice. He opened his mouth to ask a question and caught Josh's frowning gaze. Josh shook his head slightly and Ed subsided. Josh was right, Ed thought, Print Varner didn't always take kindly to questions about his past. Whatever the colonel wanted was all right by him, anyway.

The four men crossed the sidewalk, climbed the steps and entered the red brick hotel, passing close enough for the seated men to touch them. Once they were gone, Print stood and stretched. "Now you men know what to do," he said, "once you see Sam Truman leave the kitchen."

"Yes, sir," Ed said. Josh nodded as the two men rose to stand next to Print, Josh almost as tall as Print's six feet, Ed half a head shorter.

Print Varner went into the hotel. After a few minutes the other two men followed and found chairs in the lobby where they could see both the swinging door from the kitchen and the stairs leading to the hotel's upper floors. The Colonel was not in sight.

"What beats all," Ed said, "is him letting the word get out on purpose. Telling them what he means to do. Not only what but when. Telling them right to the day."

Josh shifted his chaw of tobacco from one cheek to the other, saying nothing. Ed looked for a moment at the scarr down Josh's left cheek that the graying beard was meant to cover, the scar from Bull Run. Josh had fought under the Colonel from the beginning, Ed had only been with them these last nine months. He wished he could've been along during the fighting but even then he never would've been a Print Varner. More like Josh maybe. But there was only one Print Varner.

Still and all, Colonel Prentice Varner had come up with a wild notion this time, Ed thought. And that damned Josh never would say a word. Unable to contain himself, Ed burst out, "Why Texas? Texas! It's a godforsaken country, cold as a witch's tit in the winter. And dry. The soil's good for nothing but pissweed. And even that don't grow good."

Josh spat a stream of juice into a spittoon. He stared at Ed, his gray eyes impassive. "You with the colonel or against him?" he asked.

"You know I'm with him all the way. To hell and back if he wants. I'm speculating, Josh, you know how I like to speculate, kind of turn things over in my mind."

"You speculate too much," Josh said. "You think too much and you talk too much. A good trooper doesn't talk, doesn't think. He does what he's told. *You'll* be the one to lead us to hell, Ed Quackenbush, and when you get us there we'll have no one to lead us back."

"Ah, hell, Josh," Ed began.

He broke off and stiffened as the door from the kitchen swung open and a short stout black man approached them holding a linen-covered tray over his head perched on one hand.

"Gentlemen," the black said, smiling broadly at the two men before he turned to go up the stairs. Sam Truman wore his frayed black waiter's uniform with as much pride as any soldier ever wore the Confederate grey.

As soon as he was out of sight, Ed and Josh rose slowly to their feet and headed for the stairs.

When Sam reached the second floor landing he found Print Varner waiting for him. Sam nodded but didn't smile.

"Sam," Print said softly.

The waiter was already several steps up the stairs leading to the third floor. He stopped but didn't turn. "Sir?" he said, not sounding the r.

Print climbed the steps until he stood beside the black man. Taking the linen cloth between thumb and forefinger he flicked it from the tray and breathed in the aroma of roast beef and the tang of fresh coffee.

"Nothing's too good for your friend, Mr. McCabe, is it?" he asked.

The waiter smiled uncertainly at Print. "Now, Mr. Varner, sir," he said placatingly.

"Answer me, nigger. Nothing's too good for Mr. McCabe, is it? Nothing's too good for that damn land-stealing murdering carpetbagger, is it?"

Sam shifted uneasily. "I got to serve everybody, sir," he said.

Print lifted the tray from the waiter's hand, climbed a few steps past Sam and placed it on the landing.

"I wouldn't—" the waiter began.

He didn't see Print's fist before it struck his right cheekbone. The black man grunted in surprise and pain as his shoulder thudded against the wall. Print chopped down on the back of Sam's neck with his clenched fist and the black dropped to one knee. Print hit him again and Sam pitched down the steps to sprawl on the carpet in the second floor hallway. He lay staring at Print, making no move to get up.

Print quickly took two bandanas from his pocket, gagged Sam and tied his hands behind his back. Grasping the waiter beneath the shoulders, Print pulled him to his feet and propelled him along the hallway, opening a closet door and thrusting him inside.

"If I hear a sound from you in the next hour," he said, "I'll kill you. Slow."

Print shut the closet door and stood in the corridor, listening. The hall was empty, the hotel quiet. He climbed the stairs two at a time to the landing where he picked up the tray and carried it in front of him in both hands to the third floor.

When he reached the head of the stairs he lifted the tray high enough to conceal his face. Over the top of the linen cloth he saw two of the Yankee soldiers on guard beside a door halfway down the corridor, one sitting with his chair tilted against the wall, the other standing at parade rest.

Keeping the tray between his face and the Yankees, Print walked along the faded floral carpet of the hall. When he saw the feet of the first Yankee in front of him he shifted the tray so he held it in the hand above his right shoulder.

The soldier, the one who had been at parade rest, shifted position. "You're not—" he began.

Print hurled the tray full in his face with all the force of a battering ram. The man's head slammed back against the door frame and he sat down hard as tray, dishes and silverware clattered to the floor.

Print hooked his toe under the rung of the seated man's chair, upended it and sent that soldier backwards to the floor, the man clawing for the gun at his belt.

Ed and Josh ran along the hall to Print's side, their pistols drawn. The Yankee's hand held on the butt of his gun, then dropped palm up onto the carpet. The other soldier, using his sleeve to wipe gravy from his face, stared at the three men. Print slid a knife from a sheath on his belt and held it to the man's throat.

"Stand up," he ordered.

The man pushed himself from the floor and stood facing Print. He was young, his face smooth and unlined. Print smiled when he saw the fear in the boy's eyes.

"Tell the Yanks inside to open the door," Print ordered.

The young soldier's mouth quivered. "You can just go to hell," he said.

Print's smile widened as the blade of his knife bit into the boy's neck until it drew blood.

"Tell them to open the door, sonny," he said.

The soldier hesitated and before he could answer Print heard the rasp of a sliding bolt, then the click of a key turning in a lock, and the door swung open.

"What's going on?" the bluecoat in the doorway asked.

Josh pointed his pistol between the man's eyes. When the soldier stepped back, Josh kicked the door open and Print herded the two guards into the room.

"Tie them," he told Josh and Ed.

Across the room McCabe had risen from an armchair, a cigar in one hand, his face flushed with anger. "Do you realize who I am?" he asked Print.

"I do," Print said.

McCabe stared, recognized Print, and his cigar dropped to the floor. "You," he said. He drew in a deep breath, seeming to recover some of his poise. "If anything happens to me, Varner," he said, "you'll face a firing squad. You realize that, don't you?"

Print grunted, saying nothing. Josh and Ed finished binding and gagging the three soldiers. They left them on the far side of the room, their eyes bulging as they strained to free themselves.

"You two men," McCabe said, appealing to Print's companions. "If I'm harmed, your lives won't be worth a Confederate dollar. I was sent here from Washington by President Johnson himself."

Ed and Josh said nothing. Print began to laugh. Something in the sound of the laugh made McCabe pale and he glanced desperately at the door behind the three men and then over his shoulder to the window where the curtains billowed in the breeze.

Now the anger was on him, and when the anger was on Prentice Varner, he was seeing a face from long, long ago. It was an ordinary face, except for the fleshy mouth and the piercing, darting eyes. It was the face of a man with a buggy whip in his hand, driving a young woman and a little boy across a room, out the door into the chill blackness of the night. It was the face of hate, the face of the devil incarnate, and when the anger came over Varner, it was the face of every man who stood in his way.

Print suddenly stopped laughing, taking a chair from beside the four-poster bed and placing it in the center of the room under the gas-jet light fixture. Standing on the chair he grasped one of the fixture's arms with both hands. Kicking the chair away, he hung suspended in midair. The fixture held. Print let go and dropped the two feet to the floor.

Eyes wide, McCabe backed away. He turned and bolted for the window, thrusting up the frame, but as he swung his leg over the sill Print grabbed his shoulder, yanking him back into the room. Print's fist slammed into McCabe's paunch and the Yankee screamed, his voice high and afraid as he doubled over with his hands clutching his stomach. Print viciously kicked his shin and McCabe lurched sideways, keeping his balance only by grasping the back of a chair with one hand.

"Gag the bastard," Print said. "Tie his wrists behind him."

McCabe cried out once more before the cloth bit into his lips and stiffled his protests to muffled moans. A man's voice called out from somewhere in the hotel below them and Print heard footsteps pounding along the corridor, stopping outside the room. A fist banged on the door. "Everything all right in there?"

"Your damn clumsy waiter dropped a tray in the hall." Print's voice was calm and self-assured.

"I'll send someone to clean up." Footsteps receded from the door and faded into silence.

Print smiled and picked up the overturned chair. "The rope," he said.

Josh handed him a coil of grass rope and Print climbed on the chair and tied one end over the light fixture. He jumped down and fashioned a noose, slipping the loop over McCabe's neck, tightening it until he heard McCabe begin choking, the sounds muffled by the gag. At Print's nod, Ed and Josh lifted McCabe onto the chair.

Print stood back, looking at McCabe who stood flat-footed, afraid to move for fear of toppling the chair. He unhooked McCabe's suspenders and pulled his trousers down his legs. Taking the waist of McCabe's underwear in his fist, he pulled down, leaving both pants and drawers tangled around the Yankee's feet. Print slid his knife from its sheath, running his thumb over the blade and looking at the man's exposed penis and testicles.

Josh put his hand on Print's arm. "No," he said. Ed stood gaping at them.

Print shrugged Josh off.

"No," Josh said again and Print swung around to face him. "There's no need," Josh said.

"The bastard comes down here," Print said, "like an almighty conquerer, like the lord of the earth, and he makes kings out of the niggers and he takes our women, killing and raping 'cause there's no one to say him nay. Except me. Except Print Varner." Spittle formed on his lips.

"I know you got the right to do for McCabe," Josh told him. "I know what happened between you and him when he took your land. But he ain't an animal. If you do it"—Josh nodded at the knife —" there'll be only the two of you traveling to Texas, you and Ed. I'll have no part of it."

Print took a long breath and resheathed his knife.

"Didn't you know I was funnin'?" he asked. "I'd of thought you'd been with me long enough to be able to tell."

"I have been with you long enough to tell," Josh said darkly.

Print glowered at him for a moment before turning and drawing back his boot. He kicked the chair, sending it thumping across the room and McCabe fell free, kicking, trying to cry out, his feet flailing a foot above the carpet. The fixture wrenched partly free from the ceiling and sent plaster showering on thee men below. The noose tightened, McCabe's eyes popped, and his face, turning blue, seemed to bloat before their eyes as his body jerked and twisted at the end of the rope.

There was a pounding on the door.

"Let's go," Print said.

Pushing aside the curtains, he stepped through the open window onto a small balcony and climbed onto the railing. The next balcony was five feet away. Print poised, leaped, and easily cleared the far rail. When Ed and Josh joined him, Print opened the window and stepped inside. With its shades drawn, the room was dark though the sun had not yet set. There was no one to be seen, but the bed was creased as though someone had recently lain on top of the coverlet.

Print crossed the room, unlatched the door and stepped into the corridor with Ed and Josh behind him. The hotel clerk stood at the door to McCabe's room futilely twisting the knob and calling for someone to unbolt the door.

"What's all the commotion?" Print asked him, stepping around the food and broken dishes still scattered on the carpet.

"Something's wrong in there," the bespectacled young man said. He stared at Print and then the other two men. "What are you-all doing in thirty-five?" he asked suspiciously. "That's Mr. Jensen's room."

"Just passing the time of day with Jensen," Print said. He walked past the clerk to the head of the stairs where he paused to look back over his shoulder.

"If you happen to see Mr. McCabe," he told him, "tell him Colonel Prentice Varner said hello."

The three men walked down the two flights to

the lobby where men stood aside to make room for them. When Print heard his name he went on without turning his head. He led Josh and Ed from the hotel and along the street to the livery stable where they retrieved their horses.

Riding at a steady pace they were soon out of the city.

"By God, Print," Ed said. "I didn't know you meant to brazen it out in front of all of them the way you did. Saying your name as plain as day to that clerk and leaving three witnesses behind. You never said we'd leave three witnessess."

"Four," Print said. "You're not counting the four-eyed clerk."

"Before the week's out the whole state of Georgia will know you hung the bastard."

"You got a word wrong," Print said. "They'll know *we* hung the bastard. Don't worry, we'll be heroes to them that count." He reined in his horse on a rise and swung about in the saddle so he faced the distant city. Standing in the stirrups he called out, *"Sic semper tyrannis.* Death to the tyrants."

"Print," Ed said, his voice almost a whine. "Why did you walk out of there like that? In front of everybody and his uncle."

"Print Varner's not afraid of any man."

"We'll be outcasts," Ed said. "Hunted men with a price on our heads."

"I've heard tell," Josh said quietly, "that it's called burning your bridges. Print's burned ours as well as his."

Print looked quickly at Josh, then raised his arm. "Let's go," he said. "We've a long ride to Kincaid's. We've got better things to do than sit here palavering."

He spurred his horse and they rode in the gathering dusk beneath the overreaching branches of the trees. Ed was a fool, Print thought. Ed would serve his purpose and then he'd have done with him. Josh was another matter. Josh didn't talk much, he was loyal, and he was also dangerous. Ed could be handled easy while Josh could be trouble, big trouble. Print would never trust him, not completely.

Josh is dangerous, Print told himself, because he's too much like me.

4

It was past midnight when they rode between the stone pillars and up the curving drive of Four Oaks, the Kincaid plantation. Or, Print thought bitterly, what was left of the Kincaid plantation.

The three horsemen circled the dark house to the stables where they dismounted and searched for one of the stableboys. They found none so they unsaddled and put up their horses themselves before they made their way across the moon-silvered ground to the house. Print glanced at the back door but instead of knocking he led the others along an overgrown path to the front. He'd be damned if he'd come to any man's back door, not even W.K. Kincaid's.

Print lifted the brass knocker on the front door and rapped once, twice, three times. The men waited on the veranda in the cool of the April night listening to the tree frogs croaking all around them. Finally they saw the glow of a light through a window beside the door and heard footsteps

approach the door and stop. Print rapped the
knocker again.

"It's Print Varner," he said loudly.

A key squeaked in the lock, the door inched
open and a flickering candle was thrust toward
him. Print waited. The candle was lowered and the
door swung open. Print, followed by Ed and Josh,
stepped inside.

"I'm here to see W.K.," Print said to the old
black man holding the light. The man was stooped,
his hair iron-gray, his dark eyes rheumy.

"Mister Kincaid's been expecting you-all," the
black said.

"The kitchen's back yonder," Print told Ed and
Josh. "Go hunt up some grub and put coffee on if
you can find any. Probably have to rouse one of
the house slaves."

"I'se all that's left," the black man said. "The
others done run off when the Yankees come."

"This is a mighty big place," Print said, "for
just you and old man Kincaid."

"Me and Mr. Kincaid *and* Miz Vivian. And I
ain't a slave no more. I'se a servant. I'se paid."

Print snorted and followed the black past the
sweep of the stairs into the west wing of the house.
In the rooms along the corridor he saw only a few
scattered pieces of furniture shrouded by dust-
cloths.

The black stopped in front of a dark oak door
and knocked. A man's voice answered faintly but
Print couldn't distinguish his words. The servant
swung the door open and stood to one side.

"Mr. Varner," he announced.

The library was lit by only a single lamp on a
table on the far side of the room so it was several
seconds before Print grew accustomed to the

gloom. When he did, he saw the dark mass of a high-backed chair directly in front of him.

A deep rumble came from the chair and Print recognized his own name, slurred yet understandable. He stepped forward and looked down at the old man's face half-hidden in the shadows.

Print reached out to grasp William Kent Kincaid's right hand. Kincaid's left hand lay useless in his lap and he lifted his right hand slowly, as though with effort. Although he couldn't see it, Print knew the left side of the old man's face sagged.

"Sit down, Colonel," Kincaid said. By listening intently, Print was able to make out the words. He found a chair, pulled it forward, and sat a few feet from Kincaid.

"Ed and Josh and me finished the business in the city I told you about," Print said. "We'd appreciate staying the night before we set out for the West."

"Of course," Kincaid said. "The pleasure is mine to be able to help. You'll find my house somewhat understaffed but what I have is yours, Colonel."

"Thank you." Print paused, wondering how best to bring up the subject of the money.

"There's a paper on the table behind me," Kincaid said.

"A paper?" Print stood up and walked to the table where he saw a legal-appearing document beside the lamp.

"The agreement. I stake you to two thousand dollars. In ten years time, half of all you have is mine." Kincaid sighed. "Not mine by then. Vivian's. I'm an old man, Colonel."

"W.K., you'll outlive us all."

"Not if I have a say in the matter, Colonel. Not if I can help it, I won't."

After reading the document, Print picked a pen from a rack on the table, dipped it in an inkwell, and scrawled his name at the bottom.

"Hand it here," Kincaid told him.

Print brought the document to the old man and laid it in his lap.

"Nate," Kincaid said. The servant stepped into the room and took the paper. "Bring Colonel Varner the money."

Nate nodded. After he left, Print sat down again and stretched his legs. The library smelled musty, like a parlor used only on Sundays and for funerals. Seeing Kincaid sitting helpless like this depressed Print and he shifted restlessly in his chair.

"I hope there's nothing more on your mind," Kincaid said.

"More?"

"Besides the money and Texas. And what happened in Atlanta today, of course."

Print leaned forward, the lamplight glinting from his eyes. "Do you want me to tell you about Atlanta?"

"No," Kincaid said. "It's best I don't know."

The old man sat silent for such a long time that Print thought he must have dozed off.

"Vivian," Kincaid said. "I thought you might want to talk to me about Vivian."

Print tensed, feeling a flare of desire as he thought of Kincaid's daughter, her jet black hair, her ivory beauty, her full figure. He pictured Vivian as he'd seen her in the first year of the War at the ball in Atlanta—the creamy white hooped dress that made her lovelier than a magnolia blossom, the men gathered around to pay her court, her flirtatious laugh, the way she pouted when she was displeased.

And none of it for him—he wasn't good enough for a Kincaid, not then and, as far as W.K. was concerned, not now. Things had changed since the War, didn't the old man realize that?

"You know I've always admired Miss Vivian," Print said, choosing his words with care.

"Texas is no place for a lady." Kincaid's voice had become slurred and indistinct.

"Might be just what Texas needs. I get the feeling your daughter could make a place for herself most anywhere."

The old man struggled to straighten his slumped body but remained sagged to the left. "She likely could, she very likely could. But not with you. You're a man who'll never be concerned with anyone except Print Varner. And there was that terrible business when your wife was killed."

Print felt the color drain from his face. He clenched his hands, relaxing them only by force of will. He smiled. "The truth is that nobody thinks more of another person than they do of themselves. And as for Lucy . . ." He broke off, his smile fading. Suddenly he slammed his hand down on the arm of his chair, making Kincaid jerk. "Don't ever mention her name to me again," Print said, his voice steel.

Kincaid began coughing in deep shuddering spasms. Watching him, Print relaxed. There's no danger in this old, sick man, he told himself. How long's he got left? Another year at the most. A sound from the doorway alerted him and he swung around. The door remained closed.

"I heard something," Print said. "Nate?"

"My servants . . . my servant does not listen at

at doors," Kincaid gasped, wiping his lips with a handkerchief.

Print settled back, shrugging. What did it matter, after all?

"Vivian's changed, changed a great deal," Kincaid said after a few minutes. "I doubt you'd know her. She's had to run this place as well as take care of me these last years. She saved Four Oaks."

"I'd know her," Print said. Best not to see Vivian at all, he decided.

"I think it best if you don't see her while you're here," Kincaid told him, echoing his thought.

Print didn't reply. He'd do as he saw fit, who was to stop him? Yet Kincaid was right, he shouldn't see her. Not only did he feel almost shy about the prospect of facing Vivian, but she wasn't fit for the frontier despite what he'd said to Kincaid. Texas needed women who could stand on their own feet, women who weren't afraid.

Best let her remain a dream, he thought. And how often he'd dreamed of her during the War, all those times when he thought he'd never live to return home, dreamed of riding into Atlanta in triumph, of Vivian rushing to meet him, of marrying her.

Plenty of women found him attractive; he'd never lacked for women. Yet he'd known, even when he dreamed of her, that Vivian wouldn't open her arms to him on his homecoming no matter how triumphant. He was surprised she hadn't married one of the dandies who'd clustered about her, though he also knew it wasn't because she was waiting for him. Kincaid was right—Vivian was a lady. She'd never wanted Print Varner and she didn't want him now.

He might be able to take her anyway but that would spoil the dream. Print shook his head, dismissing all thoughts of her. He was here for more important reasons.

There was a tap on the door and Nate came in and handed a thick leather belt to Kincaid. The old man smoothed the belt on his lap with his right hand, his fingers caressing the leather and, Print realized belatedly, the gold coins underneath. He handed the belt to Print.

"Take it," he said.

Print buckled the belt around his waist.

"Don't you want to count the money?" Kincaid asked.

"I trust you, W.K."

Print glanced from the old man to the servant, noticing that the document he'd signed was nowhere to be seen. Evidently the old man didn't trust *him*. Print smiled. He couldn't say he disagreed with Kincaid's judgement.

"Pinto County, Texas," Kincaid said. "The KK brand. We grazed thousands of acres there before the War."

"How much land did you own?"

"In those days not many men owned Texas land or if they did I hadn't heard of it. The land belongs to the government. Not the federal government, the state. It's Texas land, first come, first served."

"Sounds like my kind of operation. But you know I'm no rancher, W.K. What I know about cows is next to nothing."

"Any fool can herd cows. You've got something that can't be taught, Print. You've got a need gnawing inside you, a need to be somebody and you're not going to let anything or anyone stand in your way. That's why I'm letting all my chips ride on you."

Print's hand rested for a moment on his pistol.

"You're right," he said, "nobody's going to stand in my way. What I want, I go after. Land, money, a woman. Makes no difference."

The old man sighed. "You can't ever really have a woman who doesn't want you. Haven't you learned that by now?"

Print said nothing, waiting. After a time, Kincaid said, "Nate." The black man came into the room. "Two brandies," Kincaid told him.

When Print and Kincaid raised their glasses the old man proposed a toast. "To Texas," he said.

"To Texas," Print echoed.

They drank and as he sipped the brandy, Kincaid began to cough again. Nate stepped forward and Print got up, suddenly sickened by the dead smell of the room and by the slowly dying man. He nodded to Kincaid, walking from the room and leaving him to Nate.

The corridor was dark and he cursed himself for forgetting to bring a candle. He hadn't even asked where he and Josh and Ed were to sleep. He turned to go back into the library when he heard a whisper from behind him.

"Print."

His hand was on his gun before he realized the voice was a woman's.

"Miss Vivian?" he asked.

He felt her hand on his arm and then her fingers closed over his. "Come with me, Print," she said so low he could hardly hear her.

His breath caught, then quickened as she led him to the foot of the curving staircase. She released his hand. "This way," she said. He followed her up the steps, followed the faint yet heady scent of her, the scent of lilacs in April. As he climbed the stairs he felt a tremor rise in his

legs, not of fear but of anticipation, of wonder
and surprise.

The upper hall was even darker than the lower
and Print stopped at the head of the stairs, un-
certain which way Vivian had gone. He breathed
the scent of lilacs. He heard a door shut below him
and Ed's laugh came from the farther reaches of
the house. And then the house, the great mansion
that was all that remained of the Kincaid plantation, was silent.

"Here."

Light shimmered from an open doorway to
his right. Print walked along the thickly carpeted
hall to the door where he stopped, staring into the
room beyond. He saw heavy white and gold drapes
on the windows, a mirrored stand with a white
chair in front of it, and a canopied bed covered
with a white and pink spread. Vivian Kincaid,
dressed in a pale filmy wrap, stood holding a
candle above a high curved-leg table.

When she looked up and saw Print in the doorway she blew out the flame and the room was dark.
Print stepped forward and paused, reaching behind
him to noiselessly close the door. In the blackness
in front of him he heard the rustle of clothing and
a moment later Vivian's hand touched his arm,
sliding down his sleeve to seek and find his hand.
She led Print into the room and when the back of
his hand brushed her side he drew in his breath.

He had touched the bare flesh of her hip. She
was naked.

She let go of his fingers and he heard her pull
down the covers of the bed and slide between the
sheets. Now he could hear only his own heavy
breathing in the quiet of the room. And all around
him, intoxicating him, was the scent of lilacs.

I'll be damned, he thought, not moving. I will be God damned.

He sat on the bed and, once he had tugged off his boots, he stood to remove his clothes, letting them lie where they fell. He grasped the bed-clothes and flung them back.

"Print," Vivian said. He smiled at the tremor in her voice. "Print," she said, "be gentle."

He had never had a virgin. Women, yes, whores in New Orleans and Atlanta before the war and, in Vicksburg, the widow of a man recently killed, a woman who was no better than she should be, little more than a camp-follower.

And Lucy.

There were two kinds of women, he knew, whores and the others, the respectable kind. Like Lucy. He'd not had her until after they were married, never dreamed she wasn't a virgin.

Virgins were better, or so men said. Print had no doubt at all that Vivian was one. She was smarter than Lucy, a survivor like himself. And a real lady.

Print ran his hand over the sheet, reaching out and finding Vivian huddled far away from him. Feeling himself harden, he took her by the arm and drew her to him, caressing her hair with his hand while he buried his face in her hair amidst the fragrance of lilacs.

He turned her face to his and kissed her. Finding her mouth closed, he forced her lips and teeth apart with his tongue. She turned her head away and he felt the dampness of tears on her cheek. She murmured words he couldn't make out.

Impatient, he grasped her thigh with his left hand, pushing his fingers between her legs and upward along her inner thigh until he found her sex, dry and uninviting. He knelt above her and forced her legs apart, thrusting between them with his sex, trying to enter her, failing at first then inserting himself inside her, thrusting with short vicious stabs, making her cry out in pain, her head twisting back and forth on the pillow until his lips closed over hers and he pressed down to pinion her head. His hands sliding along her sides to the fulness of her breasts. When he pressed them against the side of his body, she moaned.

Print felt a sudden surge rising within him. His hands closed on her buttocks, grasping them, urging her body to his, and he came in three violent spasms while she lay beneath him, unmoving, her hands clutching the sheet at her sides.

Print groaned and rolled off her, feeling her wetness on him. When he heard her sobbing in the darkness his hand went to her hair, smoothing it for a moment.

Print swung his feet from the bed and stood up. Groping in front of him he located the table, found a box of lucifers and used one to light the candle. He looked down and saw that the wetness he'd felt was blood and he smiled to himself, then shrugged, his eyes darting back to the bed, alert and wary. He'd never wanted a woman as much as he'd wanted Vivian and yet now he felt, not exactly disappointed, but cheated in some way. As though he'd lost something.

He found a cloth on the washstand beside a pitcher of water. He cleansed himself and dressed. Holding the candle over the bed he saw that Vivian was facing away from him with only her black hair visible above the white and pink spread.

"Your father," Print said. "Does he have a safe?"

She turned her head and looked at him with wide brown eyes reddened from crying. "What?" she asked.

"A safe," he said, raising his voice.

Vivian threw the covers aside and sat up, staring at him. She put her feet over the side of the bed and stood facing him, her head coming to his shoulder. He drew in his breath as he looked down at her white breasts with their dark red nipples.

She swung her hand with all her might, her palm striking his cheek and snapping his head to one side. Startled, he stepped back, then recovered and grasped her wrist and yanked her to him.

"You bastard," she said.

Print's eyes widened and he smiled. Dropping her wrist he took her chin between his thumb and forefinger and tilted her face up to his. He kissed her gently, his lips closed but moving over hers and for an instant he thought he felt her respond but then she twisted away and crossed the room. With her back to him she took her robe from a chair and put it on, gathering the cloth together and looping the belt before she turned to face him.

"Yes," she said quietly, "my father has a safe. It's in his office behind a false drawer of a desk."

"Do you . . . ?" he began before she silenced him by raising her hand.

"I know the combination of the safe," she said, "if that's what you were about to ask." The candlelight glinted from her dark brown eyes.

"Here's what I want you to do," Print said. "Wait until you're sure your father's asleep and then go down there and open the safe. I signed a paper tonight and you should have it."

"*I* should have it?"

"Your father's staking me and Josh and Ed. We're starting a ranch in Texas."

"I know. I was listening at the door."

"You? I thought it was Nate."

She said nothing, waiting for him to go on.

"Your father's a sick man. He'll be here in Georgia and you'll be in Texas. The agreement guarantees your inheritance and you should have it with you."

"I'll be in Texas," Vivian repeated. She frowned. "As your wife, Print? I don't intend to go unless I'm your wife."

"You'll be my wife," he said.

"What good will this agreement do me? After we're man and wife?"

"The money will be yours, separate and apart. I give you my word on that."

She looked at him until his gaze fell away from hers. "I'll say goodnight to my father," she told him. "I'll get whatever it is you signed."

Print stepped to her and spread apart the top of her robe, his hands swooping down until they held her bared breasts. As he caressed her nipples with his thumbs, he heard her gasp. Vivian's mouth was slightly open, her eyes closed, and when he kissed her she put her arms around his neck and strained against him.

Suddenly she broke away. Pulling the robe together, she walked quickly to the door.

"Do you still think I'm a bastard?" he asked.

She turned to stare at him. "Yes," she said, closing the door behind her.

Print smiled, smoothing his moustache as he breathed in the scent of lilacs. Damned if I haven't made a good bargain he told himself.

They rose early the next day and rode until sunup, stayed the following day with a friend of the Kincaids, departing at nightfall and riding westward. Two nights later they were in Alabama.

Only then did Print call a halt to buy a wagon and stock it, buy two oxen and then locate a minister to marry them.

From then on they made their way west by day and camped at night. The first night they camped, Print sat smoking a cigar beside the embers of the campfire. When he was sure the others were asleep, he rose, butting out his cigar.

He took a glowing brand from the fire and blew the end until it flamed. Reaching into an inner pocket of his jacket, he removed a paper and, holding it in the light of his torch, he read his agreement with W.K. Kincaid.

When he finished reading he held the flame to a corner and watched fire spread up the curling paper. Dropping the blackened agreement to the ground he trod it into the earth with the sole of his boot.

That night Print Varner slept the deep, dreamless sleep of the righteous.

5

THE VARNER party ferried across the Mississippi and journeyed west into Texas, heading for the Trinity River and the small settlement known as Dallas. With Print leading the way, they traveled at a fast, steady pace.

The trees fell away behind them and they were on the prairie, the sky opening up overhead with the stars brilliant at night, the wind strong and constant, the land grassy yet dry. It was a vast, open, empty country where they could travel for days without seeing another human, a land of prairie dogs and rabbits, the ground dotted with pink and yellow flowers, the air clean and good.

They saw no buffalo. Farther west, they were told. The only visible Indians were in the towns, dirty, disspirited bucks and squaws learning the white man's ways.

Two days out of Dallas, Print rode to the top of a rise and, as the sun lowered ahead of him, scanned the prairie looking for a camp site. He held, spotting a trace of white to the north. He swung his bay stallion in that direction and after a few minutes saw a covered wagon ahead of him and the body of a horse on the ground nearby. There was no sign of life.

Print circled the wagon warily, keeping a goodly distance. No one stirred. He rode past the dead horse, brushing away the flies that rose in a buzzing swarm to circle his head. As he neared the wagon, the flap at the rear was pushed open and a man clambered unsteadily to the ground. He stood next to the tailboard staring disbelievingly at Print.

Print slouched over his saddle with his arms folded on the horn.

"Thank God you came," the man said. "Another day and we'd all been goners." He leaned weakly against the wagon and Print saw that his fair face had been burned a dull red by the sun.

"What happened?" Print asked.

"The other horse broke down and I had to shoot him. We couldn't make good time so I took a cutoff from the trail and a rattler bit the horse you see there and he died and we're afraid to eat him for fear of the rattler poison. There's no food left."

"Couldn't you hunt?"

"I used my last bullet on the rattler. The food's been gone for three days and we're 'most out of water. I walked miles searching for water but all the holes are dry."

"You could've set a rabbit snare," Print said.

The man wiped his perspiring face with his sleeve. "I don't rightly know how," he admitted.

"Or you could've dug Indian turnips."

"Indian turnips?"

Print made no effort to keep the disgust out of his glance as his eyes probed the desperation on

the man's face. Print wasn't from this country but
at least he'd learned all he could before setting
out. The war had taught him to do that much.

"Take us with you," the man said. "I'll do anything."

Print heard hoofbeats behind him and, looking
over his shoulder, saw Ed and Josh riding toward
him with Vivian following in the wagon.

"You said 'we.' Who you got with you?" Print
asked the man.

"There's me for one."

A woman climbed down from the wagon and
stood on the ground looking up at Print with her
hands on her hips. She wore a faded blue calico
dress and had a shawl over her head. Her hands
were red and raw and her face, like the man's, had
been badly burned by the sun.

And yet she was the most beautiful woman Print
had ever set eyes on. Her hair was reddish-gold
where it curled below the shawl, her eyes a gray-
green, her skin pale where it wasn't burned.
Though she was short—she stood perhaps an inch
or two over five feet—her figure was full and
pleasantly curved.

"I'm Tamar Swanson," she said.

Print swung to the ground and swept off his hat,
realizing as he looked at her more closely that she
was young, probably no more than sixteen. Her
eyes widened as she watched him, yet he knew she
was unafraid.

"This here's my wife," Print heard the man say.
"I'm George Swanson."

Print ignored him. He heard Ed and Josh rein
in behind him; he ignored them. Vivian called to
him from the seat of the wagon and he ignored
her.

"And who be you?" Tamar asked. Her eyes held

his and Print thought he saw her smile but he couldn't be sure.

"Print Varner. My given name is Prentice but they all call me Print."

"I like Prentice better than Print," Tamar said. "I think I'll call you Prentice if you'll allow me." This time she did smile.

"Call me what you please," he said as the color flooded his face. By God, he was blushing; this young girl had flustered him. He turned away from her to see Vivian walking toward them from the wagon.

Tamar ran to Vivian and took her hand in both of hers. "I'm so thankful you came when you did," she said. "We couldn't have lasted much longer, the rattler killed the horse and we didn't know what to do, whether to leave the wagon and set off afoot or stay here and hope and pray someone would come. We didn't know, we didn't realize . . . We're from the East."

"They can join up with us," Print said. "We need all the men we can get."

Vivian looked from Tamar to Print. "We'll talk about it later," she told her husband. "Right now I'll get them something to eat."

"There's Eli besides," Tamar said. "He's been sick with the fever these last five days."

She returned to the wagon but before she could climb aboard the canvas flap swung open and a boy jumped to the ground. He staggered and kept from falling only by catching hold of Tamar's skirt.

"This be Eli," Tamar said.

The boy must have been twelve or thirteen, a masculine version of Tamar, short, well-built, with red hair and freckles and serious hazel eyes. Eli took off his black broad-brimmed hat and bowed

to Vivian, then walked up to Print and held out
his hand. Print shook hands with him.

"I'm pleased to meet you, sir," Eli said.

Vivian ran forward, kneeling in front of the
boy and holding out her arms. He stepped to her,
letting her enfold and draw him to her.

Print looked from the boy to Tamar. "He can't
be your son," he said. "You're not old enough."

"He's my brother. Our ma's been dead for years
and pa died in New York of the influenza last year
and I married George and my brother and I came
west with him."

"We'll adopt all three of you," Print said. "Now
go get some victuals."

As he swung into the saddle, Print was aware of
someone watching him. Looking down he saw Eli
staring up at him with the look he had first seen
years ago on the faces of some of the young soldiers he had led into battle. They would have
followed him anywhere, Print thought, to the fires
of hell and back again. And that was where he
had led most of them; he could count on his fingers those who'd survived the war.

Looking down at the boy, Print raised his hand
to his hat in a salute. Eli saluted back, holding his
fingers to his forehead with his eyes on Print until
George Swanson took the boy by the hand and led
him to the Varner wagon. Vivian walked behind
them with her arm linked in Tamar's and as Print
watched the young girl glanced back and Print
thought he saw the hint of a smile cross her face.

That night Vivian took his hand in hers and
led him to their wagon. After they were undressed
she guided his lips to her breasts, moaning as he
circled her nipples with his tongue. Not waiting
until he entered her, she urged him onto his back

and knelt above him, taking his sex into her and rhythmically raising and lowering herself on top of him. When he sat up, taking her in his arms and pushing her onto her back, she clung tightly to him, holding him within her even after he had erupted in the series of spasms which always left him sated.

Afterward, he lay on the wagon floor staring up into the darkness. While Vivian had become more responsive since that first night at Four Oaks, she had never held him so passionately before, never guided him into her, never mounted him. He shook his head, thinking he'd never understand her, never understand women.

He heard the sound of men talking around the campfire and the quick, lilting laugh of a woman. Tamar. He sat up and reached out, lifting the canvas flap so he could look toward the fire glow but he saw only huddled dark shapes in the distance.

He'd have Tamar, he vowed, and keep Vivian as well. He lay back again, drifting toward sleep, feeling a sense of power greater than any he'd known since the days when he led men into battle. He was Print Varner, by God, and no man—or woman—could say him nay.

When they passed through the next town all the talk was of the Comanche raids on the ranches of the settlers to the west. The frontier had retreated eastward in the early '60s when the men left to join the Confederate Army and, despite the Rangers, the emboldened Indians had swept down from the high plains, out of their hiding places in the mountains and canyons beyond the Staked Plain, raiding the settlements, stealing cattle and horses, killing and scalping men and women, and carrying other women and children away into captivity. Some of the captives had been returned after ransom was paid but others were never seen nor heard from again.

Print Varner led his party up the Brazos into Pinto County where they made their final camp along the Keechi River. The open valley of the Keechi was flanked by low wooded hills that were part of the Upper Cross Timbers, a series of forest belts of post and blackjack oak. They discovered that the old Kincaid log house had burned and been abandoned and that the few cattle still bearing the KK brand were scattered over hundreds of miles of countryside.

Leaving Ed, Josh and George Swanson to build a new ranch house from the plentiful timber, Print rode off to reconnoiter his new land. The grass was still green and the creeks and rivers ran strong as he made his way to Fort Worth, to Weatherford, to Charlie Goodnight's ranch at Black Springs, to Palo Pinto and Fort Belknap.

Wherever he stopped for the night he was welcomed, fed and given the use of a bunk or a space on the earth floor of a cabin. Print said little as he rode the range with the cowhands but he watched and he listened. Once in a blue moon he might ask a question and when he did he listened intently to the answer with his hands crossed on top of his saddle horn, his small brown eyes never leaving the face of the man he questioned.

Print found there was more to cowherding than he'd bargained for, certainly more than old man Kincaid had led him to believe. As he watched the cowhands he'd nod with appreciation, admiring men who liked their work and were good at it to boot.

He sat on corral fences as wranglers busted untamed cow ponies, breaking their wild spirits with lariat, spurs, and quirt; saw other hands cut cows and their calves from a bawling herd and battle yearlings as they dragged them across the dusty Texas earth to the branding fire; followed them as they located their stock, driving cattle out of the brush along the river bottoms, "brush popping" they called it, at times having to sew the cows' eyes shut to gentle them until the longhorns willingly followed the rest of the herd.

He marveled at the skill of cowhands who returned rebellious herd quitters after busting them by roping their horns and then wrenching them to the ground by twisting the rope beneath their hind legs; he joined the herders as they began their long drive up the Chisholm Trail to Kansas, scouting far ahead of their cattle to locate water and pasture; he listened to old men who sat around campfires talking of days long past, of buffalo hunts, of men bigger than life like Houston and Bridger and Bowie, spinning yarns as they smoked and whittled; he listened as they told him how to find his way without the aid of sun or stars, how to make fire, how to find and kill game, how to find water and shelter, and how to slaughter and skin cows for food and hides.

When he was satisfied he'd seen and heard enough, Print returned to the ranch and saw that someone had burned the word Varner onto a slab of wood and nailed it to the gate of the new corral behind the log house. Who the devil . . . ? he wondered, then half-smiled. The boy, he thought. I'll bet Eli made that sign.

Vivian rushed out to greet him and he swung from his horse to take her in his arms. Home. He savored the word in his mind. It was good to be home. That night they built a campfire and after

supper the men, Ed, Josh, and George and Print
sat smoking and drinking coffee.

"I suspect we're ready to begin herding," Ed
said.

Print saw a movement beyond the circle of the
fire. "Come sit with us, boy," he said and waited
until Eli emerged from the shadows and joined
them.

"No," Print told Ed, "we'll wait till spring. The
rest of the summer we'll hire out where we can.
We got an awful lot to learn. More than I
thought."

"There's thousands of head of cattle out there
for the taking." Ed swept his arm around him.
"Unbranded mavericks. They say no one worked
the range during the War and there's the widows,
too, not able to herd their cows."

"We'll wait till spring," Print said. "There'll be
time enough then. Don't fret, Ed, we'll get our
share. And more."

Ed nodded and the men sat silent, smoking.
When Print got up and walked toward the house,
he heard footsteps behind him. He turned and
found Eli following him, taking long strides, his
eyes on the ground. Print waited and caught the
boy under the arms and lifted him high into the
air.

"What were you doing, boy?" he asked.

Eli looked away, reddening.

"Answer me, boy," Print said. "What were
you doing just now?"

"Trying to put my feet in your tracks."

Print lowered Eli to the ground, turned him in
the direction of the log cabin a quarter mile away
where the Swansons lived, and pushed him gently
homeward. Print saw a light appear in the Swan's
cabin and heard a woman's voice calling the boy's

name. Eli broke into a run and Print followed, walking rapidly.

Tamar was silhouetted in the cabin doorway with the lamplight haloing her red-gold hair. She shooed Eli past her into the cabin. Seeing Print, she walked to him, leaving the lightfall from the cabin door and coming into the darkness.

"You been gone a long time, Prentice," she said, stopping a few feet from him.

He said nothing, trying to read the expression on her shadowed face.

"I missed you, Prentice. Missed seeing you around. Did you like the sign we made for you?"

"Tammy!" The voice came from behind her. Looking over her head, Print saw George Swanson standing in the cabin doorway. "Tammy," he called again, "where are you?"

Tamar reached out and touched Print on the hand, turned from him and ran across the yard to the cabin. Print watched her until the door was pulled shut, then he walked slowly to the Varner ranch house, feeling the excitement building in him. He had thought it would take time, a lot of time, before he had Tamar. Now he wondered if he hadn't been wrong. Be patient, he warned himself, he didn't want any trouble with George Swanson. Not yet.

George was a failure if there ever was one. He'd failed in his father's haberdashery business in New York, he'd told Print, and Print had no doubt but what he'd fail here in Texas no matter what he turned his hand to. Print suspected he was a failure as a husband as well. The man didn't deserve a woman like Tamar.

If George wasn't around, Print thought, he'd have Tamar all to himself. If George Swanson just happened to get himself killed . . .

* * *

The next day Print Varner hired on with the
Goodnight outfit at Black Springs.

"Most of my hands are north on the Chisholm,"
the black-bearded Goodnight told him, "and the
god-damned rustlers are stealing me blind. If it
keeps up there won't be a CV-brand cow left on
the range. I don't mind losing a longhorn here
and there to the Indians but I'll be damned if I
can abide white men coming in and branding my
mavericks and running off my cattle and driving
them north to sell as their own."

Goodnight pointed west. "My range goes to the
bend in the Brazos north of Palo Pinto," he said.
"If you come across any damned rustlers on my
land, I want you to deal with them. Do you understand, Varner?"

"I understand," Print said.

At the end of his first week with Goodnight,
Print circled down to his own place on the Keechi,
spent the night, and after breakfast rode up the
hill through the timber. As he left the woods he
saw a wisp of smoke over the next rise. The fire
was on Goodnight's land, he knew.

Print topped the rise and looked around him.
He could no longer see the smoke. When he heard
a cow bawl in the brush of a nearby creekbed he
rode that way, staying on the high ground. He
pulled up on top of a hillock above the dry creek.
Below, his back to Print, a dark-outfitted man was
kicking dirt over his fire. A yearling cow lay hog-
tied a short way off and on the ground at the man's
feet Print saw a branding iron. A horse waited
nearby. Print slid his Winchester .44 from its
saddle scabbard and eased his horse down to the
creekbed, cradling the gun under one arm.

Hearing the clatter of loose rocks, the man

whirled, his hand held when he saw the muzzle of Print's Winchester aimed between his eyes.

"What are you about?" Print demanded.

The man grimaced in what might have been a tight-lipped smile. He had a two-day growth of black beard, his plains hat was old and battered.

"I'm Beatty," he said. "Jack Beatty. Everybody around here knows Jack Beatty."

Print looked again at the yearling and the branding iron. The yearling had been branded with Beatty's running iron, and iron that was able to copy most any brand.

"*I* don't know you," Print said. "And this is Goodnight's land all the way to the Brazos."

"You're mistaken, friend," Beatty said. "Goodnight might run a few of his cows here but it's not his land. This here's government land where I got as much right to be as anybody."

"You got no right to brand another man's cow."

"I'm branding one of my yearlings. As any fool can plainly see."

Print felt a rage rise in him, a blind unthinking anger. No man called Print Varner a fool and got away with it.

He studied Beattie's face and somehow, it wasn't Beattie's face anymore, but that face from long, long ago—the face of the man with the buggy whip, beating the young woman and the little boy. Now the anger coursed through him like a fever.

"Drop your belt to the ground," he ordered.

Beatty hesitated and for a moment Print thought the other man would make a move. "Don't," Print warned.

Beatty stared at Print as though trying to size the horseman up, then let his gunbelt drop. Print edged his horse to one side until he was near the tied yearling. He saw a freshly burned 8X on the cow's flank.

"My brand," Beatty said. "You're new in these parts, ain't you? I reckon you got a lot to learn."

Picturing Goodnight's CV and Beatty's 8X in his mind, Print saw how easily the one could be changed to the other. He smiled, looked down at Beatty, and then began to laugh. The other man smiled and after a moment he, too, laughed.

"Get on your horse," Print said.

Beatty stooped to retrieve his gun.

"No," Print told him. "Leave the gun lay. Get to your horse."

Beatty shrugged and, turning, started to walk to where his bay was hobbled in the brush. Print raised his Winchester and shot him in the upper back, the force of the bullet hurling Beatty forward. The man screamed as he sprawled face-first on the ground.

Print dismounted and walked to the fallen man, using the toe of his boot to turn him onto his side. Beatty moaned. Print knelt beside him and studied the wound. He'd meant to kill the bastard; with a grimace he realized he hadn't and that Beatty would live. The yearling bawled and all at once Print smiled.

"A man ought to be mighty careful who he calls a fool," he said.

Beatty's eyes blinked open and he stared up at Print. His lips moved but no words came.

After taking a coil of rope from his saddle, Print turned Beatty on his face and hog-tied him. By the time he was done, Beatty was unconscious. Taking his knife from its sheath, Print went to the yearling and thrust the blade into the steer's throat above the jawbone. Blood spurted out in a sudden fountain and then subsided to a slow trickle.

Print grunted. The sun was already high and hot, there was no shade, and he felt the sweat gather on his face. Well, there was no help for it. A man had to do what he had to do.

Using the knife, he cut a furrow down the center of the yearling's belly from jaw to anus.

6

THREE DAYS later Jason Briscoe rode along the north bank of the Brazos heading for the Goodnight ranch. He owed Charlie Goodnight a favor, owed him several favors, in fact, so he meant to tell him about the canyon of the Palo Bueno and the good grazing it promised.

He saw a horseman coming toward him making slow back and forth loops through the brush beside the river, cutting for sign. Jason reined in and hailed the man.

"Seen anybody back the way you came?" the other rider asked Jason as he drew beside him.

"Nary a soul. Comanche trouble?"

The cowboy shook his head. "Boy got hisself lost so all us Goodnight hands are out searching for him. The kid's been missing four days."

"He from a wagon passing through?"

"Naw. It would make more sense if he was. He lives up on the Keechi, six miles further on. One day he was there and the next day he was gone.

69

Can't understand it, he's thirteen, practically a man. Goodnight himself's tracking to the east, back along the way his folks came this spring. Charlie thought he might have taken a notion and headed for home. They're GTT's."

Jason knew he meant the boy's people had pulled up stakes in the East, perhaps posting a sign on their abandoned house, "Gone To Texas" —GTT.

"The boy afoot?" Jason asked.

"Naw, riding a gray mare name of Star, last he was seen. Horse probably broke her leg in a prairie-dog hole, but where's the boy? Eli's his name, a carrot-top, lived on the Varner place. Charlie Goodnight found his tracks east of the river but they went in circles and he lost them."

"I'll keep my eyes peeled," Jason said.

He rode on, intending to go to the Goodnight spread and wait for Charlie. He looked across the empty prairie. How long could a boy last out there on foot without food or water? 'Specially in this heat.

Jason swerved his horse to the northeast in the direction of the Keechi. When he saw the cabin he rode up the slope from the river. A girl with golden hair braided down her back came out of the door and stood with her hands on her hips watching him. Jason drew in his breath as he came close enough to see her high cheekbones and her green eyes. Even though she looked drawn and harried, she was about the prettiest girl Jason had ever seen.

He dismounted and touched the brim of his hat. "This Varner's place?" he asked.

"Swanson's. I'm Tamar Swanson. Varner's is another quarter-mile up the river."

"I hear a boy's missing from Varner's."

"No, from here. He's my brother. Eli. Have you any word?" The girl's anxiety touched Jason, made him want to comfort her, but he had to shake his head.

"I'd like to help," he told her.

"Then what are you doing here? Why aren't you out there?" She swept her arm around her to include the wooded hills and the prairie beyond.

"I wanted to start at the beginning," Jason said quietly, ignoring her outburst. "Why don't you simmer down and tell me what happened?"

"I'm real sorry," Tamar said, "for flaring up like that at you. *I* ought to be out there searching is what I meant. I can't abide sitting here doing nothing while Eli's lost, maybe hurt or dying."

"This is where you ought to be."

"A woman's meant to wait, is that what you mean?" Her voice rose in anger, her eyes flashed.

Jason looked down at her standing in front of him with her fists clenched at her sides, thinking she couldn't be much more than fourteen herself, her body rounded yet still boylike with only the first hint of a bosom. He smiled.

"Don't laugh at me," Tamar cried out. She shook her head impatiently. "You're all the same."

"Easy," Jason told her. "What I meant was that someone has to stay here. In case the boy finds his way home on his own."

She turned away from him and walked to the cabin door, keeping her face averted as she leaned with one arm on the rough-hewn logs. Jason went to her and touched her arm gently and when she didn't shy away he took her by the shoulders and turned her to face him. Seeing the tears in her eyes he took her in his arms and drew her against his chest, feeling her body shaking with sobs. Pulling a bandana from his pocket, he dried her tears and then held her away from him. Again he smiled.

"I'm smiling because it's such a pleasure to look at you," he said. "You're an awfully pretty girl. You'll grow up to be a mighty beautiful woman."

"I am a woman." Her voice was low and husky the anger seemed to have drained from her. "What's your name?" she asked after a moment.

"Jason Briscoe. I've a spread northwest of here. I'm stopping by on my way east to visit with Charlie Goodnight. I'm traveling to New York."

"I'm a York Stater," Tamar said, "born and raised in a little town on the Barge Canal. Canajoharie. Why are you bound for New York, Mr. Briscoe?"

"Do you always ask so many questions?"

"Yes, if there're answers I want to know. What's wrong with that?"

"Where I come from men don't ask questions any more than they have to. Too often the answers they get aren't to their liking." He let his hands fall from her shoulders. "I'm heading east to find me a wife."

"Oh," she said, staring at him. He thought he'd never seen eyes the color of hers before.

"I wouldn't think a man would have to travel so far to find himself a wife," Tamar said. "Know what I think? Men never can put their finger on what they want and even when they're lucky enough to get it they don't appreciate what they've got." She shook her head. "Why are we standing here passing the time of day when Eli's lost out there? Come inside, Mr. Briscoe, and I'll give you a cup of coffee. Then you can go."

When they were seated at the table with a steaming pot between them, Jason said, "Tell me about the day you last laid eyes on your brother."

"Nothing special happened. Eli was here working around the place in the morning. He rode east beyond the river after he'd finished his chores and he never came home." She brushed a stray wisp of hair from her forhead. "He's never done this before. What I mean is that some of the men think he might have lit out for the East, heading back to where we came from, but that's nonsense. There's nothing for him in Canajoharie. I'm here. And Prentice is here."

"Prentice?"

"Print Varner, they call him. Eli worships the ground Print walks on. Eli's the age where he would."

"And where's this Print?"

"Out searching like the others. I haven't seen him since . . ." Tamar frowned, standing and walking slowly to the door. Jason came up behind her and saw that she was staring into the woods behind the cabin.

"Since when?"

"Since the morning Eli disappeared. I was carrying water from the river and I saw Prentice ride up the hill and into the trees. I watched him till he was clean out of sight." She turned to Jason, her eyes alight. "Eli must of seen him, seen him from across the river and followed him. He didn't head east like they think, he rode west after Prentice. I know it now, I can feel it in my bones."

"I'll ride that way and take a look."

"I'll go with you," Tamar said.

"No, I mean to cut for sign. I work best alone."

"I'm going with you. Eli's my brother, not yours, and I can sit a horse as good as you or any other man." She swung away from him and went out the door, her two braids whipping to one side, and Jason saw she was headed for a small corral behind the cabin. He ran after her, grabbed her roughly by the shoulder and spun her around.

"You need a good spanking," he told her.

"You wouldn't dare." She faced him, hands on hips, head tilted up, a challenge in her green eyes.

He stepped quickly to one side of her, grasped her about the waist and pulled her down across his upraised knee. He slapped her buttocks, hard, his blow softened by her skirt. She squirmed against him, turning so she stared up at him.

He couldn't read the look in her eyes, the meaning of the slight curling of her mouth. Anger? Rage? Fear? None of those. He raised his hand again but before he could bring it down on her buttocks she twisted free, shoving him backwards while thrusting her leg behind his.

Caught unaware, Jason tumbled onto the ground. Before he could recover, Tamar sprang at him, her fingernails clawing at his face. He grasped her wrists, wrestling her away until he felt her go limp. When he released her she came for him with clenched fists and he pushed himself along the ground away from her. Tamar reached toward him, her hand curving behind his head and she drew him to her, kissing him, holding him.

She drew back, shaking her head, and he could hear her rapid breathing as she scrambled to her feet and began brushing herself off. Jason, still lying on his side, rested his head on one hand and watched her.

"Well," she asked, "are you just going to lie there for the rest of the day?"

"I go looking for Eli alone or I don't reckon I'll go at all."

Tamar drew in her breath and he could see the anger in her eyes. All at once her shoulders slumped. "You win, Mr. Briscoe," she said. "For now," she added under her breath.

Jason walked to his horse and mounted, riding back to where she stood near the back of the cabin. Tamar's face was dirty, wisps of damp hair lay on her forehead, and her calico dress was streaked. As he stared down at her he suddenly felt the quickened beating of his heart. How pretty she looked! All at once Jason frowned.

"Are you a married woman?" he asked. The thought hadn't occurred to him before.

"Yes," she said, staring up at him with the sunlight glistening from her eyes.

"You don't wear a wedding band."

"Because I don't choose to."

Jason nodded, not being able to imagine her doing anything she didn't have a mind to do. She was a hellion, Tamar was, even at her age. What will she be like when she grows a bit? he wondered. He pitied the man who was married to her. *He'd* never want a wife the likes of Tamar, Jason told himself. He meant to marry a lady.

Why then, Jason asked himself, had he felt a stab of disappointment when she'd told him she was married?

"Come with me," he told her, "and show me where you last saw this man Print."

Tamar walked beside his horse to the first of the trees where she stopped to point up the hill along an animal trail, "He rode that way, best I can remember," she said.

Jason touched his hand to his hat and spurred his horse up the slope. He heard Tamar call and he turned to see her wave to him.

"Find him," she called to Jason. "Find Eli." She watched him until he was out of sight among the trees.

Walking slowly to the cabin, Tamar smiled. He'll be back, she told herself. He'll find Eli and he'll be back. She said his name half aloud, "Jason Briscoe," liking the sound of it. Still smiling, she idly kicked a pebble. Following the pebble with her eyes as it bounced over the hard earth, she saw a pair of boots.

Tamar looked up and gasped. Print Varner stood slouched against the corner of the cabin staring at her.

"You sure did give me a start." She faced him trying to decipher his faint smile. Tamar smiled at him, hesitant and unsure.

"What are you doing back here?" she asked.

Print's smile broadened and he began to laugh, throwing his head back. Fear knifed up through Tamar's body.

"No," she said.

She turned and ran toward the corral, hearing Print's pounding steps behind her, and she looked over her shoulder just as he caught her around the waist. He lifted her onto his shoulder and carried her back to the cabin.

7

JASON BRISCOE knelt beside the hoofprints. There were two sets, both heading west and both almost a week old. He remounted and, leaving the trees behind, looped back and forth searching for sign. He found none. The horses had left the timbers and disappeared on the open prairie.

He widened his sweeps, riding north to south and then south to north and still he found nothing, no prints, no tell-tale broken twigs on the low-lying brush, no horse droppings, nothing. He rode on under the blazing sun, patient and careful, trying to let nothing escape his glance.

Jason raised his head and sniffed the wind coming out of the north, recognized the stench as the reek of putrefying flesh. Eli? Yet the air smelled of rotting animal flesh, not human.

He spurred his horse in the direction of the smell. As he crested a hill, three vultures rose from the ground ahead of him with a great flapping of wings. Jason sighed with relief as he saw the remains of a cow in the creekbed below him, and then frowned when he realized that the cow had been butchered and skinned some days before. Shaking his head at the waste, he rode into the draw. Off to his left, partly concealed by boulders, he saw the hide. Puzzled, he dismounted and climbed between the boulders and looked down.

He drew in his breath in horror. The hide had been wrapped tightly about a man's body. Only the man's face was visible, the eyes bulging, the mouth twisted in a death's-head grimace of pain.

The skin, drying in the sun, had contracted, crushing the man to death. The Spanish "Death of the Skins." Jason had heard of the torture, though he had never seen it used. He shuddered and looked away.

Around the long-dead fire he found signs of two men but no trace of the boy. He picked a running iron from the ground, studied it and tossed it to one side. Someone, Print perhaps, had found this man rustling cattle and killed him, murdered him.

Or had it been the other way around? Was this Print he had found crushed in the cowhide? Unlikely, what with the iron left behind, unless Print was the rustler. But what did this dead man have to do with the missing boy, with Eli? There must be a connection but what the link was he couldn't fathom.

Jason rode on westward with the questions nagging at him. When no answers came, he thrust thoughts of the murdered man from his mind and concentrated on his search. The reason for Eli's disappearance came second; finding him was the important thing.

The sun was low in the west when he found the next hoofprint. He knelt and examined it. No, this wasn't one of the horses from the creekbed though it matched a print he'd found in the timbers. Probably Eli's then. The horse had been heading into the setting sun.

Jason followed the tracks until it was too dark to see. When he made camp he built a larger fire than necessary, hoping the boy might sight the glow of the flames and follow the beacon to his camp. Jason woke in the night to see the firelight glinting from a circle of animal eyes watching him from the surrounding darkness. Eli, though, didn't come.

Jason was up before dawn, found water, and rode on. He ate nothing. He'd wait before he ate, he told himself, wait and see what developed. He knew he should have stocked up at the Swanson's but it made little difference. After the first forty-eight hours, he'd discovered, his craving for food lessened.

He found a creek, drank his fill, and rode on, the trail growing fresher, the rider in front of him still heading west for the most part though lately his route had wavered as though the rider was unsure of his direction.

The following day the track swerved to the north, swinging around in an arc to head back the way it had come. Jason spotted the horse at midday, a riderless grey standing with its head down in the shadow of a wind-swept shelf of rock. He spurred his horse ahead and stopped beside the grey, swinging to the ground and looping his reins on a mesquite bush. The boy lay on his back in the rock's shadow with his face up and his eyes closed. Jason's first thought was that the boy was dead.

Print carried Tamar into the Swanson cabin and threw her on the bunk built against the far wall. He returned to the door, shut it and secured it by sliding the wooden crossbar into place. Taking off his gunbelt, he draped belt and guns over a peg on the wall.

Tamar's gaze followed him as he came toward her. "Don't touch me," she told him.

"I saw you rolling around in the dirt a few minutes ago with whoever the hell that was," Print said. "I saw you kissing him. You've been teasing me ever since I saved your life when I found you on the prairie and brought you here. The time for teasing's over."

Tamar crouched on the far side of the bunk. Thinking she was afraid, Print smiled. As he neared her, she lunged from the bunk and scrambled across the room, snatching a butcher knife from a rack on the kitchen wall. She faced him across the table, the knife raised. Print eyed her warily, shifting a bench to one side as he edged around the table after her. Tamar kept her distance, circling as he circled, keeping the table between them.

Print brought his foot up, put the sole of his boot on the table edge and shoved. The table crashed down, striking Tamar's shin and scattering tin plates and cups onto the wooden floor. Print leaped over the fallen table and Tamar sprang to one side. His hand grasped her wrist and he twisted her arm, sending the knife clattering to the floor. He wrenched her arm behind her back and pushed upward until Tamar screamed in pain. Holding her arm behind her back, Print shoved her to the bunk and pushed her face down on the blanket.

Still gripping her arm, he said, "Are you ready to do what I tell you?"

"Go to hell," Tamar told him.

He pushed up on her arm and again she screamed.

"Are you?" he demanded.

Tamar said nothing, biting her lip to keep from crying out. Print seized her other arm and thrust it behind her.

"Are you?" he asked again.

"Yes," she said through clenched teeth.

Print released her arms, grabbed her braids and yanked Tamar from the bed, slamming her against the cabin wall.

"You son-of-a-bitching bastard," she said.

"Take off your clothes," he told her.

Tamar stared at him. He slapped her, first with his palm and again with the back of his hand. Her face whitened, then red flooded into the welts on her cheek.

"Do as I say," he told her.

"George will . . ."

Print laughed. "George," he repeated scornfully. "If he finds out, if you tell him, you know damn well what will happen. He'll come after me and I'll kill him. You know I will."

She lowered her head as though in assent. Print reached for her, bunching the front of her dress in his fist, pulling her to him until her face was inches from his. He saw her draw in her breath and let it out in what he read as a sigh of surrender.

"Let go," Tamar said resignedly.

He dropped his hand and stood back and watched as her fingers went to the button at the neck of her dress. She twisted the button and it came free, revealing a vee of pale white skin. One by one she undid the buttons, shrugged her arms from the sleeves and stepped out of the dress. She reached down, taking the hem of her chemise and drawing the thin white cloth over her head.

Print stared at her tightly bound breasts. "George made you do that?" he asked.

Tamar nodded and, reaching behind her, she loosened and unwrapped the binding until she stood naked with her hands crossed over her sex, her white breasts exposed.

"Damn but you're a beauty," he said, smiling as he hastily pulled his shirt over his head to reveal his hairy chest. He undid the buckle of his pants, pushed them down, watching her, his eyes seemingly fascinated by her breasts with their pink nipples.

Suddenly Tamar ran to the door but Print was ready for her. Holding his trousers with one hand, he caught her around the waist with the other and carried her to the bunk. Keeping her down with one hand, he yanked off his boots and kicked his trousers to one side. Naked, he stood over her.

He grasped both of Tamar's wrists in one of his hands, raising her arms high above her head. Lying on the bunk beside her, he used his other hand to force his way between her thighs. Print paused, remembering the urgency of his desire on his first night with Vivian at Four Oaks and the way he had hurried her when she wasn't ready. It won't be that way with Tamar, he vowed, and so, despite his growing need, he forced himself to move slowly.

His fingers sought and found her damp and slippery sex and he pushed his fingertips inside, stroking her, caressing between the lips of her sex as he felt her struggle to free herself from him. She tried to turn away but he was too strong and the more she fought the more her breasts slid against his bared chest, her nipples rubbing against him, fanning his desire.

He heard her breathing come quick and heavy,

felt her struggles change to a writhing, heard her moan. Still holding her wrists, the fingers of his other hand caressed her between her legs, moving rhythmically up and down, up and down.

"Prentice," she gasped. "Prentice, don't. Please don't force me."

He smiled, his face to her neck—he had not kissed her, fearful of her teeth. His tongue trailed down from her throat to her breasts and he took one in his mouth, holding the nipple between his teeth, circling it with his tongue while at the same time stroking her sex with his fingers.

"Prentice," she said. "Print."

His lips left her breast and he looked up to see her head moving slowly from side to side, her eyes closed. He released her wrists and lowered his hand to the nape of her neck, drawing her to him until his mouth covered hers.

Print parted her lips with his tongue and his tongue slid into her mouth, entwining with hers as, at the same time, he spread her legs, his hot distended sex sliding between her legs and entering her, plunging deep inside her. Tamar groaned, her mouth open to his, her hands clutching his shoulders so hard that her nails dug into his flesh.

He slid his sex up and out of her body, holding himself poised above her with the tip of his penis at the lips of her sex. She moaned and he felt a trembling begin in her legs and run through her body until she was quivering uncontrollably. Her legs came up and circled him, forcing him inside her again. He plunged into her while her body trembled beneath him as she came again and again.

The excitement built in him, rising higher and higher until he could no longer hold back and he came inside her, thrusting into her as deeply as he could while her legs clutched him to her. She shuddered against him. Sated, he lay unmoving on top of her but it was many minutes before her trembling stopped. When it did she slid from under him and he rolled onto his back, limp. He glanced across at Tamar and saw her lying with her eyes closed, her hands clasped between her legs while her breasts rose and fell as she breathed in short quick gasps.

Tamar opened her eyes and looked at him with a mocking smile on her face. She pushed herself up and knelt beside him on the bed with her hands on her thighs.

"Is that all, Print?" she asked. "I expected more from you than that. Can't you finish what you start? Is that all the man you are?"

Dumbfounded, he stared at her.

Tamar's hand trailed along his legs and her fingers fondled his penis. Releasing him, she reached behind her, undoing her braids and shaking her head as her golden hair fell free, bending forward so her hair cascaded onto his chest as her hand again found his sex, teasing him. He felt the excitement growing, felt himself harden.

"That's better, Print," she said. With her hand still holding him lightly, she lay on her back beside him.

"All right, Print," she taunted, "show me what kind of a man you are."

Cursing, he rose to his knees, spread her thighs and, in a fury, thrust himself into her, feeling her quiver against him as her legs and arms enfolded him and her body rose to meet his, thrust for thrust.

8

JASON SHOOK the boy by the shoulder and Eli opened his eyes.

"Are you all right, son?" Jason asked.

Eli nodded. "I'm hungry. And thirsty." The boy's face was drawn, his neck was burned a deep red and his eyes looked larger than normal, but he was alert and coherent.

Jason went to his saddlebag and returned with beef jerky and a canteen of water. "Drink slow," he said to the boy. "Drink real slow."

"You were lucky," Jason told the boy as he ate and drank. "I knew a soldier during the War out on the Staked Plain who was lost no longer than you. He'd gone clean loco by the time we found him. Course he wasn't a Texan, came from the interior, Ohio or somewheres like that."

"I had food with me. And the streams were running and I ate berries from along the creeks." Eli looked shyly at Jason. "I'm intending to be a scout."

"Maybe you will be. Course you can't allow yourself to go around getting lost like you did if you're a scout. What happened?"

Eli looked away so Jason couldn't see his eyes. "I was riding and not paying mind to what I was doing and pretty soon I didn't know where I was or how to get back home."

Jason was about to say that surely he knew enough to tell east from west; he must have ridden several days before he changed his mind and headed back. For whatever reason, the boy was clouding his story. Jason said nothing, though, putting his hand on Eli's shoulder. "Can you ride?" he asked.

"Course I can ride."

Eli pushed himself to his feet and walked slowly, determinedly to his horse. When he tried to mount the grey he swayed and Jason grasped the boy's boot in his hand and boosted him into the saddle. Eli held on to the horn for a moment before he lifted the reins.

"Good boy," Jason said. "We'll find us some water for the horses before we do anything else. Looks to me like we'll come on a creek if we head over that way." He nodded across the prairie.

They rode slowly, keeping their horses to a walk, and after a mile came to clumps of mesquite and a few miles farther on to a creek that had cut a deep meandering swath in the earth.

"How did you know there'd be water here?" Eli asked. "I had to ride blind till I came on a creek."

"Some men will tell you they can smell water," Jason said as he stooped to fill their canteens, "but I never took much stock in that. I could never smell water though of course longhorns can. I've known them critters to smell a creek from ten or fifteen miles away and then if they're thirsty it's the very devil to hold them from stampeding.

"It was the mesquite told me this time," Jason said. " 'Bout the only animal that eats the mesquite out here is the wild mustang and after the seed soaks up awhile in the mustang's bowels and gets dropped it starts to grow more often than not. Now mustangs seldom ever graze far from water, maybe three miles at most when they have the country to themselves. So when I see mesquite bushes in open country I know water's within three miles."

"I never heard tell of that," Eli said, staring at Jason with wide eyes.

"As I remember, it was Charlie Goodnight first told me. He was a great scout with the Rangers, Charlie was. None better."

They mounted and followed the creek eastward. A great beating thunder filled the air ahead of them and with a roar thousands of pigeons rose and darkened the cloudless sky.

"Birds can lead you to water, too," Jason said. "In the evening you can follow the course of the doves when they go in the breaks to water. Or you can watch for the dirt-dauber, the mud swallow some calls it. He flies low and if his mouth has mud in it you know he's coming straight from water and if his mouth is empty he's most likely going straight to it."

"Did Charlie Goodnight tell you that, too?"

Jason smiled. "Most of what I know I didn't learn by listening but by watching. When there wasn't nothing much to do and the other cow-hands would spend their time sitting around the campfire smoking and spinning yarns and whittling, I'd go out on the prairie and watch the birds and the animals and learn their ways.

Mustangs, now, water daily while antelopes sometimes go for weeks and months without any water at all."

"When I got thirsty I sucked on a pebble," Eli said.

"That helps. A bullet is better and if you take and peel a prickly pear that's the best of all."

"Maybe when we get back to the Keechi you could stay with us," Eli said. "With me and my sister Tamar and George, and you could teach me how to be a scout."

"I'm mighty pleased to have you ask me, Eli, but I can't. I'm traveling on east soon's I can 'cause I have to get back to my spread. I'm intending to trail a herd to the railroad up in Kansas come next spring."

"We came from the East, from New York, along the Mohawk."

"I'm heading for New York City," Jason said.

"You won't cotton to it, there's too many people and too much noise and smoke and everybody milling around like spooked steers."

"I'm going to the City to find me a wife."

"If it weren't for George, you could stay here and marry my sister Tamar."

Jason glanced quickly at Eli for the boy's words almost echoed his thoughts. "Your sister's a real spunky little girl," he said. "I liked her."

Jason closed his eyes and pictured the woman he meant to find in New York. Her hair would be the yellow of sunflowers, her eyes blue as a rain-washed sky. She'd be tall and elegant and know how to read and write. Maybe she'd be a school-marm, in fact, though she'd like to dance and have a good time. He pictured her waltzing with her bare arms and shoulders glowing in the gaslight.

He smiled to himself. You're a fool, Jason Briscoe, a woman like that wouldn't look at you twice, let alone once. You're a big clumsy cowhand who doesn't rightly know how to navigate once you're off your horse. What would a woman like that want with you?

I've got twenty thousand dollars left from selling the beeves, Jason reminded himself.

So you're looking for a woman who'll marry you for a bit of gold, is that it? She'd leave you, that kind would, as soon as she laid eyes on a man with twenty-one thousand. You're a fool. You'd do better to stay where you are, where you belong, in Texas among your own kind. What good will knowing how to brand a cow or being able to find water do you in New York City?

Damn, he thought, I can do whatever I set my mind to. If I mean to marry a lady, then it's a lady I'll marry. He nodded his head vigorously.

Opening his eyes, he saw that Eli was staring at him.

"You were talking to yourself," the boy said.

"When you're out on the Plains alone as much as me you get into the habit of conversing with yourself. When I get bored with what I got to say, I read. Once I read the history of Rome while I was in the saddle."

"The history of Rome? Rome in Italy?" There was disbelief in Eli's voice.

"I'll tell you how that happened. You may think it unlikely, but it was because of the Comanches. The Indians raided the settlements around Fort Belknap and when I rode out the next day I found the body of Jamie Cameron. He'd been scalped and his wife and daughter had been carried off. I rode on to old Moses Lassiter's place and he was dead and his wife, too, but they hadn't been scalped."

"Why not?" Eli asked.

"Well, they were Negroes and the Comanches never scalp black men. They'll kill them soon as not but never scalp them, I can't rightly say why. Well, sir, I located the Comanches' trail and about four of us set out after them and we had a skirmish near a woods and one of the Indians was about to shoot an arrow into me when I shot him in the arm. He got away, not that it did him much good 'cause he lost his shield and when a Comanche loses his shield he has to leave the tribe, they mean that much to them. Well, we followed them Indians for four days till they joined a bigger war party, maybe a hundred or so braves, and there were only four of us so we gave it up and came home, being outnumbered like that."

They rode in silence for a time. "What about you reading the history of Rome?" Eli asked.

"I was getting to that. Well, sir, like I say, that Comanche had lost his shield and I took it back to the ranch and just out of idle curiosity I took it apart. They make their shields by bending a piece of wood and stretching a buffalo hide over it, heating the hide in the fire to tauten it. Inside the hide they put whatever they can lay their hands on to stop arrows or bullets. Now it's a fact that thick paper stops bullets about as good as anything and inside this Comanche shield what did I find but a book all split into parts. It was the history of the rise and fall of the Roman Empire, so for the next two months while I was riding herd I read the history of Rome."

Eli looked at Jason with his mouth slightly open.

"Now that's God's own truth," Jason said. "Texans are accused of bragging and once in a great while we do stretch the blanket a mite, but on the other side of the coin we're prone to admit it when we're wrong. I was wrong about fighting the Indians in the winter. I told Custer it wouldn't work and Jim Bridger said the same but Custer and old Phil Sheridan went ahead anyway and gave the Kiowas and the Cheyennes and the Arapahoes a licking in spite of the snow and cold. That's the time I was scouting with Carleton in Comanche country."

Jason spurred his horse ahead. "We'd best make tracks," he said. "I'd like to reach the Brazos by nightfall."

They rode on at a trail lope, the man and the boy, as the sun lowered in the west behind them, the man talking, the boy listening and nodding, until, with the sun throwing their shadows far across the prairie ahead of them, they came to the river and made camp for the night.

In the morning Jason led the way to the north, heading for the Keechi. When he came in sight of the Cross Timbers, he rode in the direction of the creekbed where he'd found the body of the man wrapped in the cowhide. Eli lagged and Jason had to motion to him, hurrying him on. At last the boy stopped and would go no farther.

"What's troubling you, son?" Jason asked after he rode back.

Eli shook his head, clamping his mouth tightly shut.

"Don't go circling around things," Jason said. "Meeting them head on has always been my way."

Eli stared at him, his mouth twitching, and Jason saw that the boy was close to tears.

"Tell me about it," Jason said.

Eli drew in his breath and let it out with a sigh. All at once his words were tumbling over each other. "I rode out following behind Mr. Varner and I came to the hill and saw him in the draw with this blackbearded cowhand. Mr. Varner shot him. Shot him in the back. It wasn't right. It wasn't fair. He didn't give him a chance."

"The man was a rustler, like as not."

"Makes no matter. Mr. Varner shouldn't of shot him in the back. And then he skinned that yearling and I saw he was going to wrap him in the hide and him still alive. I didn't know why he was doing it but I didn't want to find out so I made tracks and headed west, intending to ride to the frontier. When I got there I don't know what I was going to do, but I wasn't about to stay around Mr. Varner no more and then I did get lost on the prairie like I told you."

Jason gripped the boy's shoulder. "Texas is just like everyplace else," he said, "only more so. There's good men and bad. And weak men and brave men and cowards. And men who're mixtures of good and bad and weak and strong, like most of us. The worst ones are those that are brave and bad together and maybe this Print Varner's like that or maybe there's more to the killing than you or I know. There's usually more to a story than you figure, surprises you aren't ready for, and when you can you got to wait until all the twists and turns are right out there in the open for you to study before you make up your mind as to the right or wrong."

"Print shouldn't of shot him in the back. He never gave him a fighting chance."

Jason said nothing, couldn't think of what more to say. The boy was dead right, he'd never shot a man in the back and didn't ever intend to. And the business with the hide was just plain lowdown, he couldn't find any excuse for that. Jason reined his horse around, circled the draw, and with Eli beside him entered the trees and rode down the slope of the Keechi Valley to the cleared land where the Swanson cabin stood.

Tamar ran to meet them, laughing and crying when she saw Eli. A fair-haired man stood at the cabin door, watching. Like as not her husband, George, Jason thought. Tamar walked beside her brother's horse with her arms around Eli's leg and when he dismounted she began hugging and kissing him. Eli looked at Jason, raising his eyebrows, looking kind of exasperated and proud at the same time.

"Tamar can fight like a wildcat," he told Jason, "when someone riles her." Meaning, Jason knew, that his sister didn't spend all her time hugging and kissing.

"I can believe you," Jason said.

Tamar released Eli and looked up at Jason. "How can I ever thank you?" she asked.

"I reckon the boy would have found his way home by himself if he'd had the time."

"We can't ever repay you," Tamar said.

She looked different, Jason realized, though he couldn't put his finger on the difference at first. Then he saw that her red-gold hair was unbraided and fell loose around her shoulders and her breasts strained against the fabric of her dress. She must have had them bound when he first saw her. Yet the change was more in her face, in her green eyes and something about the set of her mouth. She seemed older, more a woman.

"That's right, never." George Swanson had come up behind Tamar and put his hands on her shoulders. "We're mighty grateful to you for finding the boy."

"I'll ride on to the Varner place," Jason said, "and let them know the boy's home. I sort of want to meet this Print Varner."

"Come back this way," Tamar said, "and stop and have supper with us."

"I thank you, but I can't. I'm riding on to Goodnight's and then I'm heading east."

Jason swung his horse away from the cabin and rode down the slope in the direction of the river. He heard his name and turned in the saddle and saw that Eli had run after him.

"Jason," the boy shouted. "Jason, come back."

"I will," Jason told him. "Someday." He looked past the boy and saw Tamar watching him; George still held her by the shoulders. Jason turned and headed up the river.

He reined in a hundred feet shy of Varner's log house. "Varner!" he called.

A tall cowhand with a grizzled beard partly covering a scar on his left cheek came from behind the house.

"Print Varner?" Jason asked.

The man looked Jason up and down. "I'll get him," he said.

Jason sat his horse, waiting, and in a few minutes Print came out of the house and walked to him.

"You wanted me?" Print asked.

"I came to tell you the boy's been found. He's back at Swanson's place."

"I just now rode in from looking for him," Print said. "I thought sure he was a goner." He showed no emotion.

"The boy saw what you did to that rustler in the draw west of here. The man you wrapped in the skin."

"You're loco. I don't know what you're talking about."

"The tracks in the draw matched your tracks on the hill back of Swansons'. And the boy saw you."

"Nobody can prove nothing," Print said.

"I don't care about proving or not proving. Whatever I might think, one less rustler in these parts is all to the good. The boy saw you, that's what I'm telling you, Varner. That's why he ran off and got himself lost and near died in the bargain."

"Eli's got to learn what the world's like sooner or later. Better it be sooner."

"What you did isn't what the world's like, Varner. Leastways, it shouldn't be."

"What business is it of yours? Who are you?"

"Jason Briscoe; my spread's northwest of here. It's my business 'cause I don't want that boy hurt. He'll have enough hurts to get over later on when he's full-growed. I don't want his sister hurt, either."

"Tamar?" The way Print said her name made Jason look sharply at him. "Tamar sure as hell ain't no business of yours."

"If you hurt that boy more than you have already," Jason said, "I'll come back and I swear to God I'll kill you."

Print's eyes widened slightly and he smiled. "You talk mighty big," he said.

The two men's eyes locked and held until Jason swung his horse away and rode off. He could sense Print watching him and he tensed, half expecting to feel the slam of a bullet in his back. He fought off the urge to look behind him, stifled the urge to hurry his horse.

He rode slowly into the trees and only then did he glance over his shoulder. Print stood where he had left him, his hand on the butt of his pistol, watching him. Jason shrugged and rode on, heading for the Goodnight ranch.

He had gone perhaps a mile when he heard

hoofbeats behind him. Still thinking of Print, he pulled his horse into the trees and waited. The other rider came along the trail toward him and suddenly Jason drew in his breath in surprise.

Tamar. He came out onto the trail and she reined in beside him. Her face was flushed and before she spoke she had to wait to catch her breath.

"Take us with you," she said.

Jason stared at her in astonishment.

"Me and Eli. Take me and Eli with you."

"Aren't you forgetting someone? What about your husband?"

"It's high time he learned to look after himself."

She spoke of George Swanson, Jason noticed, as though he were a child. "No," he said, "it wouldn't be right."

"I've never begged nobody for nothing." She reached out and touched his sleeve. "I'm begging you now. Take us with you. I'm afraid."

All at once he made the conection. "Of Print Varner?" he asked.

"Yes, of Print."

"Print won't hurt the boy."

She shook her head. "Not Print and Eli. I'm scared of me and Print. Of what I might do because of Print, for Print. I know you don't understand and I don't rightly understand myself. I'm afraid. Didn't you ever come up against something you didn't understand but you knew was wrong yet you couldn't do nothing about it? Nothing except run away?"

"I didn't take you for a woman who ran away."

"I never ran away from anybody or anything in my life. Not before this. Now I want to run, to hide. I know I can't hide from myself but I'd be all right with you. I got the feeling inside of me. In here." She laid her hand on her breast. "Take me with you."

He was tempted. God but he was tempted. Yet he couldn't take another man's wife. Besides, this wasn't the kind of woman he wanted and he knew that if she came with him she'd end up as his woman; he didn't want to spend the rest of his life fighting and brawling. He was tempted, though, by God he was.

"No," he said flatly.

She drew her horse close to his and stared into his face. Without warning she struck him across the cheek so his face jerked away.

"God damn you to hell, Jason Briscoe," she said. She swung her horse around and without another word rode off in the direction of the Varner place.

Jason stared at Tamar riding away from him. He almost spurred his horse after her, came within a hair's-breadth of following her. Don't be a fool, he warned himself. That woman's trouble, trouble for her husband, for Print Varner, and for anyone else unlucky enough to want her. He wanted her, Jason knew, and cursed himself because of it.

He listened to the hoofbeats of Tamar's horse until he could no longer hear them. He wanted her and he couldn't have her and he was going to leave it at that. With a sigh he urged his horse on toward Goodnight's.

9

JASON WALKED slowly along 34th Street with the crowds pushing past him, making him feel as though he was caught in the middle of a buffalo stampede. He sought shelter in a bookstore where he walked up and down long rows staring at the books before finally selecting a new volume from a stack on a table near the door.

He began to read and was soon engrossed in the adventures of a bootblack from the back alleys of New York.

"That's by a new author who's going to make a name for himself, mark my words."

Jason looked up and saw the balding proprietor nodding at the book in his hand. Jason glanced at the cover: "Ragged Dick; or Street Life in New York," by Horatio Alger, Jr.

"A boy I know back home in Texas would sure enjoy reading it," he said.

He paid for the book and, back in his hotel room, finished reading it. When he had turned the last page, Jason nodded to himself. Now that was a real interesting story, he thought, with a moral—hard work and honesty are rewarded—and a happy ending to leave you feeling good. He packed the book in his suitcase.

The next morning Jason presented himself at the Wall Street office of the Manhattan Trust and Savings with a letter of introduction from his Kansas City bank in his hand. He was ushered into the thickly carpeted office of a vice-president.

"And what may I do for you, Mr. Briscoe?" Harvey Von Wantoch asked. "A loan, perhaps? I have English clients who are extremely interested in entering the cattle business. Only last week I was talking to Sir Charles Montgomery . . ."

"No, sir," Jason said. "I didn't come to New York for money, I came to find me a wife."

"A wife?" Von Wantoch raised his eyebrows.

"Yes, sir," Jason said.

Von Wantoch's face quickly became impassive again. He opened a humidor on his desk and offered a cigar to Jason. The two men lit up and sat for a moment watching the smoke rise toward the room's high ceiling.

"Raising money wouldn't have been a problem." Von Wantoch steepled his hands on the desk in front of him. "A wife's another matter entirely. Why don't you tell me what you have in mind."

"I'll lay my cards on the table." Jason leaned forward. "I have twenty thousand dollars, cash money, in the bank in Kansas City, the one that gave me the letter. I've never been sick a day in my life if you don't count the time I took an arrow in my right leg on the Staked Plain. I own a ranch in Pinto County, Texas. I've been known to take a drink and sit down to an occasional hand of poker but I'm a sober man and I'm not a gambler. I've come to the time in my life where I need a wife and I've come here to find one. I came to New York because I mean to marry a lady."

"I see." Von Wantoch tapped the ash from his cigar into a tray shaped like a railroad coal car. "You have a higher opinion of New York women than many men do. Aren't there any suitable women in Texas?"

"They're as scarce as peace-loving Comanches." When he saw Von Wantoch's puzzled stare, Jason added, "And peace-loving Comanches are hard to find."

"I would suppose they were. How long do you intend to be in New York, Mr. Briscoe?"

"I'd be obliged if you'd call me Jason. Two months, Harvey."

"Only two months?"

- "I have to get back to Texas for the spring round-up. That's when we brand and castrate the cattle so's to have them ready for the drive north."

"I see. You've presented me with a unique problem, Mr. Briscoe. Pardon me. Jason." He looked past Jason and out the window at the horse-drawn cabs hurrying past on the street. "I'll discuss your problem tonight with my wife. I can tell you this, though, Jason. The old money in New York marries its own kind, or else the young heiresses sail to Europe looking for a title, a count or a prince. The new money first tries to marry into the old money and ends up marrying its own kind. As you can see, that doesn't leave much in the way of suitable marital prospects for you."

"I don't think I'm making myself clear, Harvey. When I said I wanted to marry a lady I didn't mean she had to have money; she just has to be a lady. She might be right off the boat from Europe or she might be a schoolmarm or whatever women are in the city."

"Maybe you'd better tell me exactly what you do mean by a lady, Jason."

"Well, to me a lady's a woman who's interested in books and probably understands about history and politics, a woman who won't take sass from nobody, me included, and will stand up to you and tell you what she thinks come hell or high water. She . . ." Jason paused, realizing that once he'd got past the books and politics he'd started describing Tamar. He shook his head impatiently. "She's somebody," he went on more slowly, "who wouldn't ever consider marrying a cowhand and leaving the city to live where men spend their time castrating beeves."

"Since you're a cowhand or the next thing to it, you're presenting yourself with something of a dilemma if you want to marry who wouldn't want to marry you."

"She might not want to marry a cowboy but she'd sure as hell want to marry Jason Briscoe. I'm not just a cowhand, I'm a rancher, a small rancher, sure enough, but I'm going to be a big rancher some day and then I'm going to be something else, I can't say what because I don't rightly know yet, but I know as sure as I know I'm sitting here smoking this ten-cent cigar that I will be. Some day. And maybe not too long from now."

"The cigar cost twenty-five cents," Von Wantoch said.

Jason held it in front of him, frowning. "Well," he said, "I guess that shows I may be an ignorant son-of-a-bitch. But I'm not dumb."

"I'm sure you're not, Jason. So you must understand that to advance from being a small rancher to being a big one you'll need capital. At least let me introduce you to Sir Charles Mongomery while you're in New York. He's not your typical Englishman. He fought in the Crimea, he's worth over a million pounds, and he came to the States after the war and married a lovely Boston girl twenty years younger than himself. You'll like Montgomery and he'll like you."

"How much is a million pounds in American money?"

"Five million dollars, more or less."

Jason whistled. "I'd sure be willing to sit down and pass the time of day with him after I've found me a wife. But not before."

"You drive a hard bargain, Jason. Are you prepared to eat more than's good for you?"

"I never refused seconds in my life. I figure you have to get ahead with your eating when you have the chance to make up for the times you have to do without. Why?"

"Polite society in New York spends most of its time eating and drinking. As you'll soon see."

When he gained ten pounds in three weeks, Jason, for self-protection, began visiting a livery stable on 59th Street where he hired a horse named Chauncey. He rode as often as he could in the open country on the northern half of Manhattan.

And still one dinner party followed another. Jason talked little, even when a considerate hostess encouraged him to explain the intricacies of the cattle business or describe life on the Western plains. And he was at a loss whenever a dinner companion commented on the failed impeachment of President Johnson or on Seward's purchase of Alaska for seven million dollars.

"General Grant will be one of the greatest presidents this country ever had," one of his hosts told him over cigars. "How do you view him, Mr. Briscoe?"

"The country could have done better," Jason said. "We could have elected General Lee."

There was a long silence.

"Surely you're not serious," one of the men said. "Confederates can't legally hold office."

"I'm mighty serious. I hold no brief for slavery myself but I'm sure as hell a Southerner like most Texans. Remember, Texas was the last state to surrender to you Yankees. As for Grant, I'll concede he's stubborn as hell, but Lee's a better man."

When Jason left the party to walk to his hotel, he guessed he wouldn't be invited back. Nor did he care.

He did better at another dinner where the talk turned to the ancient world during the time of Christ.

"Caesar was dictator of Rome at the time," a mutton-chopped newspaper editor said.

"No, sir, I beg to differ," Jason told him. "During the time of Christ, Octavian was emperor. He was also known as Augustus and that means the highly honored."

"He's right, you know, Horace," another guest put in. "How did you happen to remember that, Mr. Briscoe?"

"Once when I was fighting the Comanches I happened on one of their war shields," Jason said. And he told them of the book on the history of Rome he'd found packed in the shield and how he'd read the book while riding herd.

"That sounds like one of those tall tales that Texans are supposed to be partial to," the editor said. "Do you happen to be a Texan, sir?"

"That's a question you don't often hear asked

in the West," Jason said, "but I don't mind telling you. Yes, I'm a Texan and mighty proud of it."

"Why don't you hear that question in the West?" one of the women asked.

" 'Cause there's so many men on the dodge along the frontier. That means they're hiding from the law. And like I always say, in the West it's not polite to ask where a man's from. If he's a Texan, he'll soon enough let you know and if he isn't, why should you want to embarrass him?"

The guests laughed uncertainly. That's the trouble with people in the East, Jason thought, they never know when you're pulling their legs.

The next day, as he strode along the path to the livery stable for his daily ride, a woman approached riding a gray mare. Jason stopped and stared. Her black hair was piled high on her head and crowned by a feather hat with a small veil falling over her forehead. She sat her horse easily, riding sidesaddle, and when she passed him he touched his hand to his hat and she smiled down at him.

A stout gentleman rode up beside her, staring at Jason from eyes set deep in his florid face. "Miranda," he said sharply to the woman and she nodded and as he rode on she followed him to the bridle path.

Miranda. Jason turned her name over in his mind, liking the sound of it. He asked the stable owner who she might be.

"Miss Miranda Myerson," he answered. "The gentleman with her is Major Burnett. They ride together regular as clockwork, twice a week, Tuesdays and Thursdays, always at the same time."

Jason nodded. This was Thursday and so, he told himself, he'd have to wait until the following week to see her again. Miranda Myerson. She was a fine-looking woman and, he thought, he'd never heard a better-sounding name.

On Friday he was a guest at a dinner on Park Avenue; on Saturday he dined out again; on Sunday he re-read *Ragged Dick;* and on Monday he took a cab downtown to see Harvey Von Wantoch.

"Have you had any results yet?" the banker asked him as they puffed their twenty-five cent cigars.

"Not yet, Harvey. No results but I have hopes. Yes, sir, I do have hopes."

"Won't you let me introduce you to Sir Charles Montgomery? He's determined to locate in Denver so he won't be in the City much longer. I advise you to talk to him. It would be to all of our advantages, Mr. Briscoe."

Jason shook his head stubbornly. "Not till I find me a wife," he said.

On Tuesday he was at the livery stable an hour before his usual time. He saddled Chauncey, a bay, then watched while the gray was readied for Miranda Myerson. When she came into the stable wearing a handsome pale green riding dress, Jason touched his hat with his hand. Miranda smiled at him, or he thought she must have because the Major definitely frowned and seemed about to speak but then shook his head as though thinking better of it.

Jason swung into the saddle and followed the couple as they rode north. All at once Miranda's horse reared, the gray's forefeet pawing the air. She clung to the reins, trying to soothe him, but when the gray's feet struck the ground the horse bolted. The Major shouted a warning, urging his horse in pursuit but Jason was already spurring Chauncey past him.

The gray raced along the path with Miranda clinging to his neck. Slowly Jason overtook them, leaned low in his saddle and took the gray's reins in his hand and pulled the horse's head toward him, slowing Chauncey at the same time. When the gray stopped, Jason swung to the ground and held the protesting horse while Miranda slid from the saddle to stand beside Jason. Her pale face was flushed and she was breathing hard.

"You saved my life," she said.

"You would have stopped him without me, Ma'am," Jason told her. "You weren't in danger; you're a fine rider." He heard the pounding hoofbeats of the Major's horse. "May I call on you?" he asked.

She nodded as the Major dropped heavily to the ground and walked to her. "Are you all right, Miranda?" he asked.

"It was just like a story from a book," she said. "The way this gentleman, Mr. . . ." She paused.

"Jason Briscoe," Jason said.

"The way Mr. Briscoe came riding to my rescue."

"Too much like something from a book," the Major said, eyeing Jason narrowly.

He downright doesn't trust me, Jason thought. Still holding the gray's reins, he maneuvered the horse so she was between himself and the Major. Running his hand beneath the gray's saddle, Jason removed the burr he'd placed there and let it fall unnoticed to the ground.

10

Jason CALLED on Miranda Myerson the next day. She lived in a stately house on Washington Square, a wide-fronted mansion with a large balcony and a flight of white marble steps ascending to a doorway also faced with white marble. Jason sent in his card and after a few minutes a maid ushered him into the back parlor.

Miranda smiled at him over her knitting needles. Jason sat on an overstuffed chair facing her with his eyes roving from the pale beauty of her face to the green yarn in a basket on the floor beside her.

"I'm knitting Mother a sweater." Miranda smiled at him expectantly. Jason smiled back. He hadn't the slightest idea what he should say to her.

Miranda's needles clicked. "Tell me all about the West," she said.

Hesitatingly, he told her of his ranch and something of the years he had spent in the Texas Rangers.

"It all sounds so dreadfully exciting," she said. "And so dangerous." The needles clicked and the ball of yarn in the basket dwindled. Again there was silence.

When the ormolu clock on the mantel chimed four times, Jason stood and wished her good day. She smiled and nodded and said she hoped he'd call again.

He waited until Tuesday before he returned to the house on Washington Square. He walked past the ailanthus trees in the park, climbed the marble steps and knocked on the Myerson door. The day before he had sat for an hour at the desk in his hotel room preparing a list of subjects to talk to her about and on the way to her house he had carefully rehearsed what he would say about each. Again he was ushered into the parlor and again Miranda smiled at him over her knitting. The yarn, blue and white today, lay at her feet.

"I finished the sweater," she said when she saw him looking at her handiwork.

He nodded, staring into her dark eyes. He couldn't remember one word of what he had intended to say.

"Do you enjoy horseback riding?" he stammered at last.

"No," she said. "It's sad but true that I don't. Not really. The Major says riding's good for me but I can't say I enjoy it. I find riding dreadfully boring."

"It can be," he said. "Do you like reading?"

"No," she said, "not awfully. You'll think I'm dull, I'm afraid, but I do have my enthusiasms. I like to knit as you can see and I like going to dances and parties and I like to ride uptown in our carriage." She smiled at him over her knitting. "I know you must read a great deal yourself," she said. "I've heard you're an authority on ancient Rome."

"I know a bit about it."

"Pray tell me about Rome, Mr. Briscoe. I find history dreadfully fascinating."

For the next half hour he told her all he knew about the rise and fall of the Roman Empire. When the clock struck four, he rose, bowed, and made his way from the room, pausing uncertainly in the hallway. He must have made a wrong turning because when he opened the door he thought led outside to the Square he found himself in another room. A lamp with a shade of multi-hued glass burned on the table, the walls were lined with dark-covered books, and through the twin windows opposite him he saw the bare branches of trees.

He was turning away when he was stopped by a girl's voice.

"Mr. Briscoe?"

He looked into the gloom and saw, settled deep in a high backed chair, a girl with a book in her lap. She smiled at him and he noticed her hair was brown and curly, her nose small and snub. Laying the book on the table beside her, she got up and came toward him, taking his hand in hers and leading him into the room. She wore blue slippers to match her high-necked blue and white gown, and though she was of slight build her breasts rounded out the wool of her bodice and he saw she was not a child as he'd thought at first but a young woman.

"You're the heroic Mr. Briscoe, aren't you?" she asked, her tone mocking him all the while she smiled shyly at him. "I've heard all about how you raced your horse and overtook Miranda and saved her life. And how angry Major Burnett was because you saved her, not him. The Major's rather pompous, don't you think?"

"I really don't know the Major well enough . . ." Jason began.

"You don't have to know Major Burnett well to tell he's pompous. At least that's what I think. I'm Janine Jamison, by the way, the poor country cousin living with my rich relatives in the city until they manage to marry me off. My parents are both dead." She paused for breath. "And how do you like New York, Mr. Briscoe?"

"I've been awful impressed by how people scurry about, as though they'd just backed against a hot stove by mistake. Most of them have treated me . . ."

"I love New York," Janine interrupted. She turned her head away and coughed. "Though as you can see it's not good for me. You wouldn't think to look at me that I've been sick, would you?"

"You appear to be the picture of health." She did, Jason thought, for her cheeks were flushed a pale pink and her eyes were lively. Her dancing eyes were brown, the same color as her hair.

"Yet I've been sick and Dr. Jenke says the city's not the best place for me. The cold winters and the soot are supposed to be bad for people with consumption. That's what I have, Mr. Briscoe, or what I did have. Consumption."

Jason nodded, not knowing what to say. Consumption meant she had weak lungs, he knew. His mother's older sister had died of consumption years ago.

"Won't you sit over here, Mr. Briscoe?" Janine asked. "Miranda can surely spare you for a few minutes. I want to find out all about you."

He sat on a sofa across from her and told her of his boyhood in Illinois, his father's death and how his mother and his stepfather brought him by wagon from Illinois south to Texas. When he began to talk he half-expected her to interrupt, to tell him of herself, and when she didn't he stretched out and crossed his legs, talking more easily than he had since he'd arrived in New York.

"Why don't you smoke?" she asked. "I see you have a cigar in your pocket."

"You don't mind?"

"I adore the smell of cigar smoke."

He clipped one end and put the cigar in his mouth. When he took matches from his pocket Janine sat beside him on the sofa, the scent of lilies-of-the valley filling the air around him. She took the match from his hand, struck it and lit his cigar, smiling up at him as he settled back at the far end of the sofa, clasping her hands together in her lap.

"Ad then what happened?" she asked. "After you got to Texas?"

So he told her of his stepfather's farm, how his mother had died in childbirth, the way his stepfather seemed barely able to tolerate him after she died, and how he ran away when he was fifteen, drifting west to the Pinto country where he'd hired out as a ranch hand and then, when the War Between the States began in '61, how he joined the Rangers and scouted for them on the frontier as they fought back against the ravaging Comanches.

A clock began to chime. Jason realized with amazement that it was seven. Through the twin windows he could no longer see the bare branches of the ailanthus trees; the city was dark.

Janine walked with him to the door where she stopped, reaching out and touching his sleeve. "Please come again," she said. "I can't remember ever meeting such an interesting man."

Jason waited until the door closed behind him before he ran down the marble steps, crossed the street and walked beside the park holding the end of his cane to the palings of the fence, making a rat-tat-tat-tat. Ahead of him a lamplighter raised his torch to a lamp and a gas flared into a circle of light.

Something wet struck Jason's face. He looked up and saw large flakes whirling in front of the light, the snow quickly covering his black coat and hat. Jason raised his head so the flakes struck his face where they melted and ran down his cheeks. He tapped his cane exuberantly on the wet pavement, then tossed it into the air. When he reached out to catch it, the cane eluded his grasp and clattered to the walkway.

He glanced around him, wondering if anyone had seen his antics, before he picked up the cane and walked sedately toward Fifth Avenue and his hotel, humming to himself. He meant to see Janine Jamison again, would see her again, he had no doubt of that. He wondered if the next day would be too soon, wondered what she thought of him.

Jason Briscoe and Janine Jamison were married four weeks later.

The winter had been mild and the riverboats were still running so Jason and Janine took passage on the paddle-wheeler *Alexander Hamilton*, honeymooning at a sprawling inn at Cornwall in the shadow of Storm King Mountain.

The first evening, as they ate in an almost deserted dining room overlooking the Hudson, Jason ordered a magnum of champagne. He raised his glass, proposing a toast—"To our life together in Texas."

As Janine sipped the champagne, she began to cough. She raised her napkin to her mouth, finally turning her head away when the coughing would not stop.

Jason looked at her in alarm. "Is there anything I can do?" he asked.

Janine shook her head and, after the spasm passed, she said, "No, the coughing spells come and go. It's nothing. The doctor thinks Texas will be good for me."

Jason covered her hand with his. Her eyes, he saw, were glistening and her cheeks had a feverish flush. He felt anguished, as though a hand had gripped his insides and twisted.

She looked across the gleaming silver, the sparkling crystal, the red-hooded candle, and smiled. "I don't ever want to be a burden to you, Jason," she said. "If that ever happens, I'll leave."

"You could never be a burden to me," he said.

She smiled and he realized with a start of surprise that while she knew a great deal about him, he knew very little about her. Well, he thought, there'll be time enough to find out; they had a lifetime ahead of them.

He noticed she spoke little during the rest of the meal, glancing distractedly around the room and down to the dark river below. When he rose and offered her his arm she looked at him with what seemed to him to be almost a plea in her brown eyes. He had the rest of the magnum of champagne brought to their suite and, after Janine took her nightgown and went into the adjoining room, he filled two glasses, then undressed and slid between the sheets.

She'll get over her modesty soon enough, Jason told himself. He took a glass from the bedside table and sipped the wine as he waited for her. Damn, but she was taking her own good time. Finally he threw the bedclothes aside and stood up, going to the door leading to the adjoining room. He'd started to open the door when he realized he was naked. With a sigh he returned to his trunk and rummaged inside until he found a robe and slipped it on.

He opened the door and went into the next room. It was dark as pitch.

"Janine?" he said.

He heard a movement on the far side of the room and he walked that way only to strike his shin on the leg of a table.

"Damn," he said.

"Did you hurt yourself, Jason?" she asked. Following the sound of her voice, he found her sitting in a chair by the window. He knelt on the floor beside her.

"I was wondering what was keeping you," he said.

"I'm afraid, Jason," she said. "I didn't want to be but I am."

He touched her hair, caressing the curls. "There's naught to fear," he told her.

"I can't help the way I feel. Do we have to . . . ?" She let her voice trail away.

"Not till you're ready," he said. He found her hand and took it gently in his. "Now come to bed," he told her. She let him lead her into their bedroom. When they were beside the bed she stood on tiptoe and kissed his cheek.

"Thank you, Jason," she said.

As he bent over to blow out the candle on the table, he noticed the two glasses of champagne. He finished his, then picked up hers and drained it as well.

They consummated their marriage in the same bed three nights later, Janine pulling the skirt of her nightgown above her hips, Jason caressing her until he felt his own desire surge and, even though he knew she wasn't ready for him, penetrating her, hearing her moan beneath him as he thrust inside her. And then it was over and he lay back looking up at the dark ceiling as, under the piled blankets, she smoothed her gown over her legs once more.

"Jason?" she said.

He didn't answer. When she repeated his name he turned to her and took her hand in his and raised her fingers to his lips and kissed them.

"I'm sorry, Jason," she told him. "Give me time. Everything will turn out all right."

"I know it will," he said without conviction.

She snuggled her head against his shoulder and in a few minutes she was asleep. We'll work this out once we're in Texas, he told himself the next day as they sailed down the ice-strewn Hudson to New York. He began to think of Texas as a talisman, a magic charm. Once we're at the ranch, he assured himself, Janine will be healthier and she'll relax. That's what's wrong here. It's this damn city with all the filth and grime. Once she's feeling better, it'll be better between us.

Before he and Janine left New York for the west, Harvey Von Wantoch introduced him to Sir Charles Montgomery. Von Wantoch left the two men sitting over brandies at Sorrento's each silently appraising the other. Montgomery, Jason guessed, was about forty, his blond hair was thinning and he had a thin blond moustache which he fingered nervously as he talked.

"My dear Briscoe," Sir Charles said in an English accent that forced Jason to listen carefully in order not to miss his meaning. "I've heard an awful lot about you and I don't mind telling you that all I've heard has been to your credit."

Jason nodded but said nothing. All he knew of

Sir Charles was what Von Wantoch had told him, that the Englishman had fought in the Crimea and was worth five million dollars. Oh yes, and was married to a young American beauty from Boston.

"I'm interested in having my money make money, of course," Sir Charles said. "You'll be saying to yourself that this blighter could do that in England or here in the East and I'd have to say of course I could. I might invest in railroads, in textiles, in shipping, the opportunities are boundless. Let me tell you why I haven't. I traveled to Denver last year, by train to Kansas City and by stage across Kansas and I hunted antelope on that Great American Desert of yours, even saw a few red savages, and quite frankly I fell in love with the West. There's danger and adventure and romance there. Your West is a place where a man's mettle can be tested. Do I sound like a young boy?" Sir Charles paused, frowning. "My wife tells me I remind her of someone who's not grown up yet."

"I make a habit of avoiding danger, Sir Charles, not seeking it out."

"You're a prudent man, then. In the Crimea . . ." Sir Charles' eyes glazed and Jason saw the right corner of his mouth twitch involuntarily.

"I never served in the Army," Jason said. "I was a scout for the Texas Rangers. One of the best times of my life, all in all."

"I don't know why I mentioned the Crimea," Sir Charles said, shaking his head. "Our commanders made blunder upon blunder. To tell you the truth, Briscoe, I'd rather not discuss it." Sir Charles abruptly changed the subject. "Do you require financial backing in your cattle endeavors?" he asked.

"No, not now, though I can see where I might in a few years. I'm planning to drive cattle north to the rails, not only mine but herds from other Texas ranches, and not only to markets in Kansas, maybe even to New Mexico and north to Colorado and Wyoming."

"You're a man with dreams, I see. I'm a bit surprised you can't use my money, though. The impression I've received here in New York is that all of your countrymen could use money. Preferably someone else's."

"When I need your money I'll ask for it and when I do ask I won't want just a few thousand dollars."

"What sum do you have in mind, Mr. Briscoe? Ten thousand? Fifty?"

"When I'm ready I figure I'll need half a million dollars, give or take."

Sir Charles hooked his thumbs under his vest and stared at Jason. "I can see why Von Wantoch wanted me to meet you," he said. "You not only dream, you dream Texas-sized dreams."

"I intend to return to Denver," Sir Charles went on. "When you're ready you can get in touch with me there. Write me or if you're ever up that way call on me. I think we may be able to do business."

The two men shook hands and parted on the sidewalk outside Sorrento's. Something about Montgomery bothered Jason, something he couldn't put his finger on. Von Wantoch had spoken highly of the Englishman and there seemed no doubt he was what he claimed to be. Jason wondered what had happened to him in the Crimea . . .

When, on the train heading west, he told Janine about Sir Charles, she said, "He sounds like a man who isn't as sure of himself as you might think. Even with all his money."

"And what do you mean by that?" Jason looked past Janine to the telegraph poles flicking by outside. Beyond the poles he saw the last traces of the winter's snow clinging to the Pennsylvania fields and hills.

"I'm not sure," she said. "He talks as though he thinks the West is an Eton playing field where a man can prove something to himself. Didn't men join the Army during the War to find out who they were? What they were?"

He shook his head. "They joined to fight for a cause they believed in. This Montgomery fought for his country in the Crimea, by the way."

"I wonder what happened to him there?" Janine said, echoing Jason's thoughts of the day before. Her attention was caught by the vista outside the window.

"Look, Jason." She pointed and ahead of them he saw the engine of their train rounding a curve with the smoke pluming into the winter air. Two boys skated on a pond below the railroad embankment and on the far side four or five others stood warming their hands at a bonfire.

"Every mile brings us closer to home," she said. "Closer to Texas. I can't wait till we get there and you can show me our ranch."

Jason felt a sudden misgiving. Janine had been gay, almost giddy ever since they boarded the train in New York, talking more, acting much as she had the first day he'd met her, her face brightly animated as she skipped from topic to topic.

"I don't want you to be disappointed," he told her. "When you're living at the ranch you won't have any close neighbors."

"How close will they be? Two or three miles away?" When she saw him frown, she asked, "Five miles?"

"Well, there's the Goodnight ranch, that's maybe thirty miles from my place. Charlie's not married; his mother lives with him. Then there's old man Overholt's place, that's maybe twenty-five miles the other way." He brightened. "New Folks moved in last spring, the Varners and the Swansons, both married. They're forty miles east of my place." He paused to correct himself. "Our place," he amended. "I met Mrs. Swanson once," he said. Tamar, he thought. Tamar. He took a deep breath and went on. "I haven't met Mrs. Varner yet."

Janine hunched in the corner between the window and the seat of the swaying train, staring at him. "Forty miles," she said, "I didn't realize it would be so far."

"Forty miles isn't far in Texas."

She clapped her hands together. "I know what we'll do," she said. "We'll have a party and invite all of them, the bachelors and the married couples, everybody within a hundred miles of us. You'll have them to our place to meet your new wife from the East. We'll have the biggest and gayest party Texas has ever seen. We'll dance all night."

She smiled hesitantly at him. "That's all right, isn't it, Jason?"

Jason nodded despite a faint misgiving. It *was* a good idea. He should have been the one to think of having a barbecue to introduce his new wife. And, he realized with a tingle of anticipation, he'd see Tamar again. He was a married man now, he told himself, so he shouldn't be thinking of Tamar. In fact he'd thought marriage would erase his desire for her and he was surprised to find it hadn't.

They'd have the barbecue next month, he decided, soon enough to give him a chance to talk to the other ranchers before the spring round-up; they'd do better going in together on the round-up this year, not every man for himself like in the past. And he'd sound them out about contracting with him to drive their cattle north to Kansas after the cattle were gathered.

Yes, Janine's idea was a good one. She had a head on her shoulders, sure enough, and she could maybe size up people better than he could. Every day he discovered another side to her that delighted and surprised him. He smiled at her.

"We'll have the best damn party Pinto County ever saw," he told his wife, pushing away his vague feeling of apprehension, of lurking danger.

Again she clapped her hands. "Jason," she said, "I'm going to love Texas whether we're four miles from our next door neighbor or forty." She took his arm in both of her hands and leaned toward him to press her head against his shoulder.

Jason circled her with his arm. Janine, he thought, when I married you I hardly knew you. But I will get to know you, I'll take the time after we're home. You were right, everything's going to be just fine once we get to Texas.

11

Isaac "Ike" McLeod knocked at the door of the Varner house. When Vivian opened it he smiled at her and handed her a sealed envelope.

"From Jason Briscoe," Ike told her. He was a black, born a slave in Tennessee some thirty years before, who had taken the name of his former master, Floyd McLeod.

Vivian tore open the envelope and stood in the doorway reading the letter as Ike mounted and rode off toward the Swanson place. A party. She'd almost forgotten what a party was. She closed the door and leaned against it, remembering the balls in Georgia, the lilting music, the young men clustered about her begging for a place on her dance card.

Vivian sighed and walked to the stove. Those days had vanished with the Confederacy. She had chosen to marry Print Varner, chosen wisely. And she'd come to love him, she'd become eager for the way he made her feel. If he'd never be the gentleman her father was, why, she could bear that.

Vivian replaced the invitation in the envelope and laid it on the table, ruefully noticing how red and chapped her hands looked against the clear white of the paper. I'll get out my hoop, she thought, and there's my peach satin that I haven't worn since I left Georgia . . .

That night when Print Varner clumped into the house he found the single sheet of paper beside his plate. "What in tarnation's that?" he asked.

"We're invited to a barbecue," Vivian told him, "to meet Jason Briscoe's new wife from New York. I'm fixing over my peach satin dress to wear with a hoop."

Print studied the invitation and tossed it aside. "What makes you so damn sure we're going?" he asked.

"Print!" she exclaimed in surprise "Print," she said, her voice softening. She came to stand behind him and put her arms around him, leaning forward so his head rested between her breasts.

"It's been a long winter, Print," she said, "with just the two of us and only the Swansons for company. And you know how impatient George Swanson makes me with his hemming and hawing, the way he can never make up his mind."

Print half-turned to reach up and cup one of her breasts in his hand, finding the nipple through the cloth and tweaking it. "I sort of had the notion you kind of liked the way it was with just you and me here alone," he said.

"Oh, Print."

He smiled to himself when he heard the tremor in her voice. Vivian's hands trailed down his sides and into his lap. He released her and started to get up but she pushed him back.

"We'll eat first," she told him. "You must be starved after being out since six this morning."

"I could stand a bite to eat," he said. "First."

She hurried to the stove, humming to herself, and ladled stew from the pot onto his tin plate. Print picked up the invitation, folded it and tucked the letter into his pocket. They'd all be together at the barbecue, he told himself, him and Vivian, George and Tamar, Jason and his new wife. What had the invitation said her name was? Janine.

Not for the first time he wondered if Jason was getting suspicious, whether he'd been missing any of his cattle, the Briscoe mavericks Print had been branding as his own. Probably he hadn't been back from the East long enough to get a handle on what was going on. And with a new wife and all . . .

The barbecue. How could he use the barbecue to give him more time? Print wondered. Enough time so he wouldn't have to worry about the likes of Jason Briscoe? And George Swanson, though George was more a nuisance than threat. George must be more of a fool than he thought, not to suspect about him and Tamar.

There must be some way he could turn the barbecue at Briscoe's to his own advantage.

"You were only teasing, weren't you?" Vivian asked as she set his plate on the table in front of him. "About not going to the party?"

"Course I was only teasing," Print said, circling her hips with his arm and squeezing her. "Wild mustangs couldn't keep me away."

Smiling, Vivian removed his hands and sat across from him "I expect you'll like my dress, the peach, once I've fixed it. It's got a round neck, rather high—that's what I'm changing.

Tamar will help me with it, she's good at sewing."

Vivian frowned, pondering. "Tamar's been acting strangely of late," she said.

Print looked up quickly, eyeing her narrowly, but his wife seemed preoccupied with her food, as though she attached little weight to her words.

Print decided to push it a bit. "What do you mean by strangely?" he asked as casually as he could.

Vivian glanced at him. "Well, you recall how she was at first, friendly enough but sort of distant, like she was afraid of me. And then when you were away, Tamar and I were busy helping each other set up housekeeping in the new cabins the men built and we became friends, or so I thought. After you came back, of course, I didn't see Tamar so much." Vivian stopped, remembering. "I thought for a time she might be expecting, because she acted like she had a secret but her figure hasn't changed so that's not it."

Vivian paused as she recalled how envious she'd felt when she thought Tamar might be pregnant. As though it would be wrong for Tamar to bear a child before she herself did. How she longed for a baby!

Print shrugged. "Sounds like it's all in your head."

"No, it's not. Lately I've noticed Tamar smiling at me as though she were years older, almost as if I were, well, Eli, for instance."

"She's like a young heifer," Print said. "There's no telling what flighty notions run through her head."

"She might be young but that girl has a mind of her own. She'll give that husband of hers a merry run for his money before she's much older or I miss my guess."

Print, scowling, shoved his plate away and stood up. Coming around the table he reached across Vivian's shoulders with both hands and began unbuttoning the top of her calico gown.

"Print!" she said in mock reproof.

She stood, pushing his hands away and continued unbuttoning the dress herself until it was open to the waist. She drew his hands down so they crossed in front of her, one on each of her breasts.

Washday. Tamar knew she'd spend the entire day doing their laundry—she'd be lucky to finish before dark because she'd run out of soap and George wouldn't get to the store in town until a week from Saturday.

She soaked a batch of hardwood in a kettle of water from the river. Once the water boiled, becoming lye, she dropped in pork rinds, boiling the mixture in a big iron kettle and stirring so the lye soap would set properly.

There was a knock on the cabin door.

It was Ike McLeod. Tamar tore open the envelope he handed her and read the invitation to the Briscoe barbecue.

"Don't go riding off," she called after Ike who was remounting his horse. "Come in and visit awhile. I'll put coffee on."

"I'd best not, thank you all the same," Ike said. "I got a heap of riding to do."

"Tell Mrs. Briscoe we'll come to her party," Tamar said. "Tell her I'm just dying to meet her."

"I'll tell her that, Miss Tamar," Ike said, swinging his horse away. That little lady's a hell of a woman, Ike told himself as he rode off.

Holding the invitation aloft, Tamar ran to the rear of the house, past the corral, across the yard and down the hill to the bottom land near the river. She hailed her husband who was plowing the dark earth. He stopped, looping the reins of his horse over the plow handle, mopping his forehead with a bandana as he squinted into the sun at Tamar.

"A party," she called to him. She looked about for Eli but he was nowhere to be seen.

She ran along the furrow until she stood in front of George waving the invitation in his face. "To welcome the new Mrs. Briscoe," she said, panting for breath. "You'll have to buy me material for a dress when we go to town. Green. Yes, I think pale green would look lovely. What do you think, George?"

"Whatever you say is all right with me, Tamar. You know I like the looks of you no matter what you wear."

"Green then, if they have any at the store." She whirled around in front of him, almost falling on the new-plowed earth.

"Print stopped by a while back," he said.

"Oh?" Tamar was suddenly alert. "I didn't see him. What did he want?"

"He asked me to ride over to Goodnight's tomorrow morning to take back that axe he borrowed. I should be home by supper time."

Tamar nodded. Suddenly she put her arms around George and hugged him to her.

"You'll dirty your dress," George said.

"I don't care," Tamar told him. "I don't care, I don't care, I don't care."

She let go and ran back along the furrow, turning to wave to George from the edge of the field before she ran up the hill to the house. As she neared the cabin she saw Eli snaking in firewood by dragging a branch behind his horse. Inside the cabin she began stirring the soap as she sang, "The Girl I Left Behind Me."

The next day when George stopped at Varner's for the axe, Print drew him aside.

"Something's been troubling me, George," Print told him. George said nothing, curious but waiting for Print to come out with what was on his mind.

"It's rightly none of my business," Print went on, "and I'm not usually one to meddle in what don't concern me, but I thought you ought to know. Seeing as how you're probably going to this barbecue at Briscoe's."

"We're going, Tamar and me, that's right," George said. "Going to take Eli, too."

"Now, I'm not saying there's anything wrong and I'm not saying Tamar has done a thing out of line, I know she hasn't. I just figure you ought to keep a weather-eye peeled when she's around Jason Briscoe."

"Tamar and Jason?" George sounded puzzled. "They only seen each other the once."

"I saw them the day he set out searching for Eli, the time the boy got lost," Print said. "And they didn't do nothing, I'm not saying they did, but it was the way he looked at her I'm talking about."

"All men look at Tamar that way," George said with a touch of pride. "Leastways most of them do. I even seen you, Print, casting glances her way."

"Maybe it was more the way she looked at him," Print pushed on. "Now I'm probably reading a whole lot into nothing and as I say, nothing happened. This is just a notion I had at the time that I've been pondering ever since and when the invite came from Briscoe I thought I'd best speak my piece and have done with it. I don't mean you to take offense, George."

"I rightly thank you, Print. There's naught to it but I'll keep an eagle-eye out during the doings at Briscoe's, don't think I won't."

"Good," Print said. "I'm telling you for your own good, George, and 'cause I don't want trouble on my place, 'specially the first year we're operating. Understand what I mean?" When George nodded, Print clapped him on the back. "Give my best to Charlie Goodnight, now. Hear?"

"I'll do that, Print." George tied the axe on his saddle, mounted and set off.

As soon as George was gone, Print strode across the yard to the back door and called to Vivian. "I'm riding along the river," he told her. He mounted and rode south, looking for cattle caught in the brush along the banks. After he'd gone two or three miles he circled back, making a wide loop around his place. As he neared the river again he spurred his horse, impatient.

He saw an overgrown calf nursing an emaciated mother and knew he should stop to blab it by clipping a piece of wood to its nose so the calf could graze but not nurse, but instead he rode on.

He entered the timbers near the spot where he'd found and shot the rustler the year before. Jason had told Charlie Goodnight about finding the body wrapped in the skin and they'd buried Beatty in the town graveyard. Though there was talk that the killing was Print's work, Eli had said nothing about what he'd seen and no one dared lay it on Print, no one even mentioned the shooting in his hearing.

Print followed the animal track leading down to the Keechi and the Swanson place. After going a hundred yards he swung his horse to the right into scrub growth. Once out of sight of the track he tethered his horse to a tree near a big oak and walked through a thicket, the branches catching at his clothes. He pushed the last of the undergrowth aside and stepped into a forest glade where sunlight coming through the new-budded trees dappled the grass.

The glade was empty. Print took a tobacco pouch and papers from his jacket pocket, rolled a cigarette, and sat smoking with his back against a tree. When he heard the sound of someone pushing through the brush he didn't look up. Even when the sound stopped and he sensed that someone stood across the glade watching him, he kept smoking, his eyes following the slow upward drift of the smoke.

"Print." She said the word almost as a command, ordering him to look at her.

Print stood up and ground his cigarette beneath the heel of his boot. Smiling, he looked at her at last, standing with his hands on his hips just as Tamar, on the far side of the clearing, stood with her hands on her hips. She realized he was mocking her, taunting her.

"You son-of-a-bitch," she said, smiling

Print crossed the clearing and put one arm around her, lifting Tamar so she pressed against him with her feet off the ground. She gasped.

"You," she began, "son," and her lips twisted away from his, "of," and then his lips covered hers and their mouths opened, their tongues meeting. She put both of her arms around his neck and clung to him, kissing him. Finally she drew her mouth back from his. "A bitch," she said.

He swung her about so he cradled her with one arm under her knees and the other around her back and carried her across the glade. He laid her on the sunlit grass and knelt beside her.

When he leaned down to kiss her she covered her mouth with her hand. "Print," she said, "I don't want to hurt anybody. Not George, not Vivian."

For a moment he remembered Vivian as she'd been the night before at the table with her breasts bared to him. Looking down now at Tamar, seeing the glint in her green eyes, seeing her need for him, he felt his power and he smiled.

Tamar's nails raked his face. "Don't smile that tomcat smile at me," she said. "Do you think I'd be here if I could help myself? Do you think it's you? Is that what you really think?" She sniffed disdainfully. "Don't you know most any man would do?"

He slapped her hard enough to make her head jerk to one side. When he brought his hand back to slap her again Tamar didn't flinch but faced him and his slap turned into a caress, his fingers stroking her cheek where he'd struck her. She kissed his hand, first the fingers and then the depths of his palm.

"That's what I like about you, Print," she said.

"What's that?"

"You *are* a son-of-a-bitch."

She lifted the corner of his bandana from his neck and used the end to dab at the blood-red slashes streaking his cheek. "I don't want to hurt you, either," she said. She kissed him gently.

With one hand he stroked the back of her head, with the other he held her breast, all the while kissing her lips. Tamar raised herself up against him, then pulled him down on top of her, returning his kiss, her body writhing under him. His hand left her breast and slid from her knee over the man's pants she wore to her thighs, caressing the soft flesh through the cloth.

"Oh!" she gasped.

She felt a trembling grow in her, the now-familiar mounting warmth spreading through her body. She shut her eyes, her lips leaving his as she clenched her teeth, her hands covering his hand on her thigh as the trembling shook her in one last spasm and was gone.

"You just have to touch me," she said, "and I start." She lay against him so they touched along the length of their bodies, feeling the hardness of him. "It's never been this way before," she whispered. "Never like with you, Print. Never, never, never."

She felt his hands leave her as his body pulled away, heard him fumbling with his clothes. Impatiently she yanked off her boots and tore at her own clothes, throwing aside her shirt and pushing the pants down over her legs. Tamar had worn nothing underneath.

She knelt facing him, looking up at him. His back was to her and he was naked now himself. He turned to stand over her and, closing her eyes, she rubbed her cheek against the hard maleness of his sex, feeling his heat. He knelt in front of her and took her bare body in his arms.

"Tell me," she said.

Print smiled, saying nothing.

"Tell me," she said again.

He leaned forward to kiss her quickly, still saying nothing. She pummeled his chest with her fists until he took her wrists in his hands and held her arms wide apart. He kissed her mouth, a long kiss, and when she closed her eyes he kissed her eyelids. She sighed, murmuring, and they fell together to the grass, his hands releasing her wrists and moving to cup her buttocks while she led his sex to her with her hands, holding him off as he was ready to enter so she could fondle him, so she could feel the hardness of him.

Print groaned and she put her arms around him, letting him enter her; she felt him stroking inside her, and again the surging warmth mounted within her, became a storm, shaking her, not stopping, and she opened her eyes, startled, her body no longer hers to control, and she was afraid so she pushed at him, trying to make him stop but instead he held her buttocks tighter and his rhythm increased and she pulsed against him again and again and again.

He seemed to burst inside her. He groaned and lay still and her trembling lessened and finally stopped. When she felt him begin shifting his body from hers, she clutched him tighter and whispered, "No, Print, hold me. Just hold me in your arms."

He lay beside her with his arms around her, their bodies touching lightly.

"I love you, Tamar," he said. She looked at him and saw he was staring over her head.

"It took you long enough to get up the nerve to say it, you son-of-a-bitch."

Print frowned. "You know I don't like you to talk that way," he told her. "That's three or four times you've called me that just today. It's not proper."

Tamar trailed her fingers down along his side to his legs. "And this is?" she asked him. She drew away. "You mean, you have mighty peculiar notions as to what's proper for a woman and what isn't. Seems to me it all depends on what pleasures you and what doesn't."

"You know damn well what I mean." Print paused and then said, casually, "I was talking to George when he stopped for the axe."

Tamar raised herself on her elbow and looked down at him. "What are you up to now, Print Varner?" she asked. "Don't think you're fooling me, I know that tone of voice. You're trying to spring something."

"I'm trying to say that George acted sort of peculiar. He looked at me sidewise and once or twice I figured he was ready to say something, getting his nerve, and then he thought better of it."

"I don't think he suspects about us," Tamar said. "Nothing's happened to make him think everything isn't like it's always been."

"You mean you're still bedding with him?" Print's tone accused her.

"That's none of your business. What I do is for me to decide."

"How did you happen to marry up with George? He's not the kind of a man I'd suspect you'd marry."

He lifted a strand of golden hair from Tamar's forehead and tucked it behind her ear. She smiled at him. One minute Print was violent while the next he was showing a streak of gentleness that he kept hidden from everyone except her. She coveted this secret knowledge of him.

"Knowing you like I do," Print went on, his fingers going to the nape of her neck.

"Why I married George isn't any of your damn business either," Tamar said, "but I don't mind saying. My father was sick and there was me nursing him and George was boarding with us. We were together all the time in the house and before long I was pregnant and there was nothing else to do but get married. I lost the baby in the sixth month, in case you were wondering."

"How old were you then, Tamar?"

"Fourteen."

Print nodded. "About George," he said. "I was thinking that with this barbecue of Briscoe's coming along pretty soon and us all going to be there, maybe you should play up to Jason while all the time treating me natural-like."

"You want me to play up to Jason? You, who's been so jealous of him?"

"I saw the way you and him were rolling on the ground and kissing the day he went looking for Eli. Then afterwards I saw the way you looked when you told me about him bringing your brother home."

"You think you can read an awful lot in the way people look, Print. The way I looked mentioning Jason, the way George looks at you. George is probably scared of you and the way he looks has nothing to do with me."

"Judging people and what they're thinking helps me stay alive. I watch their faces. Some say it's the eyes that give folks away but I watch their mouths, the way their lips twist up or down, the way they purse together."

Tamar smiled, getting up to kneel beside him, feeling the twigs in the grass sharp against her knees. "What's my face telling you now, Print?" she asked. "Go ahead, show me how good you are reading feelings from the twist of a person's mouth."

He ran his hand up the outside of her leg to her hip and gripped her there. "I don't have to read sign, I know what you're wanting."

As he started to get up she put her hand on the hair on his chest and pushed him down until he lay on his back. She straddled his legs and sat over him, leading his hands to her bare breasts, throwing back her head as she felt his thumbs caress her nipples. She moaned as his hands brought her breasts together.

She guided him into her, leaning down over him so her breasts hung pendulous above his face, and he strained upward to nip them with his teeth and circle her nipples with his tongue. She smiled and began to move over him, her hips rising and falling until she felt him grow hard within her and once more her body spasmed as he thrust up into her.

Afterwards they dressed with their backs turned to one another and when they were fully clothed they stood awkwardly, not speaking.

Print kicked a hole in the earth with the heel of his boot. "Week from today I'm sending George upriver to strip some trees for the new corral," he said.

"All right," Tamar said.

"Don't forget what I told you about Briscoe and the barbecue."

"I won't."

Print went to her towering over her, and when she put her face to his chest he lowered his head and kissed her sun-warmed hair. She leaned back in his arms, putting one hand to the nape of his neck and bringing his lips down on hers. When the kiss ended she stepped away.

Print bent over and picked his hat from the ground, set it squarely on his head, and without a word turned and pushed his way through the branches bordering the glade. Tamar listened until the sound of his horse's hooves died away and then she started down the hill through the trees in the direction of the cabin.

Her body seemed to glow with an inner warmth. She hugged herself and began to whistle. "All around the vinegar jug, the monkey chased the weasel," she sang and then whistled the tune again. She had never felt so alive, so much a woman.

She stopped suddenly, the whistle dying away, and she looked around her, sensing something amiss. Over her head a squirrel chattered at her from a branch and she saw long shafts of sunlight angling through the branches to the forest floor. She remained silent, listening, certain she'd heard something, but the forest was quiet in the heat of early afternoon.

I'm spooky is all, Tamar told herself. She shivered, though she wasn't cold. Print had no right talking of George and asking her about him, wanting to know whether she bedded with him or not. Of course she did, what kind of a wife did Print think she was? She was a good wife to George, a better wife than he was a husband, though he couldn't help being the way he was. She didn't, wouldn't, let what she did with Print affect George.

She walked on, musing. Maybe they'd best not go to the damn barbecue after all. She'd been looking forward to the party since Ike had come riding to the cabin with the invitation. She was itching to see what kind of a wife Jason Briscoe had brought back from New York. Probably a tall snobbish woman who spent all her time reading books, a woman who'd soon weary of living in the middle of nowhere. She'd counted on talking to Janine to find out what the women were wearing in the East. That would sure beat reading the walls—the newspapers used as wallpaper—on visiting a different cabin.

They'd have whiskey at the party, she was certain, and George might not be able to resist drinking. Like as not he'd break his temperance vow, she'd have to watch him. Another reason to stay home.

But Tamar knew she'd go to the barbecue, no matter what; nothing could keep her away. Yes, she'd go, but still she couldn't quiet the nagging voice that warned her to stay put, to leave well enough alone.

That had been close, Tamar'd almost seen him. What would she have done if she'd found him hiding in the thicket, watching her? Probably caned him until welts showed on the backs of his legs.

Or would she? She sure wouldn't want him to tell George about her going to meet Print and doing what they did. Not that he ever would tell George but she might not know that. Sure she'd know, Tamar knew everything

Eli waited until he could no longer hear his sister, then started north through the woods so he could circle around and approach the cabin from along the river.

12

Eli sat on the buckboard between George and Tamar for the ride to the barbecue at the Briscoe ranch. Tamar was laughing and singing and whistling and having a high old time and even George smiled now and then and joined her on a chorus of "Pop Goes the Weasel."

Eli was surprised, expecting things to be different between his sister and her husband after he'd seen her with Print in the woods three weeks ago. She seemed happy as ever, though, and nothing much appeared to have changed except maybe she was even more lively than usual, whistling a shade louder and singing when before she might have paused to catch her breath.

He didn't much like the idea of going to the barbecue with them but Tamar said he had to, she wasn't about to leave him in the cabin alone and besides it would be good for him to get out in polite society for a change and he'd said he didn't see what was so polite about it 'cause there'd be the same cowhands at the party that he heard cussing to beat the band every other day of the week.

Tamar said that digging in his heels wouldn't get him nowhere, he was going no matter what, and when Tamar said a thing in that it's-all-settled tone of voice there was no use talking any more, you just had to shut up and make the best of it even though it didn't make him like the idea any better, he'd rather be riding and practicing his shooting and learning to rope instead of sitting around watching men dance and drink whiskey and in general make fools of themselves over a lot of women.

He'd never make a fool of himself over a woman, shaving and preening in front of a mirror and combing his hair back with bear grease to make it lay flat. Then sashaying around, all smiles and polite talk, telling the women how pretty they looked with that new red ribbon in their hair when everyone knew they looked no different, homely as always.

Not Tamar. Tamar was beautiful. There'd never been anyone with looks to match Tamar's. Eli loved Tamar and he was going to see that nobody ever hurt her. He'd never marry, he'd stay home with Tamar and George and take care of her. Eli frowned, remembering her in the woods with Print.

He imagined he had his gun in a holster on his hip and practiced drawing and shooting at the long-eared jackass rabbits—jackrabbits for short—flushed by the horses. Bang, bang, he said under his breath. Got you.

"What are you doing?" Tamar asked him.

"Nothing," he said, making out he was reholstering his six-shooter.

He'd decided he wouldn't be a scout after all, like Jason had been. The only good thing about coming to the party was maybe talking to Jason if he wasn't busy with all the women. He still wanted to be like Jason and know how to track and find water on the plains and cut for Indian sign. He'd been practicing, too, and he was pretty good at tracking, hadn't he followed Tamar and found the place she met Print in the woods without either of them being the wiser?

He wouldn't be a scout, though, 'cause he meant to be a lawman instead. He was nigh unto fifteen and pretty soon he'd run away from home and join the Texas Rangers and hunt down outlaws. Any *hombre* who broke the law, who shot men in the back or branded cattle that weren't theirs, he'd hunt down and when he caught them he'd call them by name and wait till they faced him and started to draw before he'd draw himself. His draw would be lightning-fast by then and pow-pow, he'd shoot them dead.

Eli's arm brushed Tamar as he again reholstered his imaginary six-shooter.

"My land, can't you sit still?" Tamar asked.

"Are we almost there?"

"Another five miles," George said.

Tamar drew in a deep breath. "I think I can smell the beef cooking," she said.

All Eli could smell was the cologne Tamar had put on. He didn't know what it was called but he knew that Tamar smelled like flowers.

They rode up to the Briscoe ranch just as the setting sun touched the western edge of the prairie. The disc of the sun was huge and red-gold, the color of Tamar's hair, and seemed to rest on the horizon like a ball of fire spreading in all directions. Eli watched, fascinated, as he unhitched the horse from the buckboard. By the time he led the horse to the corral, only a rim of fire was left and then the sun slid out of sight and it was dark, almost night, as though there'd been no time for evening.

After feeding the horse, Eli walked from the corral to the kitchen. A whole steer was roasting over a fire in the yard and a barrel of whiskey sat on a table nearby. Every so often one of the men came out of the house and filled a tin cup, praising the size of the barrel and the size of the steer. George came to the barrel more often than anyone.

Eli sat on the ground at the edge of the circle of firelight and watched and listened.

"Whose steer you barbecuing, Jason?" he heard Charlie Goodnight ask.

Jason smiled, looking like this wasn't the first time he'd heard that question. "I swear to God that's a Briscoe steer and if you want to go down to the corral you'll see the hide to prove it."

"First time I ever heard of a man eating his own beef." Goodnight laughed and clapped Jason on the back as he went by him into the kitchen.

Men came from the house to stand about in the glow of the fire while others lounged on the ground smoking and drinking and talking. Eli saw Ike McLeod and a couple of Goodnight hands, and Ed and Josh from Varner's, and Chicago Luke, the Briscoe cook, and a couple of other cowboys he didn't know. Jason walked over and stood behind Eli, not looking at him, more keeping his eyes on the fire and the men coming and going, the same as Eli was doing.

"George Swanson tells me you're turning into a full-fledged cowpuncher," Jason said.

"I've been learning," Eli said, feeling proud. "Doing what you said. Watching them that knows."

"I remember when I was no older'n you," Jason said, "and I asked this old cowpoke who worked on a ranch near my stepdad's farm how long it would take me to be a top cowhand like him, thinking all the while I was pretty near there, and he said, 'I'm sixty years old and I'm still learning. You don't get any diplomas saying you know all there is to know.' And I guess that's the way it is. I learn something new every day."

"I'm pretty fair at shooting," Eli said, "and I'm learning to rope."

"If you're ever not needed on the Varner spread you can always ride over here and I'll find room in my bunkhouse for you. Remember that, Eli. There'll always be a place waiting for you at the Briscoe ranch."

"I'll remember, Mr. Briscoe."

A wagon drove up with a lot of laughing and helloing and Jason gripped Eli's shoulder, leaving him to go and greet the newcomers. He'd like to work for Briscoe, Eli thought, if he wasn't going to be a lawman instead of a cowhand or a scout. Jason made a man feel good, like he amounted to something. Not like Print Varner. Print made a man feel small.

The cowhands around the barbecue fire were spinning yarns and boasting, speculating about the round-up that was coming, looking forward to it after the long winter. Eli heard the fiddles tuning up in the front room of the house. He walked around where he could look through the side window and saw Ike McLeod with one fiddle and an old man Eli'd heard called Overholt with the other.

The women were sitting inside talking, Tamar and Mrs. Varner and a woman Eli'd never seen before in a yellow dress with big hoop skirts and he guessed that was the new Mrs. Briscoe everybody had been wondering about. Tamar was the best-looking by far, he thought.

Eli walked back to the fire just as Print came out of the house. Print glanced around at the men, his eyes flicking over Eli as if he wasn't there, before he went to the barrel where he half-filled a tin cup and stood sipping the whiskey, not talking to anyone, seeming content to keep his own counsel.

Eli shook his head, wondering why Tamar liked him. She wouldn't if he ever told her what he knew about Print shooting Beatty but he couldn't tell because that was a thing to be kept among men and not shared with women, not even with Tamar. Eli didn't understand how he knew this but he did and that was the end of it.

Print half-filled his cup again and went inside. A few minutes later Jason came through the door with his new wife on his arm and stood by the fire introducing her around, his wife smiling and nodding while the cowboys got up and doffed their hats saying, "Pleased to make your acquaintance, ma'am," and the like.

Jason saw Eli sitting in the shadows and brought his wife over. Eli stumbled to his feet and Jason said, "I'd like you to meet my wife. This is Janine." The slender, brown-haired woman smiled and said she was glad Eli had come to their barbecue and Eli bobbed his head and said, "Pleased to meet you," and then Jason took his wife back into the house.

The fiddles were going full-tilt now and Eli, seeing the cowboys had all gone inside for the dancing, wandered over to the barrel sort of casual-like and drew a half cup of whiskey. Holding

the cup in both hands he hurried away along the
side of the house.

Through the window he saw all the women
standing up and the men, too, waiting for the
next dance to start. There were way more men
than women but they'd mended that by heifer-
branding some of the cowhands with ribbons tied
around their arms.

"Salute your honey!" old man Overholt shouted
and the partners bowed to each other.

"First lady, center," the fiddler called.

Eli saw Print standing in the doorway across
the room. Print's eyes were on Tamar and as he
watched, Eli saw Print look from Tamar to Jason
and back to Tamar, nodding to her. Tamar must
have seen Print because she sort of shrugged
before she went on dancing with George.

The men shouted as they danced, the women
swept around and around, their smiling faces
glowing with perspiration. The dancing figures
crossed the window, back and forth, as Eli took
his first sip from the cup in his hand.

He gagged on the fiery liquor, coughed and
spat. Waiting a few minutes to catch his breath, he
drank again. The whiskey left a trail of fire
through his body. Eli shook his head and, leaving
the lighted window, made sure no one was looking
when he poured the rest of the whiskey on the
ground.

A man's voice inside the house called for a
waltz and the fiddles struck up a lilting melody.
The cowhands retreated to the sides of the room
leaving only Jason and his new wife on the floor
that had been cleared for dancing. Jason held
her with one arm about her waist, one hand in
hers, and led her gracefully around and around
the room. The men cheered.

Print Varner, Vivian's hand on his arm, came through the doorway from the other room. He bowed to his wife and she curtsied. Eli's eyes widened. He'd never seen Mrs. Varner in a hoop skirt before. She looked a lot younger and prettier, too. Print took her in his arms and they glided about as the music rose and fell.

Eli had thought Jason and his new wife were good dancers but he grudgingly admitted that Print and Vivian were better. Watching them waltz was almost like being at a show, or at least, what he imagined a show to be. The cowboys had quieted when Print started dancing and now as the music stopped they let out whoops and cheered and Eli saw that Jason and his new wife were clapping for Print and Vivian, too.

Eli looked for his sister. Tamar was standing by herself watching the two men, Print and Jason. Her mouth a little open, the lamplight glittered from her green eyes, and her face shone with the excitement of the dancing.

George came up behind her and said something but she didn't seem to hear him and Eli saw him speak to her again. Tamar gave a start and turned to George, smiling at him and looking, Eli thought, as though she'd been caught doing something she hadn't ought to.

Bored with watching the dancing, Eli walked to the rear of the house. The wind was cold off the prairie so he sat near the fire on the steps leading to the storeroom behind the kitchen. After a time, Chicago Luke came out and cut a slice of beef and tasted it. He shook his head like he thought the meat would never be cooked through.

Eli heard a muffled sound behind him but at first he paid it no mind. The noise came again and he stood up, glancing at Chicago Luke who was swearing a blue streak while he directed the turning of the steer. Eli had recognized the sound from the storeroom as somebody coughing, not the sound of a cough from a bad cold but a deep, hollow, wracking cough.

He opened the door and went in and, in the gloom, saw a woman bending over with one hand to her chest and the other at her mouth. When she straightened up, breathing ragged-like, he saw by the light coming from the kitchen that it was Jason's new wife, Janine.

Eli didn't know what to do.

"May I help you, ma'am?" he asked.

She looked at him, startled, shaking her head. When she saw who he was she tried to smile. "Wait, Eli," she said, "you can help. Pour my medicine for me, will you please? I can't hold the spoon with my hands shaking this way."

Eli saw a bottle and a spoon on the table beside her. He poured a spoonful and was about to hand it to Janine when she started coughing again, holding her handkerchief to her mouth. All at once he saw blood cover the handkerchief and trickle between her fingers.

Eli was so startled he dropped the spoon on the floor. He didn't know what to do. Should he run for help? Janine's coughing subsided, though, and again she tried to smile at Eli as she dabbed at her lips with the blood-soaked handkerchief.

"Don't be afraid, Eli," she said. "Please pour me another spoonful."

He felt along the floor with his hands until he found the spoon, wiped it on a cloth as best he could, and once more poured medicine from the bottle. Janine took his hand in both of hers and guided the spoon to her mouth, swallowing the medicine. She grimaced as though the taste was bitter, then breathed deeply.

"Please bring me some water, Eli," she said. "My hands are so sticky."

He went to the pump in the kitchen and filled a pan of water and when he brought it to her she washed her hands and face, drying herself with a clean handkerchief. She handed the bloody handkerchief to Eli.

"Will you do me a great favor, Eli?" she asked. When he nodded, she said, "Take and bury this handkerchief where no one will find it. Will you do that for me?"

Again Eli nodded and hastily turned to go out the door, awed and frightened by what he had seen.

"Eli," Janine said, "I'd appreciate it greatly if you didn't say anything about my being sick. Will you do that for me, too?"

"Yes, Miz Briscoe," he said.

He walked across the yard and buried the handkerchief behind the corral. He felt queasy in his stomach from seeing the blood and from thinking about how Mrs. Briscoe must feel with her blood coming out of her mouth. He wondered what was the matter with her.

Was she dying? A tingle ran up his spine. No, he told himself, she couldn't be that sick, hadn't he seen her dancing with Jason just a short time before? At the same time he felt sort of good because she was trusting him with a secret. Maybe one that Jason didn't even know.

When Eli came back to sit at the fire he found George nursing another cup of whiskey. "Looks like I'll never get a dance with that sister of yours," he muttered, "what with all the other men mooning over her." George sounded proud and angry at the same time. "Your sister's too damn pretty," he said.

George sat holding the cup in both hands, staring down at the liquor. Tamar wouldn't like George drinking, Eli thought. He remembered before George married Tamar how he'd come home from Bailey's Tavern and not be able to unlock the door and Eli would have to get out of bed and let him in. Tamar said drink was George's weakness and she'd made him promise to go teetote when they set out for Texas and as far as Eli knew George had kept his word. Until now.

At midnight they ate, the cowboys sitting wherever they could find space in the house, on the porch or on the ground around the fire. As soon as the plates were cleared away, the fiddles started again and Eli curled up near the dying fire, hearing Ike McLeod chanting:

Weave 'em up and weave 'em down,
Weave 'em pretty girls round and round . . .

When Eli woke, the dancing was still going on though he saw that some of the cowhands had already bedded down near the house. The fire burned low, with now and then an ember snapping to send sparks flying.

Eli walked away from the lights of the house so he could study the stars in the northern sky. The Big Dipper was so low beneath the North Star he figured it must be between two and three o'clock in the morning. When he neared the house again he heard a woman laugh from the direction of the kitchen and he knew it was Tamar. He'd recognized Tamar's laugh anywhere.

Two people, a man and Tamar—she smelled like flowers—walked past him. Eli stayed in the shadows until they were gone. Must be Tamar and

George getting some air, he thought. He shook his head, puzzled. Tamar's laugh hadn't been the laugh he was used to, she had sounded excited, like when she was with Print Varner in the woods.

Eli frowned. Tamar wouldn't do that here. It must be George she was with. He went back to the fire and was warming his hands over the embers when the kitchen door banged open and George came out.

"Where'd she go, Eli?" George's voice was slurred and he sounded real riled.

Eli swallowed. "Who do you mean, George?" he asked.

"Your sister, that's who I mean. She's out here somewhere with Jason Briscoe and I mean to find her."

"I didn't see her with Mr. Briscoe," Eli said, which was the truth, and yet now that George said the name Eli realized the man with Tamar *had* been Jason.

He didn't like to lie to George 'cause he liked him, at least he liked him whenever he felt anyway at all about him. George was somebody who was there with you and then when he was gone you didn't miss him. For an instant he wondered how Tamar felt about George. After they got married Eli had always thought of them together, as Tamar and George. But Tamar and Jason?

George kicked angrily at the ground and sent some dirt spraying into the fire, raising smoke. He set off in the direction Eli had seen Tamar and Jason take.

"George," Eli called after him, trying to think of something to say to turn his attention away from Tamar, but George paid him no heed. Eli stood looking after him, not knowing what to do.

Would he ever know the right thing to do? he wondered. He heard George's voice not too far away. George was shouting. Eli had never heard George shout before.

Some of the cowhands were rousing from their sleep, grunting and asking what all the hubbub was about. Eli heard Print's voice, real loud, from the direction of the house, saying, "What's all the ruckus?"

And then they were all running toward the commotion with somebody carrying a lantern. Eli ran after them. The men stopped, gathered around, and Eli pushed his way through the crowd until he could see what was going on.

George and Jason were fighting. Tamar stood shouting at them to stop, pulling at George's arm. It wasn't really George and Jason fighting, Eli realized after a minute, it was George fighting and Jason holding the smaller man away.

George shook off Tamar and ducked in under Jason's arm, butting him in the stomach with his head. The blow didn't seem to have any effect. George flailed at Jason with his fists, mostly hitting his arms. Finally Jason grasped George around the waist and raised him over his head and Eli heard Tamar scream and saw her run at Jason, beating him on the chest with her fists as Jason made believe he was going to throw George to the ground. Instead he set him on his feet and one of Jason's men came up behind George and pinioned his arms.

"You bastard," George shouted at Jason, "trying to steal a man's wife right out from under his nose. And you a new married man, too."

George went on like that while Jason just stared at him like he was crazy and Tamar tried to hush him, crying all the time. The cowhands stood around gawking and grinning kind of fool-ish-like.

The man holding the lantern turned and Eli saw it was Print Varner. Print had a smile on his face like he was enjoying all the fuss. Print's a son-of-a-bitch, Eli thought; he's the one George ought to be calling names, not Jason. Print saw Eli staring at him and the smile faded from his face and he looked away.

I hate you, Eli thought.

13

BY THE TIME the sun rose, throwing long shadows westward, the Briscoe barbecue was over. The fiddles were laid away, the steer had been eaten, the whiskey barrel was empty, the candles had guttered and the house was quiet.

Jason lay beside his wife. He'd thought she was asleep but now he heard her stir and, turning, saw her large brown eyes staring at the ceiling.

"Are you all right?" he asked. "I thought you looked pale when you were dancing. Toward the last."

"I'm fine. All the excitement, the noise and the dancing tired me. And meeting all those people for the first time."

As she went on, Jason listened with only half an ear. George Swanson was a fool, he thought, picking a fight in front of half the State of Texas. And Tamar—he didn't understand Tamar. Leading him outside, saying she needed a breath of air and then playing up to him like she had.

What was wrong with kissing a girl when she practically asked him to? Not asked so much, dared him was more like it. Well, of course he shouldn't have but what was a man to do?

"Jason, are you listening to me?" Janine asked.

"Yes, of course. What did you say?"

"I wanted to know what the fight was about."

"Oh, you mean my run-in with Swanson. He had too much to drink and he objected to my dancing with his wife. He tried to goad me into fighting him but I wouldn't. It was all a big fuss over nothing."

"Tamar's a pretty little thing. How I envy that red hair of hers. I imagine she leads her husband a merry chase."

"I wouldn't be surprised," Jason said, wishing she'd talk about something else.

"Jason," she said, "There's a matter I've been meaning to speak to you about."

Jason frowned. Was she going to start asking him about Tamar?

"I've meant to tell you before but I keep putting it off," Janine said. "I know the round-up starts next week and after that you're leaving for the drive to Kansas. I don't want you to worry. I'm not going to worry so I don't want you to, either."

She's sicker than she's admitted, that's her meaning, Jason thought. He'd suspected as much for some time yet he hadn't been sure and maybe he'd hoped that by acting like she wasn't sick it would turn out that she really wasn't. He knew she hid her worst times from him, never even liked him to know how often she had to take her medicine.

"I think I can guess what you're going to say," Jason told her.

"I never was one for being able to keep secrets," Janine said. "I know he's going to be a boy."

"A boy?" Jason tried to catch the drift of what she was telling him.

"I expect the baby will be born the first part of October."

For a moment Jason was stunned. Then a vast wave of joy flooded through him. "You're sure?" he asked. "There's no doubt?"

"None at all. You didn't guess after all, did you?"

He took her in his arms and held her frail body close to his as though to protect her. From what, he wasn't sure.

"I think that's wonderful news," he said.

"It was a surprise after all. What did you think I was going to tell you, Jason?"

He thought frantically. "I suspected you were—were going to say how you wanted to go about fixing up the house. Seeing you've been talking so much about carpets and curtains and the like lately." His evasion sounded feeble but maybe she'd believe him.

"I do mean to make this a more civilized-looking place after I have the baby. Not before. I want to do one thing at a time."

"Are you strong enough? I know how poorly you sometimes feel."

"I've set my mind to it, Jason, and when I set my mind to a thing, I do it come hell or high water. That first time I saw you in the library at the Myerson house, did you know I said to myself, 'Janine, that's the man you're going to marry,' even before you said a word? And marry you I did. Now I've set my mind to having this baby and I'm going to, no matter what. And he'll be a boy, you wait and see if he's not."

14

THE WINTER had been hard, even for Texas, with the blue northers driving snow down across the plains and scattering the cattle over hundreds of miles of range as the animals sought food and shelter in the brush along the creeks and in the Cross Timbers. Now spring was late in coming so it wasn't until near the end of April that the grass greened and the round-up could begin.

In later years it came to be known as the Briscoe-Goodnight round-up, the biggest in Texas up to that time, named for the two men who directed the harvesting of the cattle, though ranchers from miles around sent men to help.

The cowhands got ready by repairing their saddles and lining up good strings of horses, breaking some, for the remuda. The Goodnight chuck wagon, the first chuck wagon in the world, was overhauled, its big wooden hubs greased and the mess gear loaded.

Briscoe and Goodnight made their first night's

camp near Charlie Goodnight's ranch, intending
to swing south and west in the weeks ahead. Diego,
Goodnight's cook, was up at three in the morning
and at three-thirty he strode among the men sleeping on the open prairie.

"Come, *muchachos*," he trilled, "get up and hear
the little birds singing their sweet praises to the
Lord God Almighty." His voice changed to a roar.
"Damn your souls, get up!"

The men roused, rolled their beds and, after
lashing them, dumped them next to the bed wagon. They splashed cold water on their faces and
came to squat around the fire for a breakfast of
sowbelly, hot biscuits and coffee. Then the wrangler drove the remuda, the band of saddle horses,
into a corral formed by two heavy ropes tied at
their inner ends to wagon wheels and supported
at their middle and outer ends by three-pronged
forked sticks driven into the ground.

As the cow ponies milled and dodged, each rider
roped a good long-legged distance horse from his
string of six or seven. Each man had a morning
horse, an afternoon horse, a rope horse, a cutting
horse and two or three half-broken horses to gentle
on short rides.

George Swanson needed three passes before he
roped his horse. As he tightened the cinch of his
saddle, he glanced about him, suspecting the other
men were sneering at his ineptness. They seemed
to be paying him no heed but the night before
he'd heard snickers as he'd walked by some of the
Goodnight hands and he'd known they were whispering behind his back about his run-in with Jason Briscoe.

George joined the other men near the fire where
Jason stood facing them, his eyes flicking around

the group and passing over George as though he wasn't even there. Damn him to hell, George thought.

Jason used a stick to map out the plan of that day's campaign in the dirt, making an X at the center of the day's work. Diego nodded and mounted the chuck wagon, cracking his whip over his team and heading out for the rendezvous spot. The wrangler followed, driving the remuda along at the rear of the wagon.

As soon as they were gone, Jason divided his men into two groups of six each, sending one group to the left and the other to the right. George found himself in the right-hand, northern bunch with Print Varner in charge.

Print led his men out of the camp, heading at an angle to the path of the chuck wagon. Every couple of miles he sent a man farther out to the right in a loop of eight or nine miles to find and chase cattle back toward the center of the drive, each rider like one of the spokes of a wheel driving the cows toward the chuck wagon pulled up at the hub.

Once he was alone on the prairie, and after he'd routed a few head of cattle from a creek bottom, George reached for his canteen and raised it to his lips. The liquor burned his throat all the way down. George wiped his lips with the back of his hand before he screwed on the top of the canteen and returned it to his saddle.

He remembered the day before when Charlie Goodnight had laid down the law to the riders working the round-up.

"There'll be no liquor," he'd said, "absolutely none. And no gambling. Any man working with me who drinks or gambles will be sent packing."

What Charlie Goodnight and Jason Briscoe didn't know wouldn't hurt them, George told himself.

Fortified by the drink, he spurred his horse on. The sun was hot overhead and sweat gathered on his face. He flushed more cattle from the brush along another creek, heading them in the direction of the rendezvous. Cows were stupid, stubborn brutes, he thought. He came on a cow and her calf but he couldn't force his horse through the brush; to prod them out he'd have to climb onto the bank and around behind. The hell with them, George thought, riding on.

A couple of hours and a couple of drinks later, George had maybe fifty head herded in front of him. On both sides of him he saw puffs of dust where other riders were bringing cattle in. He joined up with Ed who was riding herd on maybe ninety or a hundred head and saw Ed look with disdain at his paltry fifty.

Ed didn't say a word, though, just nodded as though nothing was wrong. In his mind George could hear what Ed would tell the others around the campfire. "Can't expect a man who can't ride herd on his own wife to be any good at riding herd on cows." The sound of the cowhands' laughter rang in George's ears.

Tamar had laughed at him, too, once they'd gotten home from the Briscoe barbecue and Eli was asleep in his bunk.

"Oh, George," she'd said, "you're making a something out of a nothing. I don't care a whit for Jason Briscoe. Whyever would you think different?"

"I saw him," George said sullenly. "He was kissing you and I didn't see you running away."

"That's not the way it was at all, you've got it

turned around. We were out for a bit of fresh air
what with all the dancing and the smoke in the
house and Jason was boasting to me about how
he'd found a wife in New York and how he thought
it was such a shame when nobody he knew from
Texas could be at the wedding. I said I might
have missed the wedding but I could still give the
groom a kiss and he up and backed off so I told
him he was afraid of me so he let me kiss him on
the cheek and just that minute you came blunder-
ing along as drunk as a coot and started to fight."

"That wasn't the way I saw it," George said. He
wanted to believe her and he halfway did, that
sounded like what Tamar might do. He said, "I
wasn't drunk. Maybe I'd had one or two drinks
but I wasn't drunk."

"Why you picked a fight at Jason's own house
and at his own party, I'll never know. And with a
man who could beat you with one hand tied behind his back. And you *were* drunk, drunk as a
coot."

George felt his face redden. "I took him on
because he was kissing you, that's why, and he had
no right."

She turned away. He'd expected Tamar to answer him back like she always did—he knew
Tamar didn't take nothing from nobody. But she
hadn't answered back, she'd turned away and the
look on her face told him she was guilty somehow
and it hadn't happened the way she'd said.

Just when he'd been ready to believe her.

He tried to ignore her during the next few days,
talking only when necessary, but Tamar wasn't
having any of that and before long he'd given in
and it was like it had been before. At least that's
the way it seemed, but George sensed there'd been
a change between them and he blamed Jason Bris-

coe. Hadn't Jason kissed Tamar and then with all the men gawking hadn't Jason picked him up and held him over his head like he was a half-empty sack of meal?

He'd get even with Jason Briscoe, he told himself. He'd bide his time, act like nothing out of the ordinary had happened, like he'd forgotten and was going to live and let live, but when the time came he meant to even the score with Jason. One way or another.

The cattle were rumbling toward the chuck wagon with the dust rising in a cloud around them, a cloud giving no shade from the noon sun beating on the riders. While the cowboys waited for the milling to die down and for the cows and calves to seek out each other—no matter how big the herd they always did by smell or by instinct—the riders looked over the gather to see what brands they'd turned up.

As soon as the cattle settled, George and the others rode to the chuck wagon, ravenously hungry. Goodnight had ordered one of his own beeves killed because they were on his land and Diego was putting the finishing touches on the barbecuing. Besides cooking the fresh beef, he'd spent the whole of the morning preparing an assortment of pies and a plum duff pudding for the men.

After they ate, the cowboys threw the dregs of their coffee on the canvas cover of the water keg so the evaporation would keep the water cool. They shredded their cigarettes and watched as the wrangler corraled the remuda. Then the men who were to ride into the herd to separate out cows and their calves for branding selected and mounted the ponies trained for this cutting-out work.

"You'll hold down the critters for the branding," Jason told George.

That's right, George thought, give me the shittiest job going. He didn't say a word, though, not even giving Jason the satisfaction of a nod of acknowledgment. Not that Jason seemed to notice; he turned away and started giving orders left and right.

George couldn't help admiring the skill of the cutters, specially Charlie Goodnight who was working the herd himself. The black-bearded rancher dropped the reins of his pony to his saddle horn and steered his mount with his knees. As soon as he showed his horse the calf he wanted to pull from the herd, the gelding's ears twitched and his eyes stayed glued to the pursued animal while he worked it toward the branding fire, the horse going about his job without a lot of fuss and feathers so he'd keep the herd quiet and the other calves would stay near their mothers.

As soon as his pony had the calf near the fire, Goodnight used a sidearm cast to slip his rope under the animal's hind legs. He pulled the rope up and back, taking out the slack and drawing the loop tight. He stopped his pony, stretching out the running calf and toppling him to lay bawling on the ground.

George ran forward and grasped the calf's hind legs while another cowboy took hold of his front leg and jaw. Goodnight, glancing at the hovering mother cow, read the brand on her side.

"Bow and arrow," he shouted.

A cowhand took the heated bow and arrow iron from the fire and burned the brand on the calf's flank while another man cut a notch in one of his ears. By the end of the afternoon the air around the fire was acrid with the smell of burned hair from the hides of several hundred calves and other new-branded cattle.

Several times during the day, while he was being spelled by another cowhand, George moseyed over to his saddle for a quick nip. He shook his canteen; it sounded less than half full. At this rate it'd never last till the end of the round-up. The whiskey wasn't having any effect on him at all, he told himself, other than helping him get through the day.

He'd been thankful for having a couple of drinks under his belt when the cowboy from the Bow and Arrow spread, the one they called Slim who had a few words to say on every subject under the sun, grinned across a bawling calf as the branding iron sizzled on the animal's hide and said, "From what I hear, George, you'd better do a little branding on that young heifer of yours."

If he hadn't had a few drinks George'd probably have been riled enough to call Slim on it, but as it was he just laughed, passing the words off by saying something about all heifers needing branding at one time or another.

They finished the branding for the day and the men started saddling up for the ride to the night camp. George felt a little woozy, from the heat of the sun he supposed, and had trouble tightening his cinch. Then, when he was ready to mount, his horse shied and threw him back onto the ground.

With a curse he scrambled to his feet and found himself face to face with Jason Briscoe.

Jason wrinkled his face in disgust. "You've been hitting the bottle, George," he said. "You can smell the booze from here to the Rio Grande."

"That's a lie," George said.

"Don't throw the lie at me," Jason told him. "You heard Goodnight's orders about liquor on the round-up. You'd best pack your gear and head for home. And let Tamar tuck you in for the night."

"Better she tuck me in than you her."

Jason gripped a handful of George's shirt in his fist and yanked the other man to him. "Just what do you mean by that?" he demanded.

Confused, afraid despite the Dutch courage he'd had to drink, George said, "Take it however you want. I ain't scared of you. And I ain't been drinking."

Jason shoved him away and walked past George to George's horse. He began running his hand over the saddle.

"What do you think you're doing?" George asked him.

"I'm going to take a sniff of your canteen to prove one way or the other whether you've been having a nip."

"Take your hand off my gear."

George reached past him for the canteen. Instead his hand closed over the butt of the Colt he'd put in his saddle holster when he started working the calves for branding. George hesitated, then Jason pulled the canteen from its canvas sheath. George tugged the gun free and stepped back, holding it pointed unsteadily at Jason.

"Put away that shooting iron before somebody gets hurt." Jason took a sniff at the open canteen.

"Get your God-damned hands off my gear," George shouted.

Jason returned the canteen and let his hands drop to his sides. "Pack it in and get the hell out of here," he told George.

George fired. He'd meant to scare Jason by shooting over his head but the shot came closer than he'd intended, creasing Jason's hat. George blinked, astonished he'd fired at all, and when he looked again he saw that Jason had a Colt in his hand.

"Drop the gun, George," Jason said quietly.

George heard the cowhands running to see what the shot had been about and he remembered how they'd run up the same way at the barbecue when he started fighting Jason. They won't laugh at me this time, he told himself, not after they see me stand up to Briscoe.

"I'll teach you to show respect to my wife," he shouted, firing and missing badly.

Jason fired low, intending to crease George's leg to put him out of action before he hurt somebody. Just as he fired, George leaped to one side, going into a crouch, and the shot hit him full in the upper chest. George grunted as the force of the .44 hurled him back onto the ground beside his horse. His gun spun away. The horse reared and bolted.

Josh ran and knelt beside George. After a few moments he stood and looked at Jason. "George's dead," he said.

Jason holstered his gun. "I didn't mean to kill the damn fool," he said.

"We all saw what happened," Josh said. "George went for his gun first, he brought it on hisself." The men standing behind him nodded.

Print stepped forward. "Josh," he said, "you and Ed corral that horse and tie George on him. We're gonna have to take him home. I'll ride on ahead of you and tell his wife." He looked maliciously at Jason. "Unless you want to, Briscoe."

Jason stared coldly at Print until the other man looked away, shrugging. "I'll ride ahead to Swanson's place and tell Tamar," Print said.

They buried George Swanson the next day on a

rise over the Keechi a few hundred yards from his cabin. They'd called a day's halt to the round-up and all the hands were at the funeral, all except Jason who'd stayed with the herd they'd gathered the day before.

Eli, standing beside Tamar on the hillside, watched as four men used ropes to lower the plain plank casket into the ground. There was an awkward pause, the men looking at one another, before Josh stepped forward and said a few words over the grave and led them in prayer.

"Our father, who art in heaven . . ." they mumbled. At the "Amen," shovels were thrust into the pile of earth beside the grave and the men shoveled the dirt onto the coffin.

Eli looked from the corner of his eye at Tamar and saw that his sister was staring straight ahead. She'd had hardly a word to say since Josh and Ed had ridden in with the body the night before and this frightened Eli. When their father died in Canajoharie, she'd wept and carried on something fierce but now her eyes were dry and turned in as though she was studying something only she could see.

"You'll have to look after your sister now, son," Ed told him as they walked down the hill from the grave. Eli nodded.

They all went to the Swanson cabin and found Vivian already there with enough grub to feed everybody twice over. Eli thought he wasn't hungry so he was surprised when he found himself eating more than his share. Every time he looked at Print he felt cold all over. Print will come and take Tamar away, he told himself.

At last the cowhands left, Print and his wife among the last to go, and Eli and Tamar were alone. They sat at the table for over an hour with neither saying a word, Tamar staring at the lamp as though mesmerized by the flame. Eli heard a horse ride up and a minute later there was a knock at the cabin door.

When Tamar paid no heed, Eli got up, drew the crossbar and opened the door. Jason stood outside. Eli didn't rightly know what to do so he ducked his head and stepped back. As Jason passed him he put his hand on Eli's shoulder. Jason stopped beside Tamar and stood staring down at her.

"I'd give everything I have to undo what happened yesterday." Jason reached out as though to touch her but his hand held a few inches from her arm. "I know nothing I can say will help but I wanted you to know how I feel."

Eli thought his sister would nod or try to smile or maybe fly into a rage and start beating at Jason with her fists. If she did, somehow he knew it would be all right. She didn't, though. What she did was nothing. Tamar acted as if she hadn't heard Jason, as if he wasn't even there.

Eli watched as Jason stood looking at Tamar. After a long time he turned and spoke to Eli, looking awful tired. "If there's aught you need," he said, "let me know. I'll do whatever I can."

Eli nodded and Jason left the cabin, easing the door shut behind him. After what seemed forever to Eli, Tamar went to bed. Eli waited until he was certain she was asleep before he gathered a few provisions from the shelves and packed them in George's saddlebags. After saddling, he led his horse to the front of the cabin, tethering the gray before he went back inside. Tamar was sleeping restlessly behind the curtained part of the room she'd shared until the day before with George. Eli took George's Colt from the shelf above the fireplace where Print had put it when they brought George's body home. He thrust the Colt into his belt.

When Eli rode up to Varner's place, he found the house unlighted and quiet. Eli thought of Print shooting Jack Beatty in the back and wrapping him in the skin, remembered how Print and Tamar had met in the glade in the woods, not once but many times, and how Print, in some way, had seen to it that George was killed. Now with George dead, Print would take Tamar away. Hatred for Print Varner seethed inside him.

Eli dismounted, trailing the reins over the horse's head. He walked purposely onto the porch and pounded on the door. When there was no sound from inside he raised his fist and pounded again. He heard footsteps, a man's. He was glad it wasn't Vivian because he liked Vivian and he didn't want her to see what he was going to do.

"What in the hell . . . ?" Print stood in the open doorway with a candle in his hand.

Eli took the gun from his belt and shot him.

Print staggered back, the candle dropping to the floor and going out. Eli heard Print cursing and he fired again at the sound of his voice.

"That's for Tamar," Eli shouted. "I know about you and Tamar. That's for what you did to her."

Eli turned and ran. When he started to mount his gray he realized he still had the gun in his hand. He smelled the acrid odor of gunsmoke; behind him he heard voices calling from inside the Varner house. He was about to throw the gun away, hesitated, then thrust it into his belt.

He looked back at Varner's, saw a bobbing lantern and heard a man's voice shouting at him. Eli mounted and rode off into the night.

15

PRINT VARNER, naked to the waist, lay on his back on the kitchen table.

"That damn kid, that damn Eli," he muttered over and over.

"Give him another shot of whiskey," Josh said. Ed held the liquor to Print's mouth and the wounded man swallowed it, coughing.

"Hold him down," Vivian told the two men.

She took a long-bladed knife from a pan of boiling water and wiped the handle dry before she bent over Print. The wound was a dark brown hole in his upper right chest near the armpit. Vivian wiped away the blood with a damp cloth.

"Put this in your mouth and bite hard," Josh held a wooden ladle to Print's lips. Print opened his mouth and bit down on the bowl.

With a grimace, Vivian pushed her forefinger into the wound to determine the course of the bullet. She swallowed twice, her teeth clenched against the nausea that threatened to gag her.

The bullet had gone up and to the right. She pulled out her finger and thrust the knife in, opening the wound wider as she probed. Blood trickled down Print's side and he grunted in pain, beads of sweat clustering on his forehead. Vivian probed deeper, the tip of the knife meeting resistance, scraping against metal, she thought. Or against bone?

She maneuvered the knife, the blood smearing the hilt and oozing onto her fingers. There. She forced the bullet from the wound and held the small piece of metal for a moment between her thumb and forefinger before dropping it onto the floor. Dipping a cloth in the hot water, she cleaned the wound, cauterized it with whiskey, and bandaged it.

Josh took the ladle from between Print's teeth, glancing at the deep teeth marks on the bowl. When Print let out a long, shuddering sigh and opened his eyes, Vivian leaned over her husband.

"Why did he do it, Print?" she asked. "Why did Eli try to kill you?"

"I don't know. He's gone plumb loco. George. George getting killed must have set him off."

Vivian dipped her hands in the basin and washed Print's blood from her fingers, remembering how the pounding on the door had wakened her a few hours before. She had heard what Eli shouted at her husband after shooting him. Print and Tamar, he'd shouted. Eil *must* be loco, like Print said.

Yet from the beginning she hadn't liked the way Print looked at Tamar, from that first day when they'd found the Swansons marooned on the prairie. She had to admit Tamar was a pretty little thing with her golden hair. And men seemed to like the way she stood up to them, sassing them back.

Tamar must have the morals of an alleycat, she thought. Look at the way she behaved at the dance, making up to every man in sight and luring Jason off. In fact she'd made eyes at every man at the party except Print.

Vivian dried her hands on a towel. Every man except Print. Just what Tamar might do if she *was* guilty. Vivian felt her face redden with anger. After all, she was a Kincaid, she had money coming. Vivian Kincaid didn't have to dance to a tune called by a Varner.

She smiled down at Print. "Are you feeling better?" she asked sweetly.

"As good as might be expected," he said.

"That's wonderful. Before you know it you'll be up and around as good as new. Lucky for you Eli was so excited he didn't take good aim."

She mustn't act rashly, Vivian told herself. She'd make sure she wasn't imagining things before she decided what to do. As her father had always said, "When you get riled at a man, count to ten and then if you're still riled, count to ten again and then when he isn't expecting it, kill the son-of-a-bitch."

A week later, Print was dressed before dawn. After he ate breakfast he sat nursing a second cup of coffee, holding the cup awkwardly in his left hand. His right arm was in a bandana sling.

"You're a fool, Print," Vivian said, "to join the round-up again so soon." She sat across from him with her hands folded in her lap.

"I might as well. From the way you been keeping your distance, you'd think bullet wounds were catching."

"You know you'd just start bleeding all over again. As it was, you were lucky the wound didn't putrefy."

Print grunted and set his cup on the table. "I know what your trouble is," he said. "Eli shooting me's put some sort of a bee in your bonnet. You're probably thinking all sorts of fool thoughts."

"I always liked Eli. He'd not shoot a man for no reason at all."

"I wasn't intending to speak out but I can see I better. I know why Eli came a-gunnin' for me and then lit out for parts unknown."

"You do? Why didn't you ever say? All this week you've been telling me he must have gone loco because of George getting killed."

"George was part of the reason, but only part. I didn't say nothing about the other 'cause it reflects no credit on me. So I don't want you to ever let on to anyone what I'm about to tell you."

"You know I won't, Print. I'm your wife."

"You recall last year when Eli ran away? I didn't know at the time but he'd been spying on me. I caught this rustler by the name of Beatty with one of Goodnight's cows, caught him red-handed, and when he went for his gun I killed him and then I got worried how it might look, us being new in the county, so I wrapped his body up in this skin and hid it.

"Eli saw me, Jason Briscoe told me later, but he didn't see Beatty go for his gun, he must of been behind me or too far away, and he thought I shot him down in cold blood. That's why he ran away, Jason'll tell you the truth of what I'm saying, and it's why Eli came gunning for me last week, thinking maybe I had something to do with George getting killed when everybody knows it was Jason's doing."

"I don't have to ask Jason," Vivian said. "I believe you." And she did, for the story rang true. She remembered the way Eli had changed toward Print all of a sudden the year before, following him around at first and then having nothing to do with him.

And yet she had heard Eli accuse Print of being with Tamar. Could she have been mistaken? Vivian asked herself. What with waking in the night, hearing the shot, hearing Eli shouting?

Print got up and came around the table. Leaning down, he kissed her, his lips parting, and she felt herself responding. She put her hand to the back of his head and held him to her, kissing him. She wouldn't feel this excitement, she assured herself, if her suspicions about Print and Tamar were true.

As they walked to the door, his left arm encircled her waist. Vivian was relieved, almost joyous, and yet she realized she still felt a nagging doubt. And because of that doubt she didn't abandon her plan. The idea had come to her during the night when she'd been awakened by rain thrumming on the roof over her head.

"If you ride down that way," Vivian said, "will you stop at Tamar's cabin and tell her I'll be by to pay her a visit later today?"

"I wasn't planning on going along the river," Print said. "I want to swing toward Goodnight's on my way to join up with the men herding to the west of here."

"Never mind, it's not important."

"When were you intending to go visiting?" Print asked casually. Too casually? Vivian wondered.

"Not before mid-afternoon. I've a lot of washing I didn't get done, what with you being here all this week."

Print nodded and headed for the corral. "When

you see Tamar," he called back to her, "try to get her to change her mind about moving up here nearer us. She shouldn't be living alone so far from neighbors."

"I will," Vivian said.

She watched him ride off to the west, waving to him until he was out of sight. Once she was alone, Vivian breathed deeply. The air was fresh from the rain, the grass and leaves had been washed clean of dust. It was almost, she thought, as though the world had been reborn.

She went into the house and sat at the table with her hands clasped in her lap. I should start the wash, she thought. He's my husband and I ought to trust him. She stared down at the table top. Tamar and Print. No, it couldn't be true. She'd get up right now and fill the tubs.

Vivian half rose, then sank back. I have to know for certain, she told herself. Prove to myself it's not true. The washing can wait. I'll just sit here another thirty minutes and then ride down and visit Tamar.

Print rode in a circle so he approached the Swanson cabin through the trees on the hillside above the river. He looped his reins on the fence and lifted the latch, cursing when he found the door bolted.

He knocked, calling out, "It's me, Print."

Tamar opened the door and stood aside. He walked past her and sat at the table, looking up at her. She wore a green robe over a white nightgown and her red-gold hair was tousled, her eyes dulled by sleep. He caught his breath at the sight of her but when he reached for her Tamar backed away.

"You ought to move nearer to us," Print said.

"I can have Ed and Josh move you and the cabin in no time at all."

"I'm staying put," Tamar told him.

"You still think Eli's coming home?"

"No. I did the first day or two after he ran off. Not any more. I got a feeling I'll never see him again. Not alive."

"Sure you will, Tammy. Once he finds out he didn't kill me like he probably thinks he did, he'll come home with his tail between his legs."

"I'll never see him again. I tell you I've got a feeling."

Print stood up. When he saw Tamar edge away from him he went to the cabin window and stood with his head bowed, sighing a long sigh.

"This here's all my doing," he said.

"I don't rightly understand, Print."

"I know why Eli took that there shot at me. The fault's mine and it doesn't do me proud. That's why I've never said a word to no one."

"I reckoned he'd found out about you and me, Print. Or guessed."

"Had nothing at all to do with you, Tamar. It was me." He heard her take a step toward him but he didn't turn. "I don't want you to say a word of this to nobody," he said, "but you recall the time last year when Eli ran off? Well, what really happened . . ." He told her the same tale he'd told Vivian less than an hour before.

"You see," Print said when he'd finished, "it didn't have nothing to do with you. The fault's mine. And I'm sorry as hell for what it's done to you."

Tamar took his left arm in her hands and pressed herself against him. Though the softness of her breast roused him, Print made no move.

"He never told me," Tamar said. "All this time and Eli never breathed a word of it to me. I saw how different he acted but then I thought that's how boys are."

"He's not a boy, Tammy, he's fifteen, he's a man. He thought it was something between men so he didn't trouble you with it." Print sighed. "I didn't want to say nothing 'cause I knew you'd never forgive me, bringing all this down on you, especially now that Eli's run off again."

"Print, I think the more of you for telling me the truth." She buried her face against his chest.

Print groaned, twisting slightly away. "Your brother shoots a mean .44," he said.

"Here I've been acting like I was the only one with troubles," Tamar said, "and all the time you've been carrying this in your mind and in your heart. All the while it was eating away at you and you not saying a word."

Print shrugged. "A man does what he thinks right," he said.

Tamar raised her head to him and kissed him. His good arm circled her waist and drew her to him, his tongue forcing its way between her lips and meeting hers.

"Oh, Print," she said. "I've missed you so much these last two weeks. It's been like having a fever and me with no medicine to bring it down."

He took his arm from around her waist and cupped her breast through her robe. "I think I got the cure you've been needing," he said, leading her toward the bed.

"No." When he started to protest, she said, "I want to, Print, you know I do, but not here, not in this cabin, not where . . ." She paused. "Not where I lived with George."

He nodded. He watched while she took off the

robe and dressed. Then, taking her by the hand, he led her outside. The sun was up and the day promised to be warm. Tamar's bare feet made tracks across the damp earth as they walked toward the timbers.

Vivian watched them climb the hill, hand in hand, and enter the trees. For a moment she thought she'd be sick as the bile rose in her throat and gagged her. She drew in one deep breath after another, fighting her nausea until she finally calmed herself enough to swing the horse around and ride slowly back to the ranch.

Her first thought was to pack and leave. Let Print come back from the round-up and find her gone. Better yet, have him come home and find nothing; she'd burn the house and leave a mass of charred rubble to greet him on his homecoming. Yet if she left, where could she go? The last letter from home had told of her father's failing health. The old house outside Atlanta had been sold and her father was in the city being cared for by Nate.

All she had was here with Print, this land and their few hundred head of cattle. If her father died, and she knew he must soon, and she left Print, she'd have no one. Her relatives in Charleston didn't enter in for she could never abide living on *their* charity.

She had always had a man she could depend on, first her father and then Print Varner. Some women might be able to get along without a man; Tamar—she thought of the other woman with a grimace of distaste—seemed determined to live alone and probably could as long as a man was around to gratify her baser desires. She, Vivian Kincaid, needed to live with a man.

She'd bide her time, Vivian told herself. She was Print's wife, Tamar was the one to be sent packing. Tamar could go straight to hell for all she cared. She'd make the best of a bad bargain, Vivian decided. At least for now.

When she reached the ranch she searched for the agreement her father had had Print sign. Where could he have hidden it? The paper wasn't in any of the drawers, nor in the desk he used, nor hidden away on one of the shelves, nor among his ranch gear. She even searched the cabin behind the house where Ed and Josh bunked. Nothing. She'd been a fool to do Print's bidding when he told her to take the agreement from her father's safe. She should never have given it to him; she should have known Varner couldn't be trusted.

When, three weeks later, Print rode back from the round-up, Vivian listened patiently while he told her the news.

"Briscoe's already left to herd cows to the railroad in Kansas," he said. "He can't trail into Abilene this year 'cause the Kansans say Texas cattle have ticks that make their cows sicken with fever. There's nothing to it, any fool can see Texas cattle don't get the fever, but Briscoe's driving the herd west to Ellsworth anyway."

"How many of our cows is he taking?" Vivian put the least bit of stress on the "our."

"Five hundred head."

"Five hundred! I didn't think we had so many to send north."

"I bought a few and the cows from last year have been dropping more than their share of calves. One way or another we got us five hundred head all trail-branded and on their way."

"It's a shame that Jason Briscoe has to leave his new bride so soon."

"She's expecting in the fall, too," Print said. "I

heard that from one of the Briscoe hands. Jason and I don't exactly exchange confidences."

"Expecting." As she repeated the word, Vivian felt a stab of envy. If she had children, it would be different between her and Print. Men settled down quicker when they had young ones. She wondered if, even now, a baby would make the difference. God knows she'd tried. What more could she do?

"And her such a little thing," Vivian said.

"Sickly, too. Weak in the lungs, or so they say. She was hoping that coming west, the change of air, would do her good."

"Print," Vivian said, "as soon as you're settled in, maybe next week, I'm going to ride over to the Briscoe's and see Janine. I'm going to tell her that if she needs me she's to send for me. When her time nears or before."

"I don't rightly like . . ." Print began.

Vivian stamped her foot. "This has nothing to do with you and Jason, nothing at all. You're not to balk me in this. I'm telling you what I plan to do and you'll come to no harm by it. I mean to go to Janine Briscoe now and when her time comes I mean to be with her."

Print shrugged. "I don't like it," he said, "but I'll not oppose you."

That night, after Vivian put on her nightgown, Print blew out the candle and came up behind her, holding her breasts and drawing her to him until she felt his hardness against her. Print reached down and drew the gown over her head so she stood naked, then dropped his own clothes to the floor and turned her to face him. He pushed her back on the bed, taking her quickly and hungrily. Not a word passed between them.

When he was done, Vivian rolled away so her

back was to him. It was the first time she'd ever lain with him without wanting him and she felt a satisfaction, almost a joy, at this numbing of her feeling for him. At the same time she felt a certain sadness, a regret for what had been and now was no more.

Still without turning toward him, she said, "What did you do with the agreement, Print? I'd like to read it over in the morning."

"What agreement's that?" he asked.

"The paper daddy had you sign when he lent you the money to start this ranch."

Print grunted. "I burned it on our way here."

Her head jerked up. "Why did you burn it, Print?" she asked, her voice like ice.

"We already got all the agreement we need. The one saying you and me are joined by the bonds of holy matrimony. We don't need no other papers."

She bit her lip to keep from answering. If Print Varner expected her to scream like a fishwife, to berate him, he was very much mistaken. She was a Kincaid and Kincaids didn't act like that. As she lay silently beside him, hearing Print's breathing deepen as he fell asleep, her heart hardened against him and she knew that, when the right time came, she would leave him.

16

THE TEXAS SUMMER was long and hot. On one of the hottest days, in August, a letter came for Vivian from Charleston. After she read it she let the sheets of paper fall to the floor as tears blinded her. Her father was dead. And, unexpectedly, a week after her father's death, Nate had also passed away. The last links to Four Oaks, to her childhood, were gone.

Late in September the weather changed and Vivian felt the first cold wind sweep off the prairies, sending leaves whirling from the trees in the Timbers. Shivering, she pulled her shawl tighter around her shoulders.

The next day Ike McLeod rode up to the Varner house. "She needs you, Miz Varner," he told Vivian. "Miz Janine needs you bad."

Vivian went into the bedroom where she had kept a bag packed these last three weeks. Finding Print at the corral, she told him she was going. "I'll stay with Janine," she said, "until she's able to care for the baby."

Print nodded but said nothing as he bent over to kiss her goodbye. As she turned from him she wondered if he'd bring Tamar here, to her house, to her bed. I do't care what he does, she told herself, but she couldn't repress the pang of jealousy she felt.

She mounted her horse and joined Ike at the front of the house. She nodded to him and they set off on the forty-mile journey to Briscoe's. She spoke hardly a word the whole way. Ike was pleasant enough, she supposed. She didn't blame him for the way he acted—as though an ex-slave was as good as anybody—she blamed Jason Briscoe.

Jason wasn't used to blacks, she supposed, and didn't know how to keep them in their place. According to Print, Jason even trusted Ike with money from the cattle sales. She had nothing against Negroes herself, the Kincaids had owned many slaves before the War, but there was a limit, a line that had to be drawn. Negroes were different from whites, that's all there was to it, just as Indians and Mexicans were different.

When, late in the evening, they arrived at Briscoe's, Jason met her at the door. He grasped her hands in his and led her inside.

"How is she?" Vivian asked.

"Janine's in pain," Jason said. "And she's weak. She coughed up blood this morning so I gave her medicine but it didn't seem to do any good."

She followed him to the bedroom door, then hurried past him and knelt by the bed. She was shocked at Janine's appearance. Even though Janine was swollen with the child, she seemed shrunken, diminished, her face whiter than the pillow case and slick with perspiration. Vivian saw that the other woman's teeth were clenched in pain and though her eyes were open they didn't focus.

Vivian turned to Jason. "Your wife needs a doctor," she said.

"The closest one's over Dallas way," Jason said. "I sent a man there three days ago and I've not seen hide nor hair of him since."

Janine began to moan, twisting her head from side to side.

"I'll see to her," Vivian said. "You stay outside, I'll call you if I need you."

"If there's anything . . ." Jason began.

"Just leave me be," Vivian said and Jason retreated into the main room of the ranch.

When Vivian came out of the bedroom four hours later Jason was nowhere in sight. She opened the outside door and saw the glow of a cigarette in the darkness.

"How is she?" Jason asked, grinding out the cigarette and coming quickly inside. A blast of cold wind made her shiver until he shut the door behind him.

"You have a boy," Vivian said.

Jason stared at her. "How is she?" he asked again. "How's Janine?"

Vivian shook her head. "You'd best go to her," she said.

He strode past her into the bedroom and knelt at the head of the bed. Janine's face was white, her hair limp and damp; the sheets were stained with blood. Jason couldn't hear her breathe.

"Janine," he cried hoarsely, pressing his cheek to hers. "Janine," he whispered. He felt the chill of death on her cheek and he moaned.

Vivian came up behind him and when she put

her hand on his shoulder he looked at her with tear-stained eyes. "She's gone," he said.

She nodded. "Janine passed on just as the baby came. There was nothing I could do, nothing anyone could have done."

Strange, she thought, I feel nothing. Only this overwhelming tiredness. Why don't I feel anything? she wondered.

Jason buried his face in his dead wife's hair, sobbing. Vivian turned from him and went to the rough-hewn cradle and lifted the baby into her arms. She had wrapped the boy in a blanket until only his face showed.

For a moment she hugged the baby and as she did tears came into her eyes and ran down her cheeks. When one dropped to the baby's face she wiped her eyes with a handkerchief and began crooning a lullaby as she rocked the baby in her arms.

Vivian looked up and saw that Jason was standing beside the bed looking at her. She held the baby to him. He hesitated, then took him in his arms and held him awkwardly.

"You said it's a boy?" he asked.

"Yes," she said.

"Is he . . . ?" He paused. "Is he all right?"

"The healthiest baby in all of Texas," Vivian told him.

Jason held his son away from his body, staring down at him, marveling at him. "He's so small," he said. He knelt beside the bed and laid the child beside his wife. "Janine," he said, "I mean to name him Jan. After you. When he grows up he'll make you proud."

"Jason," Vivian said. He didn't seem to hear her so she said his name again. "Jason."

When he stood and turned to her, she said, "She

wouldn't have lived, Jason, even without having to carry and give birth to the boy. I know in my heart she wouldn't have lived." She wasn't sure. God forgive me for lying, she murmured to herself.

Jason didn't answer but after a moment he nodded, then picked up Jan and handed him to her. "I'd like to be alone with my wife," he said.

Vivian, holding Jan tight against her shoulder, left the room and softly closed the door behind her.

The next day Jason Briscoe buried his wife near the ranch on a hilltop overlooking the open prairie. He placed a marker in the earth with her name and the years of her life cut deep in the stone.

That evening, after laying Jan in his cradle to sleep, Vivian went looking for Jason. Not finding him in the house, she walked outside and saw him standing at the corral watching the horses.

When he saw her behind him, he said, "I've had my fill of this country. This house, this ranch, they'll always remind me of Janine and what we had and what we didn't have, what we might have had if there'd been time." He sighed. "And George Swanson getting killed the way he did. No one blames me for that, not exactly, though I hear what they say about me. 'There's the man who shot George Swanson 'cause poor George had a drink or two'—nonsense like that. I'm packing it in, bag and baggage."

"Where will you go?" Vivian asked softly.

"West. I'm taking my herd and as many of my men as'll go with me and drive through Belknap and across the plains into New Mexico. I'll winter there before I set out for the north, to the Pan-

handle. Once, when I was scouting for Captain
Carleton in an Indian campaign, I saw a valley
there, a beautiful place it was, all deep and green,
a canyon where the wind can't reach. I mean to
find that valley again and build a new ranch there,
a big ranch with maybe forty or fifty thousand
head some day, the biggest ranch in all Texas."

The vividness of his vision drew Vivian to him,
made her want to believe in him, made her want
to share his dream. She put her hand on his sleeve.

"You'll be able to do it, Jason," she said. "I
know you will."

When he turned to her she wanted to lose herself in his arms, wanted him to hold her so some
of his strength would flow to her. Jason mumbled
and she asked him what he'd said.

"God willing," he said.

She repeated his words, her hand dropping from
his arm. Jason awkwardly wished her a good night
before he turned and walked to the ranch house.
She followed, blowing out the candle and preparing for bed. They both slept in the main room of
the house for neither wanted to use the bedroom
where Janine had so recently died.

Vivian lay listening to Jason tossing on his bedroll, wanting to comfort him but fearful he would
spurn her. A horseman rode up to the bunkhouse,
a man called in the night, and a horse whinnied
in the corral. The baby cried fretfully and she got
up to hold Jan in her arms, crooning to him as
she spooned milk into his mouth.

"You need someone," she whispered. "You need
a woman to love you, to care for you, to teach you."

The child quieted and she laid him back in the
cradle, rocking it until he was asleep. By the time
she finally returned to her bed and slept it was

long after midnight and she knew what she must do.

Jason was up at dawn and, while he was outside shaving, Vivian cooked breakfast. They ate together, just the two of them in the death-hush of the house, talking little yet at ease with one another. Much like a man and wife, Vivian thought.

"I've sent Ike to town," Jason said when he was ready to leave. "There's a Mrs. Bates there, I'm told, who'll hire out to take care of the baby until we're ready to leave for the west."

"You can't take the baby with you on the trail, he's too young."

"He's my son; he'll go where I go."

"At least find a woman to go with you to look after him permanently. A bunch of cowhands can't properly care for an infant."

"I intend to." Jason hesitated as though he'd given thought to the words he was about to say, yet still found them difficult to bring out. "There's that young wife of Swanson's living all alone in the cabin near your place. Maybe she'd consider coming along to help with the baby."

"No!" She'd spoken without thinking. Vivian felt herself redden when she saw Jason staring at her.

"I mean," she said, "she'd never agree to go with you. I've talked to her some since her husband was killed and though she admits the fault's not all yours, her heart is dead-set against you. Nothing will change her."

Jason sighed. "I reckon you're right, the notion was a damn fool one to begin with. When I went to see her the day they buried George, she wouldn't even listen to what I had to say and I've had no words with her since. I sort of hoped time would ease her feelings."

"Time's hardened them instead. Tamar's bitterness is like a rock she clings to."

Vivian took Jan from his cradle and let him nestle in her arms. Jason touched the baby's cheek, then chucked him beneath the chin as Jan squirmed.

"I'll find a woman for him," Jason said. He put his broad-brimmed plains hat squarely on his head and went out to saddle up. A few minutes later Vivian, standing in the doorway with Jan in her arms, watched Jason and two of his hands ride from the ranch in the direction of the town.

Again that night Vivian lay on her bunk staring up into the darkness. Jason tossed and turned for a time but after an hour his breathing deepened and she knew he slept. Mrs. Bates, he had told Vivian at supper, would arrive the next day and then she'd be able to return home.

"I don't know how I can thank you for all you've done," he'd said.

"You don't have to, Jason," she'd answered.

Vivian rose quietly from the bed and crossed the room in her bare feet, feeling the lingering warmth from the stove that had been banked for the night. She bent over the cradle where Jan slept soundly. Leaving the cradle she went to the window and looked out at the moonlight silvering the prairie in front of the house.

She walked to the blanket that had been draped over a line to separate their sleeping quarters. Holding the blanket to one side, she ducked under the rope and stood looking down at Jason's dim form on the floor. He lay sprawled on his back with an old Army blanket over him.

She hesitated—there was still time to retreat, to return to her bunk, to try to sleep until morning and then return to Print. She shook her head. No, she'd not go back to Print Varner, not willingly. Not so much because of Tamar, Vivian told herself. She could handle that slip of a girl.

For a fleeting moment she wondered what attracted men to Tamar. With all her young prettiness she certainly wasn't a lady. Perhaps that was it. Men naturally sensed when a woman was a whore and that appealed to them. For a time. Until the woman tired of the man and started whoring after someone new.

But it wasn't just Tamar that had made up Vivian's mind for her, it was Print's burning of the agreement. That piece of paper had been her birthright, her shield against misfortune, her passport to the future. And Print had left it in ashes, left her defenseless. And for that Print would pay.

Vivian pulled her nightgown over her head and let it drop soundlessly to the floor beside her. Naked now, she shivered, not so much from the coolness of the night as from uncertainty. Biting her lower lip, she crossed her arms over her bare breasts.

She knelt beside Jason, carefully lifting the edge of the blanket, saw the paleness of him and knew he was naked. She lay on her side next to him, pulling the blanket toward her so it covered both of them, the bedroll hard under her hip. For a time she lay without moving, listening to Jason's breathing. He moaned and she wondered if he was thinking of Janine. Reaching out, she touched him tentatively on the shoulder and felt him turn toward her.

His arms found her and drew her to him and he buried his face in her hair. She moulded herself to the curve of his body, tingling to the touch of his legs on hers and the long hardness of his body against her softness. His face was still in her hair and his arms were tight around her though she knew he was still asleep.

Her hand trailed down his side to his hip, lingered there for a long moment and then found its way to his leg. She hesitantly reached between his thighs to his sex and felt him harden under her touch, and she let her hand brush back and forth against his hardness, trembling with fear and desire as she heard him moan in his sleep.

Vivian grasped him gently in her hand, guiding him to her until she felt the heat of him against her leg. Still on her side, she parted her legs so his sex slipped between her thighs and she opened herself to him and felt him slide inside her, felt him withdraw and slide within her again.

"Janine," he said, half awake now.

She murmured meaningless phrases as, with her other hand, she brushed his dark hair back from his forehead. A tenderness welled inside her and she felt tears sting her eyes. She crooned to him as she had crooned a short while before to comfort his son. Taking his head in both of her hands, she drew him to her, arching herself so his lips went to her breasts, his tongue to her nipple. She moaned, trembling with desire.

Suddenly Jason drew away and she knew he had come fully awake. His hand went to her face, his fingers touching her cheeks and hair.

"Vivian," he said in surprise, drawing back.

"I'm so alone," she said. "We're both of us alone, Jason. Let me stay and comfort you. I need you, Jason, we need each other."

"Vivian," he said again, his voice soft, as though he was pleading with her.

"Take me with you, Jason," she said urgently. "You need me, your son needs me. Let me go with you when you set off for the west."

"You're another man's wife." Jason's voice had hardened. "I couldn't do that to anyone, not even Print Varner."

"A wife in name only," she said. She drew in her breath, wanting to tell him the truth, yet too proud. After all, she was a Kincaid. Sensing Jason's hesitation, she put her pride behind her. "He's been bedding the Swanson woman," she said, "so I'm leaving Print, no matter what."

"Tamar and Print?" Jason's voice echoed his shock and disbelief.

"I saw them together. That's why Eli shot Print and then left home. I'm sure that was his reason. Somehow he found out about Print and his sister and he intended to kill him because of it. I can't live with him now that I know."

Jason said nothing. She could see the outline of his body in the darkness, he was sitting up with his legs crossed, looking at her. When she touched his leg, letting her fingers run along his bare flesh, feeling the soft hairs, she heard his sudden intake of breath.

"Jason," she whispered. "Take me with you. Please, Jason." Haven't I even a shred of pride left? she asked herself.

He stood and, brushing past her, shoved the blanket out of his way and walked into the other part of the room. She heard the rustle of clothing and when a candle flamed she saw he had taken his trousers with him and pulled them on.

Jason removed her dress and chemise from the peg where she'd hung them and came part way to her, throwing the clothes so they landed on the floor at her feet.

"Put them on," he told her.

She stood holding her clothes in one hand, her body bared to him, the candlelight glowing on her golden flesh. She watched his gaze rove down to her breasts, to her hips and the dark triangle between her legs.

With a groan of anguish he turned from her. "Get dressed," he said.

She slipped the chemise over her head. Her throat tightened and she thought she was about to cry when anger flared in her. How dare he spurn her! Seeing one of his boots on the floor she picked it up and threw it, the heel of the boot striking his bare back. Jason didn't move.

Vivian's anger drained away as suddenly as it had come. She hurriedly finished dressing and went to stand beside Jason in front of the window. A cloud had drifted across the moon and the yard outside was dark.

"I saw some cattle down in the timbers near the South Fork when I rode to town," he told her. "I mean to rout them out in the morning."

"I'll leave for home just as soon as Mrs. Bates gets here," Vivian said, thankful for the matter-of-fact tone of his voice.

"Ike will ride with you."

"There's no need," she said. "I'm quite capable of finding my way."

"Ike will ride with you just the same. After all you've done for me and Janine it's the least I can do." He pulled on his shirt and began buttoning it.

"When do you intend to leave for the west?" she asked.

"In three or four weeks," he said. "As soon as I've settled my accounts here."

He wasn't looking at her so he didn't see Vivian's quiet smile of determination.

17

PRINT GOT out of bed and stood beside it, naked.
He grasped the blankets in one hand and pulled
them down. Tamar looked up at him from the
bed, making no move to cover herself, and Print
smiled at her nonchalance, her boldness.

She watched him dress. When he was fully
clothed, she said, "Come here to me," and he returned to sit on the bed. She reached for him, her
arm circling his neck, kissing him, her lips meeting
his fiercely, passionately. He held her, then let go
and stood up.

"You act like you think you're never going to
see me again," he said.

She didn't answer. When he turned at the door
he was smiling. "You keep saying this is going to
be the last time," he told her, "and it never is.
You said we'd never use this cabin. How long did
that last? Until the first good rain, that's how
long." When still she didn't speak, he said, "You're
my woman, Tamar."

"I'm not your woman, I don't belong to anybody." Her anger flared out at him. "I'm my own woman and I intend to stay that way."

Print smiled again, touched the brim of his hat and left, pulling the door of the cabin shut behind him.

As soon as she heard him ride off, Tamar padded across the wood floor in her bare feet, intending to dress and begin packing. She stopped, her head in a whirl, and had to hold to the table to support herself. A sudden fear gripped her. Could she be pregnant? Pregnant by Print? No, she knew that was impossible for she'd just finished her monthlies.

The dizziness must be a sign, a sign that a change was coming; she sensed it. All she had to do was wait. She'd intended to be gone in the morning, heading east, back to civilization, but now she shook her head. All I have to do is wait, she told herself again. Why she thought this she didn't know, yet the feeling was strong. If nothing happens in a month's time, she promised herself, she'd leave Texas.

Vivian, accompanied by Ike McLeod, returned home the next day.

"You were gone long enough," Print told her.

"Janine Briscoe died giving birth," Vivian said. "Her baby lived and I had to stay with him until Jason found someone else."

"She was a puny thing." Print sounded mollified. "I said so all along."

When Vivian turned from him and began unpacking her carpetbag, Print came up behind her and circled her waist with his arm, pulling her to him. She stiffened and he spun her around so she faced him.

"What's the matter?" he demanded. "Are you too good for me all of a sudden?"

She said nothing, staring past him, and after a moment he turned on his heel and left the room. That night he took her savagely, rolling off her as soon as he was done. In a few minutes she heard his breathing deepen.

She waited until she was certain Print was asleep before slipping from the bed, putting on her robe and going to the peg where he'd hooked his gun belt. Taking his Colt from its holster, she walked outside and by the light of the moon removed all of the cartridges except one. With the gun held stiffly at her side she returned to their bedroom and stood beside Print. Her face was expressionless as she spun the chamber of the Colt once, twice, three times.

Vivian drew in her breath, raised the gun and pointed it at her husband's forehead and pulled the trigger. The hammer clicked on an empty chamber. Vivian let out her breath, not knowing whether she was pleased or disappointed. She heard Print shift restlessly on the bed.

"Why are you up?" he asked her.

"I felt sick," she said.

"Come back to bed."

"Soon," she told him.

She went outside, reloaded the gun and, returning to the house, replaced it in the holster. The next time he had his way with her against her will, she told herself, she'd leave two bullets in the chamber. And then the next time she'd leave three. Never more than three. She smiled to herself, surprised at the depth of bitterness she felt toward this man she had married.

But she never used his gun again. The next day Print left for the fall round-up and branding and when he returned three weeks later, Vivian was gone. She'd left him a note, telling him not to try to follow her, that she was never coming back. She gave no reason.

Print tossed the note into the fireplace and watched the paper flame up and curl into ash as the agreement with her father had burned over a year before. Follow her? There was no point in following her when he knew she'd be back whining for him to take her in. He gave her two or three days on her own before she returned. Two or three days at the most.

After a week passed, Print was still expecting to see Vivian ride up to the house at any time. When he heard of Briscoe leaving the Pinto country he was suddenly suspicious, wondering if there might be a connection between Vivian and Jason. After all, she had been with him when his wife died.

Print shook his head. Jason Briscoe wasn't the kind to try to brand either another man's heifer or another man's wife. Holier-than-thou, that was Briscoe, a man who thought he was too good for ordinary men. But after two more weeks without a sign of Vivian, Print's assurance that she'd return of her own accord began to wear thin.

One evening Ed came to the main house after supper. He and Print sat and smoked, Ed hemming and hawing as he talked of the cattle, the horses, the weather, and the speculation about Briscoe's reasons for leaving to go farther west.

"Out with it Ed," Print said at last, "tell me what's on your mind. You're acting as itchy as a stump-tailed bull in fly season."

"I happened to be over to Abe Green's place today," Ed said. Abe did occasional blacksmithing for the nearby ranches. "A stranger came by to have his horse shod. He'd just come from Fort Belknap way."

"Nothing unusual about that," Print said.

"While he was at the fort he heard talk of a woman. Seems she was traveling alone."

Print stubbed out his cigarette. "Damn it, Ed, say what you got to say right out. We been together a long time and we'll be together a lot longer if you'll just speak your mind and stop this confounded easing into things."

Actually, Print was flattered by the fear he read in Ed's eyes and in the down-curve of his mouth.

"He didn't say for sure but from what he did say the woman sounded a lot like Miz Varner."

"Now, Ed, I could have told you a good five minutes back that you had something of that sort on your mind. All right, what about her?"

"Well, she rode into Belknap by herself. And just a few days before another party with a trail herd had been there and then rode out. And then Miz Varner rode out herself, maybe headed the same direction, if you catch my meaning."

"A man would have to be deaf, dumb and blind not to. All right, Ed, you've told me all but one thing. Who was this party with the trail herd?"

"Jason Briscoe."

Print slammed his fist on the table. "Briscoe," he said, venom in his voice.

"I didn't reckon you'd be too pleased."

"Did this cowhand say where Briscoe was headed?" Print asked.

"West. Bound for the Pecos, he figured. Why anyone would drive cattle into that desert beats all." Ed talked rapidly, as though he expected the rush of his words to calm Print. "You know what they call the Pecos," he said, " 'Graveyard of a cowman's hopes.' I never been there but they say the water's gyppy and the land's as barren as a sixty-year-old spinster."

Print got up and paced to the door and back.

"What're you intending, Print?" Ed asked.

Print smiled, then began to laugh. Ed frowned for he'd found that no good came of it when Print laughed.

"They'll expect me to come riding after her," Print said. "They'll be thinking I'll be hell-bent-for-election to bring Vivian back. That's what you'd expect, isn't it, Ed? Knowing me?"

"Now, Print, this stranger sure didn't say this woman he saw was with Briscoe. That could just be one of those coincidences, them both being around the same place at the same time. That's most likely what it is, one of those coincidences."

"You didn't answer my question, Ed. When I ask you a question I don't want a lot of beating around the bush, I want a straight answer."

"Yeah, that's what I'd reckon you'd do, Print. Go after your wife fixing to bring her back. Probably take me and Josh with you."

"And because that's what Briscoe expects, that's not what I'm about to do. Never do what folks expect you to do, Ed, that's the secret of keeping them off-balance. Worry them a little first, make them wake up in the middle of the night hearing noises they can't explain, wondering if it's Print Varner come gunning for them. So do you know what I intend doing, Ed?"

Ed shook his head.

"Nothing. I intend to do not one little thing. I don't intend to so much as lift my little finger against them."

Ed nodded though he didn't follow the drift of Print's thinking; if the truth be known, he didn't care to. He'd find out soon enough what Print meant to do.

As soon as Ed was gone, Print put on his buckskin jacket and rode to Tamar's. Knocking on the cabin door, he said loudly, "It's me, Print," and heard Tamar slide back the wooden bar.

"Pack your duds," he told her once he was inside. "You're coming to live with me."

Tamar faced him with her hands on her hips. "I am? Where?"

"At my place. You're moving in with me. Ed was over to Green's today and heard Briscoe's lit out for the Pecos with Vivian following him."

"And you're intending to sit back and say 'good riddance' to both of them?" Tamar eyed him closely.

"For the time being. She's mine, God damn it, and no man's going to take what's mine and live to tell about it. But I'm a patient man. I plan to build my herd and trail a few thousand head north to the rail lines like Briscoe did this last spring. I'm going to bide my time and then when I'm good and ready I'm going to go after Briscoe and if what I hear is true I'll kill the bastard. It's as simple as that."

"And in the meantime you expect me to pack up and go live in another woman's house? In your wife's house, the house you built for her? You're plumb loco, Print."

"You can't stay here, Tamar. A lone woman can't live by herself in the middle of Texas. 'Specially not with winter coming on."

"I can manage, don't think I can't. I don't need you, Print, I don't need any man."

He took her in his arms, crushing her body to his, lifting her from the floor and kissing her. She gasped, her mouth opening to his and her body trembling against him. When he released her he stepped away from her and brought his hand to her breast, tracing the swell of her bosom with his fingers, letting his hand go lower until he gripped her between the legs, his fingers caressing her soft flesh. She moved her body against his hand, her own hands coming across her breasts to hug herself.

"Oh, Print," she said. "Nobody's ever made me feel the way you do."

He smiled. "And you're the one that says she's able to do without a man. You can no more live without me than a cow can fly."

Tamar stiffened, taking his hand from her leg and holding it in both of hers.

"You think that's all there is to a woman, don't you?" Tamar asked. "The going to bed and the giving of pleasure to a man?"

"Appears to me you do as much getting as giving," Print said.

"You think that's all I care about, don't you? You think of me as a warm body to bed down with, nothing more. Admit the truth, Print, admit it."

Again he smiled. "I wouldn't say that's all you care about. By my reckoning it's more like ninety percent of it, though, give or take."

"You're honest, at least, Print, I give you that. You're honest but you're wrong. Don't stand there laughing at me, I know me better than you ever will. Better than you'd know me in a hundred years. You're right in part, I do like the bedding with a man, the touching and the talking in bed, the lying next to a man . . ."

Print grasped her arm. "Not *a man*," he said. "Me. Me, Print Varner."

"All right," Tamar said. "Lying next to you,

you, Print Varner, and you touching my breasts and going inside me and pleasuring me."

"Don't talk like that, Tamar. You know I don't like you to talk about it the way you do. A lady just doesn't discuss them things."

"I been doing some reading these last months," Tamar said, "and I learned a new word. It's a word that fits you, Print. The word's hypocrite. Know what it means? I can see by the look on your face you don't. It means a man who looks all pure on the outside but when you cut him open he stinks like three-day-old fish. You like what we do in bed but you don't want me to talk about it because ladies aren't supposed to say such things."

Tamar put her hand to the top of her head as though holding down a wide-brimmed hat in a wind. She sashayed a few steps away from him, twirling her body as if she wore sweeping skirts. "Do you like my gown, Print?" she asked. "I ordered it from the House of Worth at number seven Rue de la Paix. That's in Paris, Print. Paris, France. Is that how you want me to act? Is that how your Georgia ladies behave?"

"You've been doing too damn much reading. All the book learning's beginning to go to your head. You're getting above yourself."

"Getting above myself? And just what do you mean by that? There's nothing in this world I can't do, Print Varner. I'm eighteen years old and I intend to live forever and ever and ever. I can learn to do whatever I want, whatever I set my mind to, do you understand that?"

"And how much schooling have you had, Miss Tamar High-and-Mighty Swanson?"

"Eight years. I can do sums and I can read and I can write. That's only a starting place. You don't need schooling, though I'd like to have more.

But whatever's been written in books you can learn as long as you can read. Then you can become whatever's within your reach. I believe that with all my heart."

He took Tamar by the shoulders and shook her. "No," he said, "you're what God intended you to be, no more, no less. You're filling your head with nonsense and all that'll come of it is disappointment. Someday you may get gowns from Paris, France, but it'll be me that buys them for you."

"Let go of me, Print," she said, her voice deadly quiet. He let his hands drop to his sides.

"I'm not going to be wearing gowns for some time," Tamar said, letting her voice slide into a Texas drawl. "I'm not about to play the lady for you. I'm going to wear men's get-up. You probably figured what with Vivian lighting out for parts unknown and me living just a hoot and a holler away, I'd be hauling my gear up there to the Varner ranch and doing a bit of cooking for you and Ed and Josh. And when I wasn't cooking, I'd do the wash for you and the darning and the mending that has to be done. Besides cleaning and toting water from the river, just to mention a few of the chores.

"And then in the evening you probably figured I'd sit around listening to you tell me stories about what a hard-working man you were, after which I'd blow out the lamp and come to bed and if you were feeling spry I'd receive my reward. That's pretty much what you figured, isn't it, Print?"

"There's not much use talking to a woman what knows all the answers before a man can get a word in edgewise."

"I'm not about to do any of those things, Print," she said as though she hadn't heard him. "I'm going to do man's work; that's a whole lot easier than woman's work any day. I'm going to take George's cows and raise me a herd. I'm intending to be a cowhand, Print; I'm going to live here by myself and when I'm feeling like it I might invite you in of a night and then again I might not. And if you don't like it, Print Varner, you know damn well what you can do."

18

"God damn!"

Sam's voice rose over the sound of the baby's squalling and Jason and Ike stopped arguing to stare at him. Silent Sam Claiburn wasn't much of a hand for cussing. As a matter of fact he rarely opened his mouth.

"I reckon none of us knows what's wrong," Sam muttered as he untied his bandana to wipe curdled milk from the baby's neck and chest. In his big calloused hands, Jan looked all the tinier.

"If he keeps on yelling like that it means he's healthy," Ike said. "I tell you what's wrong is the cow's milk we been feeding him. What we got to do is find some woman with a baby of her own so she can nurse the boy. My mama done that when I was a babe. She told me Miz McLeod's little girl fed right alongside of me."

Jason sighed. "We're not likely to find a wet nurse when we can't even find a woman of any kind who'll head west with us."

"We got to try," Ike said. "The boy's spitting up as much grub as he's putting down."

Jason shook his head. "When Mrs. Bates was caring for Jan he took the cow's milk all right. I tell you something's sickening him."

The three men stared down at the bawling baby cradled in Sam's arms. Jan's face was bright red and his arms and legs waved vigorously.

"He don't look sick," Ike insisted.

Anxiety lay in the pit of Jason's belly as heavy as a blacksmith's anvil. He looked away toward the campfire. Was Ike right? Jan's crying was sure loud and lusty. In fact, he bawled just like a starving calf. Nothing wrong with his lungs at least—he didn't have his mother's weakness there. But then why did he keep puking up his feed?

"We might try milking another cow," he said. "Can't do any harm."

"We tried three already," Ike said. "Cow's milk just don't agree with him."

"I could write and offer Mrs. Bates more money," Jason said, "but I doubt she'd come if I offered to pay her a hundred dollars a day. She just plain don't care to leave her own family for as long as it'd take to go with us to the west, specially with no sure way for her to get back home. Can't say I blame her."

He put his hand to Jan's cheek. "I reckon I ought to have left him with her like she told me to. But he's my son, damn it, and he belongs with me." He glanced back along the trail toward Fort Belknap. "I was wrong. He's too young to be raised by a bunch of dumb galoots like us."

Jan's screams subsided as he nuzzled his father's fingers.

"We're only a day out from the Fort," Ike said. "We could take him back."

"I'm not about to leave my son with strangers."

Jan, turning his head away from Jason's fingers, began to squall again.

"Seems like we got to do something," Ike said.

"I know we do. Only what?" Jason broke off as a shout came from one of the men circling the bedded herd. Jason came alert. Indians? He strode away from the fire with Ike a step behind him.

Before they got to their horses, another shout came from the rider. Not Indians, one rider coming in. Jason halted, waiting. Could be a cowboy looking for work. He could use another hand what with Sam tied up looking after Jan. He'd hated to ask Sam—nursing a baby was no work for a man.

As Jason watched the horse approach through the gathering dusk, he had a sudden hunch warning him that this was trouble coming. He didn't get this feeling often but when he did it was right more often than not. His hand dropped to his gun and he felt Ike stiffen beside him.

The rider pulled up. "I could hear the baby crying from a mile away," a woman's voice said. "What have you been doing to poor little Jan?"

Jason's mouth dropped open in surrise. He took a few steps forward and his hand left the butt of his six-gun.

"Vivian!" he exclaimed.

A few minutes later Jan lay in Vivian's arms sucking avidly at the bottle of milk she held. When she pulled the nipple from his mouth he protested loudly but, paying no attention, she hoisted him to her shoulder.

"Seems like he wants more," Jason said.

"Of course he does," Vivian told him. "But you have to let the swallowed air come out or else babies can't keep their milk down."

The three men glanced sheepishly at one another. Vivian looked from one to the other. "Do
you mean you didn't know that?" She turned her
head to Jan and began crooning to him as she
patted his back. "Poor little boy, have they been
mistreating you? Poor little Jan, it's all right, Vivian's here to take care of you."

"What about your husband?" Jason asked Vivian the next morning.

"Print doesn't know I've gone," she told him.
"Not yet. By the time he come in from the range
and figures out where I am it'll be too late for
him to ride after me." She put her hand on Jason's arm. "I'm never going back to him. Never.
I'll kill myself first. Or I'll kill him."

Jason looked down and she took her hand away.

"I came to take care of Jan," she said. "You
need me to do that. The boy needs me. That's why
I'm here; there's no other reason but to care for
Jan. And I had to have a place to go. Will you
take me with you?"

Jason drew in a deep breath, let it out. God
knows he did need her to care for Jan. But he'd
rather have almost any other woman in the world
with him than Print Varner's wife. He didn't like
the feel of it. Sooner or later there'd be trouble
with Print.

But Jan came first.

"I'll be glad to have you along," he told Vivian.

Day after day they headed west, following the
old Butterfield Overland Stage Trail as far as they
could. Jason acted as trail boss, scouting ahead for
water, grass and bed ground, doubling back to
hold his hat at arm's length to signal the direction
to the point riders. These men, the best in the out-

fit, rode on either side of the lead steer, Old Sam, named for Sam Houston. The bell around the five-year-old longhorn's neck clanged steadily, a sound the cows soon learned to follow.

Behind the point men rode the swing and flank hands, holding the herd to workable form and size, while in the rear came the dust-covered drag men, prodding the drags, the stragglers, and killing the new calves who were too young to keep up with the rest.

The steers trailed in pairs and bunches, every strong young cow gathering a following. There were a few muleys, born hornless, and after a few days they bedded down together apart from the others. And then there was a loner or two prowling along the flanks of the herd, as though searching for something but keeping their own counsel as to what they hoped to find. One cow was an outcast, hooked at by all the steers, with even the hornless muleys making a horning motion at her.

Unless all of these longhorns, the loners, the muleys and the outcast, were settled down early in the drive they ended at the rear with the drags. But the most difficult to settle, the most willful, were the two-year-old heifers. Some never steadied and Jason made a practice of killing and eating them early on.

The men and cattle rested and fed at the head of the Middle Concho before starting the final eighty-mile stretch of desert to the Pecos. Before reaching that river they had to pass poison lakes marked by whitened bones of animals killed by the alkali water.

"Give them all they can drink," Jason ordered before they left the Concho.

The men filled their canteens and the water

barrels on the chuck wagon to overflowing. Then, in the late afternoon, Jason pointed the herd in the direction of the setting sun and they set out over the hard-baked earth.

At midnight they made dry camp and pushed on again at dawn. Jason swung by Vivian's wagon where Jan was carried papoose-like on a padded board hanging in the shade of the canvas, the cow who gave him milk trailing behind the wagon at the end of a rope.

"It's five days to water that's fit to drink," he told her. Vivian nodded. "The boy's all right?" he asked.

"As long as your cows give milk," she answered.

Jason rode ahead, his horse kicking up puffs of dust behind him. He didn't know what he'd have done if Vivian hadn't joined them at Belknap. She was like a mother to the boy, treating Jan as her own. She was worth any problems he might have with Print, Jason told himself.

She'd never again approached him as she had after Janine died and he'd never mentioned that night to her. Strange, he thought, Vivian was a comely woman with her black hair and her slenderness, some men would call her beautiful, yet he didn't desire her. He felt toward her as he would if she were his sister or a young boy. He'd pondered his reaction and, when he found no answer, gave his musings up as a waste of time.

It's better all around this way, he told himself, what with her being a married woman and all. He smiled slightly as he imagined what Print would say when he found out his wife was riding with Jason Briscoe. Nothing you could write in the newspaper, he'd be willing to bet.

On the second night out from the Middle Concho the herd was too thirsty to bed down. The longhorns milled about and the cowhands had to fight to keep them from breaking back along the trail in search of water.

"This won't do," Jason said to Ike McLeod. "They're getting in enough walking in their bed ground to carry them all the way to the Pecos. Tomorrow we'll have 'em on the trail before sun-up and we'll push 'em hard."

The herd swung out onto the desert the next morning, the point men having to hold the lead steers in check while the drag riders cursed and popped their ropes and quirts to keep the weak stock moving. The herd bawled, then moaned for water, then grew silent with their dry, dusty tongues hanging out. Their eyes were sunken and their ribs showed plain. When a thirst-maddened steer turned to fight he was cut from the herd and left to die.

The sun burned down on the worn-out cowboys, shimmering on the flats ahead of them with the look of water, tantalizing them. Their canteens dried up and the water barrels rattled in the chuck wagon while the clouds of dust covered cows, horses and men.

As the riders passed by the chuck wagon, Chicago Luke handed them black coffee and then they rode on, trying to hold back the lead steers when they got a whiff of where water had been in now-dried wallows. Usually the steers themselves slowed before they reached the caked mud. When they came to the dry hole, though, they milled aimlessly, all the while bawling, unwilling to leave this place where they knew water had once been.

Most of the calves had dropped along the trail long ago and now the weaker cows began to go down. The men, tired and worn to rope's end, unable to help the cattle entrusted to their care, swore thickly, ready to drop themselves. They were silent, mostly, except for an occasional "Hi-ah! Hi'ah!" to keep the drags moving.

Night came and still they pushed on, the Pecos twenty miles away now with the poisoned holes between the herd and the river.

"Swing them south," Jason ordered when he saw the first light of the new day. "Their first whiff of water has got to be from the Pecos." He'd run the herd to the river, he decided, keeping them away from the poisoned holes, and save what he could. The alternative was losing all he had.

The sun rose and burned down from high overhead. Ten miles to go now. Jason watched, waiting, and saw it come. Old Sam lifted his head, holding his dry tongue out stiff. The lead steer broke into a stumbling run and the others followed him, the earth echoing with the rumble of the longhorns' hooves as the wind brought the smell of water and the sound of the lead bell back to the rest of the herd.

"Keep them strung out," Jason shouted to his men, the cowhands fighting to spread the cattle, afraid of them bunching and piling up to drown in the Pecos.

The cattle poured into the river valley with the leaders charging over the bank and the others cascading behind them and onto them, pushing the cattle into and across the river, some struggling out onto the far side, the thirst-frenzied animals blocking the current, damming it so the water rose halfway up the dried-out banks.

Finally the riders quirted them out of the river to keep the cows from foundering and drowning themselves. The longhorns backed from the water, stopping on the bank to blow, their swollen tongues lolling, the cowhands' snapping ropes moving them into the grass of the Pecos valley, the first food they'd tasted in days.

"We'll rest them her and hope the Indians don't find us," Jason told his men.

He was thankful they'd seen no sign of Indians for he knew they were in no condition to fight. They'd lost half the herd and three horses and the men were bone-tired. Only Jan seemed unscathed by the drive over the wastelands for he gurgled and cooed when Jason lifted him from his cradle board.

"We'll make him into a top hand yet," Jason said. Surveying the remnants of his herd, he added bitterly, "Looks like all you gotta be is kind of dumb."

"Jan's a smart and sassy baby," Vivian protested. "And big for his age." She looked across to where the men were drinking their coffee and smoking their pipes and cigarettes in the shade of the bank of an arroyo. "I hope to heaven he doesn't grow up to be a cowhand. He deserves better, he ought to have schooling. You should send him East so he can make something of himself."

"There's worse ways to live than this," Jason told her, "and worse places than Texas. This here's a broad-gauged land and it's going to need broad-gauged men to tame her."

"It's no better than a desert," Vivian said, taking the boy from Jason's arms and holding him on her shoulder. "Fit for nothing except Indians, Mexicans, coyotes, wolves and cowboys."

They rested for three days and then drove the herd up the east bank of the Pecos with the only living creatures along the way the fish in the river and the rattlesnakes. Jason planned to trail what was left of his herd to Fort Sumner, more than a hundred and fifty miles to the north.

They found grass near a large wooded tract and bedded the cattle. "I'll ride on to Sumner and find out if they're buying beef," Jason told the men as they sat around the campfire. He glanced at the cowhands, then said, "Ike McLeod's in charge till I get back." He noted a few surprised looks. "Any man's got an objection," Jason said, "now's the time to have your say." Nobody spoke out.

"Some of them men won't appreciate taking orders from a black man," Ike said to Jason as soon as they were alone.

"I don't care what they appreciate or don't appreciate as long as they do what they're told. Any man gives you trouble answers to me when I get back."

"You don't think you'll find Comanches between here and Sumner?" Ike asked.

"There's been no sign of them the whole trip. A few times I had the feeling Indians were about but nothing came of it. They don't expect a herd to be trailing out of Texas this time of year nor along this route. Besides, they're probably all at the Fort."

Ike shrugged. "You're the boss," he said, "but if it was me . . ."

"It ain't you," Jason said impatiently. "I'm the one has to decide what to do with the herd. Maybe we'd be best off keeping them here till spring to feed and fatten up. Then again maybe we can get a good enough price at Sumner right now so we can drive them there. Maybe we ought to avoid Sumner altogether and trail on into Colorado."

"Seems to me that back in Texas you were talking about taking the herd to the Staked Plain and starting a ranch."

"I've had doubts and second doubts about that

scheme. It might be too soon to ranch on the Plain, maybe we'd best wait a few years. I'll wait to hear what the troopers at the Fort have to say about the Indian situation before I make up my mind."

Jason clasped Ike's shoulder, turned, and saddled up. He swung east and north of the bluffs overlooking the Pecos, cutting for sign. He found no evidence of Comanches but, late in the day, he came on the track of a single horse.

Kneeling on the ground, he studied the print. The horse was shod, needed reshoeing in fact, so it wasn't an Indian pony. The rider was headed north, slow, his horse lame.

Jason rode north and after a quarter-hour came on a man's track, the boot sharp-pointed as best he could tell, the heel narrow. The man was walking beside his horse, leading him. Jason rode on slowly, pondering.

He topped a rise and saw the horse lying sprawled on the barren ground ahead of him. There was no sign of the rider. When he looked down at the bay, he saw that a bullet had been put through the stallion's eye. The animal appeared to have been dead only a short while. The man's track led on to the north.

Jason loped ahead, following the tracks. After a time he crossed rock and lost the trail. Even after cutting for sign, circling in wider and wider loops, he couldn't find it again. Deciding the man would continue to make his way north, heading for Fort Sumner, Jason rode in that direction.

"*Señor!*"

Jason whirled about and saw, stepping from behind a cluster of boulders, a man dressed in dust-streaked black holding a rifle in his right hand. He wore a wide-brimmed sombrero with a rawhide loop under his chin. His vest was decorated with silver ornaments and the sun glinted from the silver on his long flared pants. A Mex.

Jason, eyes wary, hand resting loosely on his legs near his saddle scabbard, watched him approach. He didn't trust Mexicans, no Texan did after the massacre at the Alamo, after Santa Anna and the Mexican War.

The horseless man stopped six feet from Jason and swept his large hat from his head. Jason saw that his hair was the color of new-minted silver. "Allow me to introduce myself," he said in flawless English. "I am Don Luis Grandez."

"Jason Briscoe. What's a Mex like you doing in these parts?" Jason asked.

"I do not claim the honor of being a Mexican," Don Luis said. "I was, until recently, a Californio residing near Monterey and, besides, a citizen of the United States of America."

"I'll be damned," Jason said, thinking that this Don Luis spoke better English than he did.

"You should have no fear," Don Luis said. "I have been watching you for some ten minutes and could have killed you and taken your horse if I had wished. In California I am considered a passable shot. As you can see, I am a man of peace, an honorable man. All I request is assistance in traveling to Fort Sumner."

Jason nodded. "Get up behind me," he said, "and I'll ride you into Sumner."

With Luis mounted in back of him, Jason set out for the north.

"As to what I'm doing here," Luis said after they'd ridden several miles in silence, "I am fortunate enough to have many head of cattle in Mexico. It is my misfortune, however, that the Indians raid my herds and steal from me. I'm seeking new land, new grazing ranges in the north."

"I thought you said you hailed from California."

"*Si,* my ranch was in a valley not far from Monterey. There it is not the Indians who steal from Don Luis but the Americans, those who came to California in search of gold. I trailed my herd south into Mexico to escape them. As you might say, I went from the fire into the frying pan."

"I suppose you have a fair-sized herd," Jason said, not believing him and intending to lead Luis on.

"Five thousand head."

Jason noticed that Luis kept looking from one side of them to the other.

"You're almighty itchy," Jason told him.

"Yesterday before my stallion was lamed I saw signs of Indians. Comanches."

"I've always considered myself a good plainsman and I haven't seen hide nor hair of Indian sign."

"I was riding more to the east. Perhaps you didn't cross their trail."

Jason rose in the saddle to look eastward. They were crossing flat, mesa-like land, open for miles, the only rise a large outcropping of rock with dust blowing above it. The size of the dust cloud grew. Jason stiffened and in that moment saw a band of horsemen charge from behind the rocks toward them.

Comanches.

19

"Hang on," Jason shouted to Luis, swinging his horse about and spurring for the river. Slowed by the double weight, they saw the Indians gain with every stride. Jason guessed there were ten warriors in the party.

They reached the river ahead of the Comanches and Jason spurred his horse down the incline, seeing a sand bank about a hundred yards away to his right with a few stunted bushes growing on top. Water from the bluff behind them had cut through the sand making a wash a couple of feet wide and two or three feet deep. As it neared the river, the wash turned sharply to the right, forming a cut visible only from the other side of the Pecos. The river here was about a hundred feet from bank to bank.

Jason took his Winchester from the saddle, waited until Luis slid from the horse, then dismounted himself and whacked his mount away with the flat of his hand. The two men raced for the bend in the wash and took refuge there behind the smartweeds and scrub oak. The Indians charged to the top of the bluff behind them and stopped. Jason saw one of the Comanches gallop down the slope and grasp his riderless horse by the bridle. Downstream three Indians were swimming the river and as he watched they scrambled up the far bank and loped out of sight.

"If they manage to shoot from over there into the open end of this ditch, we're done for," Jason said.

"Keep your eyes on the Indians on the bank behind us," Luis told him. "I'll deal with the three across the river."

Jason started to protest, objecting not to the plan but to Luis' assumption he could give orders, when an Indian raised his head over the edge of the bluff. Jason squeezed off a shot and saw the Indian twist away out of sight, wounded.

From the corner of his eye he saw a Comanche armed with a rifle crawl into the open on the far side of the river. Luis bided his time. The Comanche spotted them, raising his rifle. I hope to God Luis knows what he's doing, Jason thought.

Luis fired and the Indian half-rose, then crumpled to lay motionless on the ground. Neither of the other two warriors followed him into the open. The Comanches on their side of the river had all retreated beyond the top of the bluff and the early evening was suddenly quiet. Soon, Jason saw, it would be dark.

"We're dead men," Jason said, "if they attack. They'd overwhelm us in no time, it's nine or ten of them to two of us."

"I think they will not fight us," Luis said. "They'd lose too many men, perhaps three, perhaps more, and for what? Now that they have your horse there is nothing else they want."

"Indians attack out of pure cussedness when they're of a mind. to, maybe to count coup. This may be their hunting grounds we're on. Look." He nodded downstream where the bluff dropped almost to water level. "They're crawling toward us through the shinnery, the brush."

"Cover me," Luis said, "while I talk to them."

He took a white kerchief edged in silver from around his neck and tied it to his gun barrel and held it aloft.

"Don't be a fool," Jason told him. "If you show yourself they're as likely to kill you as not."

"Better be killed as a man than as a sheep," Luis said.

The Californio scrambled up the sand bank, Jason rising behind him with his Winchester at the ready. Two shots rang out from the bluff, a bullet tearing through Jason's left forearm. He dropped his gun and grasped the wound with his other hand as he sat in the ditch. Luis slid back down beside him.

"They don't seem to want to talk," he said.

For the first time he saw Jason's wound. He cursed in Spanish.

"I think it missed the bone," Jason said.

He scooped mud from the bottom of the ditch and covered the wound, then Luis wrapped his kerchief around Jason's arm and tied it tightly. Luckily, Jason thought, it was the left arm and he could still use the Winchester.

They heard a whirr, then another, and two arrows plummeted into the ditch and buried themselves beside Luis' leg. Though they scanned the bluff and the brush they saw no Comanches.

"They're angling them in," Jason said.

The two men hugged the side of the cut, the arrows striking the sand above them or falling harmlessly on the far bank. Luis, looking downstream, saw the tops of the smartweeds quiver, part slightly, and then close again. A Comanche, pushing the weeds in front of him to one side with his lance, was crawling toward them. Luis shifted his body to be in a position to get off a shot. There was a sudden "Whir-r-r" of an aroused rattlesnake near the Comanche and the Indian hastily backed off.

"Looks almost as though they're fighting every man for himself," Jason said. "As long as they keep that up we've got a chance."

"They could starve us out."

"Indians don't usually have the temperament to mount a long siege. They'll either give up on us as not worth the bother or they'll attack and kill us both. There's no point us both waiting here to find out what they intend. Our best bet's for you to try to get away downriver after dark."

"No," Luis said. "I will stay, you will go."

"I'd do better holding them off here, what with my arm shot like it is. I don't know how far I could get."

"If one of us can escape by the river, two of us can."

"You're not talking logical, Don Luis. Once there's no shooting from here the Indians'll know we're gone and as soon's it's light tomorrow they'll be after us on their ponies. We'll be dead men inside of a few hours, both of us."

"What you say makes sense," Luis admitted. "Do you have comrades near here?"

"They're camped to the south below a bluff over the Pecos." Jason described the place.

"They call that El Bosque Grande," Luis said. "The great woods. If fortune is with me I think I can be there in twenty-four hours."

They waited until night came and clouds scudded across the sky; the moon, low in the west, seeming to race in and out of sight. An owl hooted from across the river.

"An Indian signaling," Jason said. "They must be starting to pull together." Again the night was quiet. When at last the moon dropped below the horizon, Luis whispered to Jason.

"I will leave you my pistol and take only the rifle with me."

"What is that gun of yours?" Jason asked. "I never saw its like before."

"A repeating Henry rifle. The cartridges are of metal and will be able to withstand the water." He paused. "Good luck, my friend," he said.

"I'll stand them off as best I can," Jason said. "If they're about to take me, I'll kill myself. I've seen the bodies of men that've been captured and tortured by the Comanches."

Luis clasped Jason's good hand, then crawled along the gulley to where it met the river. Sitting on the ground, he removed all of his clothes except his sombrero, drawers and undershirt. He tied his boots together and slung them around his neck. Taking his knife, he thrust it into the river bank below water level. Luis reached into the river and found rocks on the bottom of the stream and used them to weight down his clothing under three feet of water.

He slipped into the river, his bare feet touching a gravel shoal some three or four feet below the surface. In the starlight he saw an Indian sitting bareback on a pony in the middle of the stream less than a hundred feet below him so Luis headed

the other way, staying close to the bank and its
overhanging bushes.

Without warning he stepped into deep water
and plunged in over his head. Pulling himself up
by grasping the rocky bank, holding his rifle in
one hand, he waited to see if he'd been heard.
There was no signal from the Indian downstream.
Undoubtedly others were stationed upriver but as
yet he had not been able to see them.

As he regained his breath, clouds drifted across
the sky and the night darkened around him. Recognizing his chance, Luis struck out into the river,
still carrying the gun in one hand. The weight of
the rifle, the boots around his neck, and the swift-
ness of the current running against him, pushed
Luis back and pulled him underwater so he had
to retreat to the shoal where he stood gulping in
air.

Once more Luis tried to swim upstream carrying the rifle and once more he was swept beneath
the surface. Carefully looking around him to note
the configuration of the river banks near where he
stood, he reached under the water with the rifle,
stuck the muzzle down into the bottom sand and
pushed the stock against the bank beneath the
water. The rifle hidden, he swam upstream.

When he came to where he judged the Indians
would most likely be, he swam underwater, sur-
facing next to the shore to take a few ragged
breaths before slipping into the stream again to
make his way up the river. Finally, confident he
was beyond the Indian sentries, he climbed from
the water to the bank of the Pecos and into a cane
brake. After resting a few minutes, he headed
west away from the river, turned downstream and
by daybreak was well on his way to the south and
the Bosque Grande.

He kept on in the heat of the day dressed only in his underwear, his feet sore and raw in boots intended for riding rather than walking, and with no shade for his sombrero had been swept away by the river. He stayed near the Pecos, several times swimming the stream to shorten his course. In the late afternoon of the second day, weak and feverish, he staggered to the crest of a hill and saw, in the river valley below him, a bedded herd of Texas longhorns.

Ike McLeod looked up to see a man stagger to the top of the hill behind their camp. At first he thought he was an Indian, for the Pecos was running red with mud and the man's body and clothing were as red as the river. Then he saw it was a white man and Ike rode up the hill. The man's eyes were wild and bloodshot. He had abandoned his boots and his feet were swollen; every step he took left blood in the track.

Ike dismounted, slung the man on his horse and rode him into camp where Vivian cut up a blanket, soaked it in river water and wrapped it around the man's feet. Chicago Luke cooked him a light gruel and for an hour Vivian sat beside him, alternately spooning food and water into his mouth. Only then could be talk coherently.

"*Señorita,*" was his first word. He was staring at Vivian as though he'd never seen a woman before.

"Briscoe," Luis said, turning to Ike. "Indians attacked us. I left him forty miles upriver from here."

He told the black man how Jason had found him afoot on the plains, of the attack by the Indian band, and his own flight from their hiding place two nights before.

"I want five men," Ike said once he'd gathered the hands. "We're riding north."

Every hand in camp volunteered. Ike picked his men and they mounted, leaving Luis in Vivian's care and posting the rest of the men to guard the cattle. The sun was down when they rode out and the night was cloudy but they kept near the river, heading upstream. Rain started to fall around midnight, a heavy driving rain, and the night grew so dark they were forced to halt. After an hour the storm subsided and they rode on, the rain stopping altogether well before dawn.

As the sun rose between swift-moving grey clouds, they saw they were nearing the place described by Luis as the scene of the siege. They passed Comanche tracks almost as fresh as their own and a short way farther on found a piece of paper impaled on a bush.

One of the cowhands reached down and plucked the paper from the limb. "It's a page from Briscoe's daybook," he said. "Look-a here." He held the paper aloft where the men crowding their horses around him could see.

An Indian had drawn a stick picture of a Comanche and a white man shaking hands. The white man was wearing a tall silk hat.

"What do you reckon they mean by that?" the cowboy asked. "I never seen a man wearing a two-story hat myself, 'cept in pictures."

Ike took the drawing from him, folded the paper and thrust it in his pocket. He motioned them on and, as they neared the spot where Jason and Luis had been besieged, they rode out onto the plains, meaning to sweep full-tilt over the bluff and take the Indians in the river bed by surprise. They galloped up the incline to the crest of the bluff and, guns drawn, thundered down the river side.

There were no Indians in sight in the valley though Ike saw the wet sides of the bank upstream where horses had climbed from the river. Ike, seeing the sand bank and the wash described by Luis, vaulted from his horse and ran into the gulley. The cut was almost filled with stones and the two sides were spiked with more than a hundred arrow shafts. He came to the sharp bend in the cut and looked down.

"Mr. Briscoe!" he shouted.

Jason lay at the bottom of the ditch, his eyes closed and a smear of blood on his cheek. They've killed him, Ike thought. God damn them to hell, they've killed him. He glanced at Jason's hair, thankful they hadn't scalped him as well.

Ike knelt on the ground beside him. "Jason," he said, "Jason." He'd never called him anything but Mr. Briscoe before.

Jason's eyes blinked open and he stared at the black man kneeling beside him. Slowly Jason tried to push himself to his feet.

"I'm plain tuckered out," he said and collapsed onto the rocks scattered on the sand around him.

20

"THE COMANCHES never did attack me," Jason told them once he was back in camp and had a night's sleep. "They feinted and darted around and threw rocks into the gulley and shot those arrows up into the air to angle down on me. I kept pressing off a shot here and there to let them know I was alive and then just before you came they gathered their horses and lit out."

Ike unfolded the picture of the Indian and the white man shaking hands and gave it to Jason. "What's it mean?" he asked.

"God knows," Jason said. "The daybook was in my saddle, that's how they got ahold of it. Maybe they were trying to tell us they had a treaty with the white man from Washington to let them hunt these lands and it was us trespassing, not them. That'd be my best guess."

"We found Don Luis' rifle and his knife and his clothes," Ike said, "just where he told us we would, hidden under the water in the river."

Jason stood up and sought out the Californio, finding him sitting with his back against the wheel of Vivian's wagon. Vivian was some distance away tending a kettle suspended over a fire on a potrack.

"I want to thank you for saving my life," Jason said. "If you hadn't managed to send the men for me I'd be dead by now. I sure couldn't have stayed awake much longer."

Luis nodded gravely. "Then we are even. You saved me; I saved you. What you call fifty-fifty. We are quits."

"I don't think so. You could have made your way to Sumner afoot after you lost your horse."

Luis shrugged. *"Quien sabe?"* he said. After a pause he went on. "I have many cattle in Mexico. Not longhorns such as yours yet they are well-fed and healthy. I have been thinking these last two days and I have made a decision. If you will have me, *Señor* Briscoe, I will be your partner."

"Partner?" The idea had never occurred to Jason. What did he want with a partner?

"Si, we could join our herds in the grasslands to the north, each sharing according to the number of cattle he brought with him. During my journey from Mexico I have been thinking of what I should do. I am a rancher, *Señor* Briscoe, not a man who trails herds to market. You are the herder, you have brought these cattle of yours the many terrible miles from Texas to the Pecos."

"You don't know how many head I lost crossing the desert."

"Ah, there you are mistaken. While I was here waiting for your return I talked to your men and I learned of your epic struggle against the desert. I know how many cattle you lost, I know the country you traveled, my people before me knew the country. Haven't we traveled this land for hun-

dreds of years? Isn't the Staked Plain itself named
for the markers the early Spanish explorers left
behind to guide those who followed?" Luis had
been talking faster and faster and now he subsided, sighing.

"All that is in the past," he said. "Just as this
great open country will someday be in the past. Yet
we do not live in the past or the future, we live
in the present. I know how many cattle you lost
and knowing the country I say it was a miracle to
bring so many to the Pecos alive. Whenever I find
a man who can work miracles, I become his dis-
ciple and I follow him. Of a certainty. However,
it will not only be to my advantage; it will be to
yours as well to have me as a partner."

"How so, Don Luis?"

"In this way. I do not see you as a man who will
always be satisfied with a few thousand head of
cattle. I picture you as a man who dreams of a
herd of fifty or a hundred thousand head. Who
knows, perhaps someday two hundred thousand.
And you will not be content with a few thousand
acres of land, you will want more. Each cow needs
how much land for grazing in the Staked Plain
country? Twenty perhaps? With a hundred thousand cattle you will need two million acres of
grazing land."

"I think you're the *hombre* who dreams big
dreams," Jason said. "Though I admit to being an
ambitious man."

"We are both ambitious men," Luis said. "With
a herd of great size, you will need help. I am a good
rancher. In California, my honored father, Don
Esteban Grandez, was known the length and
breadth of the state as a breeder of fine stock and
I learned much from him before his death. These
Texas longhorns of yours are tough and they trail

well, you have proved that, yet their meat is stringy and tough, or at least that is what they say in the East."

"You've been east, Don Luis?"

"Two years ago I traveled to Philadelphia and to Boston and to New York City. And I visited Chicago on my return journey to Mexico. I saw cattle in the East that were fat and sleek, cattle known as Herefords."

"Damn blooded stock," Jason said, "damn Eastern cows. A herd of Herefords wouldn't last through one Texas winter."

"Perhaps not. Yet if the Hereford was bred to the longhorn, who is to say what the result might not be? Perhaps you would retain the endurance of the longhorn as well as the fleshiness of the Hereford."

Jason picked up a stick and made random marks on the ground as he considered the idea. "I've toyed with another notion," he said. "Breeding buffalo to longhorn cattle. What do you think, Luis?"

"I think if one has an idea, one should make the experiment. The animals are similar, as much alike certainly as the horse and the donkey and they gave us the mule. What would we call one of these creatures, a buffle? A cattalo?"

"The name doesn't matter but I'd like us to try breeding them while there's still buffalo left on the plains."

"Yes, of a certainty we will make the attempt. And while I manage our ranch, you will journey to Texas and buy cattle and drive them to the north, to Kansas and the railroads, to New Mexico to sell to the Indian agents to feed the Indians who have sought peace on the reservations. And the best we will keep for ourselves, to build our herd."

"You make a good case for us getting together, Don Luis. But you haven't spoken to the biggest problem of all. My men are Texans for the most part and you, though you hail from California, you're a Mex to them. Like you were a Mex to me until I got to know you better. Could you boss Texans?"

"*Señora* Varner said to me you called yourself a broad-gauged man. Perhaps I am one as well. Is anything impossible to such men? If I hadn't seen that you chose a black man to lead your hands, I would have remained silent. Besides, *Señor* Briscoe, I do not boss men, I lead them. I ask them to do nothing I cannot do, however poorly."

Jason held out his hand and Luis clasped it. "Partner," Jason said, and it was done.

"We'll go north," Jason told him, "and find us our range and then you and I will ride to Mexico and bring your herd to join up with mine."

"It is good," Luis said. "Ah, one other matter. A delicate one, yet I must speak of it if you will permit me.

"Shoot."

"It is personal. You do not mind?"

"Go ahead, Luis. If I mind, I'll let you know in short order."

"That is the way I prefer it to be between us," Luis said. "It is the woman, *Señora* Varner. I am told her husband lives in Texas, far to the east. Yet she is here with you and she has the care of your son, as a mother would."

"What you say is true enough. I'm afraid I don't get your drift."

"I hesitate to speak for fear my words will seem like the sudden thrust of a knife. Yet I must. When a woman is the mother of a man's child, or acts in that way, it is customary for her to be the wife of the man or act in *that* way."

Jason laughed and slapped his thigh. "You speak like a gentleman, Luìs," he said, "and I'm afeared I speak like a Texan and so I suspect the two of us don't always talk the same language. I follow you now." He glanced at Vivian who had carried the kettle to the chuck wagon where she was talking to Chicago Luke.

"She's not my woman," Jason said. "Never has been. And never will be."

"Ah," Luis said, smiling. "I thought it best to be certain. I have never seen a more beautiful woman than *Señora* Varner. And the way she cares for your child, the love she bestows on him although he is not her own, I have never seen the like. I myself have been married two times and God has seen fit to take both of my wives from me before their time."

"Aren't you forgetting one important fact?" Jason asked. "Besides her being already hitched?"

"You are talking of my religion, are you not?" When Jason nodded, Luis said, "I hope you will not think the less of me when I tell you I take my religion lightly. I look into my heart for a creed to follow, not to the church. The church has not been good to the people of the country of my father's birth, Mexico. As you may know."

"I know a little Roman history but not much Mexican, Don Luis."

"The dates and the battles, perhaps not. I suspect you know much of the ways of men and that is a part of history also."

"Men I think I know. Women, now, have always been a puzzlement to me."

"Aren't they to all men?" Luis' gaze followed

Vivian as she returned to the wagon and lifted Jan from his cradle-board.

"I hope," Jason said, "you don't intend to"—he groped for the right words—"to rile her in any way."

"I will be a gentleman at all times. I intend to court *Señora* Varner, to give her small presents, a flower, perhaps, or a silver ornament for her hair, as signs of my admiration. I will court her and at first she will turn her back and ignore me. I will slowly wear away her reluctance as the Pacific Ocean wears away the shore near Monterey and when the time is right she will come to me."

"You may have a mighty long wait," Jason said. Till hell freezes over, he thought. Vivian didn't cotton to Mexicans whether they were U.S. citizens or not.

"I am a patient man." Luis stood. "We should toast our partnership. A little wine, perhaps?"

"There's no wine in the camp. I don't allow the men to drink so I don't myself."

"A good policy, though a trifle harsh. In California, we believe in enjoying the bounties of nature, the grape, the wine. In moderation."

"I'm afraid there's not much moderation in Texas. It's whole hog or none."

"'Whole hog or none,' I must remember that. The language of Texas is colorful. May we suppose we have wine, to toast our future?"

"You can make believe all you want, Don Luis."

Luis raised an imaginary glass in his hand. "To the partnership of Grandez and Briscoe," he said.

"No, you got it wrong. Sort of backwards. To the Briscoe-Grandez spread. Agreed?"

Luis smiled. "Agreed," he said. His smile broadened as he looked up at Jason. "Podner," he added in a fine Texas drawl.

*   *   *

When Jason and Luis rode into Sumner, they found that the fort was being used as the headquarters for a reservation of Navajo and Mescalero Indians. Some years before, the campaigns waged by Kit Carson had driven thousands of Indians from their own lands to the fort to seek the white man's protection. To follow the white man's road.

As an Indian reservation, Sumner was a failure. Irrigation had proved largely impractical, the soil was poor and unproductive, fuel was scarce and provisions inadequate. When Jason and Luis drove in their herd they found the Indians on the verge of starvation.

"We'll buy your steers, the twos, threes, and up," the Indian agent told Jason.

"How much will you pay?" Jason asked. He expected to be offered two or three cents a pound.

"Eight cents a pound on the hoof," the agent told him.

"Only eight?"

"If it was up to me, I'd pay more, but the Great White Father in Washington won't let me."

"If that's the best you can do," Jason said, "I suppose I don't have much choice. I'll take it."

"*We* will take it," Luis amended and Jason nodded.

When they were alone, Jason said to Luis, "I heard tell that during the gold rush men claimed they found creeks in California with the bottoms paved with nuggets so thick you just had to wade in and pick them up. These cattle cost me maybe five dollars a head in Texas and by bringing them a few hundred miles they've come to be worth eighty dollars a head. I think we've found us a creek of gold."

"Yes, for now. Creeks such as you talk of, if they ever existed, were soon picked clean of riches. I think we should move swiftly. How do you say, use the hot iron?"

"Hot iron? Oh, you mean strike while the iron's hot. True. You heard me ask about this canyon I know of, the Palo Bueno, the agent called it. Said it was a campground for the Cheyennes, Comanches and Kiowas. We'll never be able to start a ranch in the canyon, not now, not with the Indians there. So I was thinking we'd trail the cows and calves we didn't sell on north to Colorado and stock a range there and in the spring go to Mexico for your herd."

"I have a better plan. You, *Señor* Briscoe, go north to Colorado. Give me your man McLeod and one or two others and I will take them to Mexico and bring my herd north and you can meet us on the trail. We'll sell what we can here in New Mexico and then you'll lead us to the range in Colorado."

Jason lifted his hat from his head, smoothing back his hair as he pondered the idea. Luis made sense. If. If Jason trusted him with two or three of his men on the long trek south to Mexico, trusted him to return with the herd. If he really had a herd there in the first place.

Luis drew in his breath and held it, knowing this was the test of the strength of their handshake at Bosque Grande.

"Agreed." Jason smiled as he saw Luis let out his breath.

"*Compañero,*" Jason added.

21

IN THE NEXT five years, Jason Briscoe and Don Luis Grandez prospered as the herds carrying the B-Bar-G brand increased six-fold. Jason led drives from central Texas, buying and herding his own cattle and driving steers for other ranchers under contract. He trailed the cattle north to Dodge City and Pueblo on the Atchison, Topeka and Santa Fe, and into Hays and Denver on the Kansas Pacific. More and more of eastern Kansas had become off-limits becase of the nesters—the homesteaders—and the fear that Texas cattle carried tick fever.

As the cattle drives shifted west, the white hunters of the buffalo, the hide men, pushed out onto the plains as the price of hides rose in the East. When the Indians fought to save their hunting rounds, the soldiers were sent to subdue them. In early autumn the 4th Cavalry, over four hundred strong, followed a large band of Indians to the rim of the Palo Bueno where they found a trail down the canyon's side.

The Indians, taken by surprise, fled from their camps, and by the time the warriors turned and rallied the troops were in possession of tribal camps extending for two miles up and down the canyon. Holding the Indians back with long-range carbine fire, the soldiers destroyed all they could find. Tepees, robes, tanned hides, arrows and dried meat, everything that would burn or be ruined by heat or smoke went into the great bonfires. Holes were knocked in the bottoms of cooking kettles and, as the smoke rose over the canyon's rim, the Indian horse herds were rounded up.

The animals were driven to the top of the canyon and after the Tonkawa scouts—the Tonkawas had long before made common cause with the whites against their fellow Indians—were rewarded with the pick of the ponies, the rest were slaughtered. More than 1,400 horses and mules were killed since the Army had learned that the best way to fight Indians was to destroy their villages and their livestock. For the Comanches in the weeks that followed it became a matter of surrender or starve. And, except for small bands of warriors, they surrendered.

During the following year, Jason scouted the Palo Bueno canyon and found it deserted, the Indians gone. Only the herds of buffalo remained.

"It's ours for the taking," he told Luis when he returned to their Colorado ranch. "There's enough grazing land for a hundred thousand head."

"If this is to be the ranch we have talked of, the home ranch of our herds, we must buy the land so it will be ours forever."

"What with building up our herd, we don't have enough ready cash to buy land."

"Then we must borrow," Luis said.

"With the banks in Denver charging two percent interest a month?"

"Has not the time come," Luis asked, "to talk to your friend *Señor* Montgomery? The Englishman you have told me about, the man with the five million dollars."

Jason nodded. "I agree," he said. "The time has come to talk to Sir Charles."

"How much do you want to borrow?" Sir Charles Montgomery asked Jason. They were seated in the Englishman's third-floor office in downtown Denver where, from the windows, they could see the snow-capped Rockies while from the street outside came the cries of muleskinners.

"I reckon two hundred and fifty thousand dollar would do us," Jason said.

When he noticed that Montgomery didn't blink, he added, "That's for now, for seed money. We'll need another two hundred and fifty thousand in three years' time."

"You warned me when we talked in New York six years ago that you'd ask me for half a million dollars," Sir Charles said, "and by God you have. You know, don't you, you're talking full partnership money?"

"Don Luis and I are aware of that."

"And we're not talking handshake money. An agreement involving a half million dollars would have to be drawn up by lawyers."

"I hate to see them lawyers with their highfalutin' words and their whereases come into it, but I see your point. I expected as much and I'd be agreeable."

"You speak for your partner?"

"I do. Though Don Luis and I didn't need lawyers or papers when we hitched up, a shake of the hand was good enough for us. On the strength of that handshake he brought more than four thousand head north from Mexico."

"I fully understand how you Texians operated. Those times are mostly over now, we're in the '70's, not the '60's. Cattle ranching is big business today and we have to use big business methods. Accountants and lawyers and all the rest."

"If we're to be modern and all, the word's Texans, not Texians."

"Texans, then," Sir Charles said. "Now listen to me, Briscoe. If I'm even to consider doing business with you, I expect you to know how I operate. Firstly, I don't ask you to like me. Whether you do or not is immaterial to me. I've followed your ranch operations with interest, your partnership with this Grandez fellow, and I think we can make money. That's my only interest, making money, not the improvement of the breed, not the building of a cattle empire, just making money."

Jason studied the other man. Sir Charles had lost much of his blond hair since he'd seen him in New York; he was now almost bald. He'd put on weight, too, had quite a corporation, as they called it, around the middle, and his face had become fuller and redder. And not from the sun, Jason guessed. Only his thin blond moustache seemed the same.

Before, in New York, something about the man had struck Jason as being odd, something about what he'd said when he talked of fighting in the Crimea, but Jason couldn't recall what it had been. Yet he'd done some checking on his own, as he was sure Sir Charles had checked on him, and found that the Englishman was indeed wealthy and had a reputation as a square dealer. In fact, a couple of ranchers had taken advantage of Sir Charles by charging him for cattle based on inflated tally counts.

Still, Jason had to admit he didn't like the man. Maybe it was just that English accent of his. Or his attitude. Sir Charles seemed to think that God had put other men on Earth as servants to do his bidding.

"I've no great aversion to making money," Jason said.

"Good, then I think we can do business if we can come to an agreement on the terms. Oh, yes, I have one other condition. Before the papers are signed and after you've driven your herd there, I want to travel down to this canyon of yours and see what the country looks like."

"If I was spending a half million dollars on a place," Jason said, "I know I'd sure as hell like to see the lay of the land. Me and you can ride there together."

"Good." Sir Charles rose from behind his desk and the two men shook hands. "By the by," Sir Charles said, "my wife will be going to the canyon with me."

"My eyes are beginning to blur," Jason said.

"I don't believe I understand your meaning."

"From reading all the fine print you keep adding to our contract."

"Isn't your wife coming to the Palo Bueno?"

"I'm not married. I'm leaving my son and the woman who cares for him at the Colorado ranch. My partner will go on ahead of us with the cattle and we'll meet him there."

"I know you Texians think the fewer women on a working ranch, the better. My wife, though, accompanies me everywhere."

"Working women are always welcome on a Texan's working ranch," Jason said. He caught himself, shaking his head vigorously. "Accept my apologies," he said. "Here I am asking a man for a half million dollars and I appear to be setting out to insult him right and left. Somehow you bring out the cussedness in me, Sir Charles. I most humbly beg your pardon."

"Your apology is accepted, my good man," the Englishman said. "You may change your opinion of my wife once you've met her."

Jason met Paula Montgomery the following month when he came to Denver's Palace Hotel before the start of their journey across the plains to the Palo Bueno. The herd had been on the trail for five weeks and would, if all went well, be bedded down in the canyon by the time Jason and the Montgomerys arrived.

"You're to call me Paula," Mrs. Montgomery said. Her voice was light and clear but she, too, had a different way of speaking and Jason remembered she was from Boston.

She crossed the room and Jason tried not to stare at her grey twill trousers. They fit so snugly over the curves of her hips he knew she must have had them tailor-made. A plain white shirt was tucked inside the pants and she wore a black leather belt, tooled like a man's but obviously made especially for her tiny waist.

Paul shook Jason's hand, not letting go immediately, and when he felt her hand press his he drew away, the blood flooding his face.

"Why, you're blushing, Mr. Briscoe," she said, "or may I call you Jason?" When he nodded, she went on. "You're not to think of me as a woman. I can ride better than Charles and shoot better than Charles. In fact. . . ."

"Paula." Sir Charles' words sliced knife-like

across the room. "That is enough," he said, "that is quite enough."

Paula smiled sweetly at him. She was some twenty years younger than her husband, in her late twenties, Jason guessed. Her pale blonde hair was pulled to the back of her head in a bun, emphasizing her high cheekbones. On any other woman the style would have been too severe but it only highlighted Paula's femininity. She looked more female in men's clothes, Jason thought, than most women did in their frills and furbelows. She reminded Jason of someone—who he couldn't say.

Paula went to her husband and kissed his cheek. "I'm sorry, Charlie," she said.

"Quite all right, my dear," he told her. "I'm sure Mr. Briscoe doesn't care to witness one of our spats." He turned to Jason. "The wagons are loaded for the trip," he said. "Both Mrs. Montgomery and I will ride horses, however."

Paula Montgomery proved to be a capable horsewoman. She was right, Jason saw as they headed south from Denver, she was a better rider than her husband. Sir Charles sat his horse heavily, not moving with the animal and so tiring him, while Paula sat lightly in the saddle and guided her bay with a touch of her leg or the flick of her quirt.

When they reached the Arkansas River east of Fort Dodge, the stink of rotting buffalo carcasses rose all around them. The hide hunters, Jason saw, had built a line of camps along the river and shot down the buffalo, night and morning, as they came to drink. In one spot he counted sixty carcasses in the space of a few hundred feet.

"What a terrible stench," Paula said, covering her nose with a lace-edged white handkerchief.

"It's a shame," Jason told her. "Not that I haven't killed buffalo myself. I have and I will again. In fact we'll have to kill them to clear the herds out of the Palo Bueno this summer before we can graze cattle there."

They rode south from the river, leaving the stink of the dead buffalo behind. Jason slept on the ground as he always did on the trail, while the Montgomerys carried a tent in one of their wagons and each evening the teamsters unloaded and pitched it.

Fifty miles south of the Arkansas, they came on a camp of hide men as the hunters were preparing to fan out on the plains in search of a buffalo herd.

"I'm going along if they'll take me," Paula said. "I've never shot a buffalo before. Neither have you, Charles; don't you want to come?"

"Buffalo are too tame for me, my dear," Sir Charles said. "Go along with Briscoe if you want."

Jason shrugged and he and Paula followed the hide man and his three skinners onto the plains. They soon sighted a small herd of a few hundred buffalo and after riding to the lee side—downwind —the hunter signaled them to dismount.

With Jason and Paula a few feet behind him, the hide man crawled toward the herd. Once they were within three hundred yards, the sentinel buffalos became uneasy, looking about them and pawing the ground. The small black buffalo birds that followed the herds fluttered up from the sentinels' shoulders, then settled back. The hide hunter put his canteen, a supply of cartridges and an extra rifle on the ground beside him.

"The first rifle gets overheated from all the shooting," he explained in a low voice. He used a rock to drive a forked stick into the ground, resting the rifle barrel on the fork as he aimed and pressed off a shot from his Sharps .50 caliber. One of the buffalo staggered and fell.

"How do you decide which ones to shoot first?" Paula asked.

"By watching for them that are most restless. Or the one that starts leading the others away." He shot again and another buffalo fell. "They're stupid beasts," he said. "The Indians in the mountains hunt buffalo by driving them over cliffs. Do you want to give it a try?" he asked Paula, nodding to the gun in his hand.

Paula hunched up beside the hide hunter and took the rifle, raising the gun to her shoulder. Aiming carefully, she pressed the trigger and a buffalo, standing apart from the rest of the herd, dropped to the ground. Jason heard Paula's muffled cry of triumph and, looking at her, saw a gleam in her eye and a delighted smile on her lips.

Why, she liked to kill them, Jason thought, got a pleasure from seeing them go down. He had probably killed more animals in his time than she ever would, yet he never enjoyed it. He killed to eat, or to give his cattle grazing room, or to destroy predators, never solely for the sport. He didn't rightly understand a person, man or woman, who found so much pleasure in killing a buffalo.

They were magnificent brutes, he thought. For hundreds and hundreds of years they'd withstood the blue northers and the blizzards of winter, the droughts and dust of summer, the windstorms and the prairie fires. Even the Indians. And here they were being slaughtered so a stinking hide man could collect his dollar for the skin and his two bits for the tongue. Jason shook his head, saddened.

As they rode south, he remembered coming to the rim of a canyon years ago and seeing, far below, an old buffalo surrounded by a pack of six large grey wolves. When the buffalo made a dive at the nearest wolf, tumbling him over and over, the rest of the pack pounced on the buffalo's hind legs, snarling and snapping, tearing at his hams.

Jason fired at the wolves, killing two; the others retreating and the buffalo hobbled off, bleeding so profusely that Jason doubted he could survive for long. Years had passed but the memory of the wolves and the old buffalo had stayed with him. These hide men, he thought, were a thousand times worse than any pack of wolves.

That night they made camp along a creek far from the stench of the dead buffalo. After Jason helped the wagon driver build the fire, Sir Charles came to sit with him as they waited for Paula to join them for supper.

When Jason looked up and saw her walking toward them from the tent, he gaped. Gone were the men's trousers; she wore a full skirted black dress with red piping at the waist and crimson slippers peeped from under her skirts. The gown's neck scooped low and the contrast between the black of the dress and Paula's white skin was startling. She had loosened her blonde hair so it fell in soft waves over her shoulders.

"You look dazzling, my dear," Sir Charles said. "Simply dazzling."

She nodded to her husband as she came to stand in front of Jason. "And you, Jason," she said, "how do *you* think I look?" She smiled up at him.

His gaze couldn't avoid the pale curves of her breasts above the dress. "Magnificent," he said, blushing, and her smile changed as though they shared a secret. Or soon would.

"Thank you," Paula said, "both of you."

Sir Charles brought a chair for his wife from the

tent and, since the night was beginning to cool with the setting of the sun, he laid a white buffalo robe across her lap.

Jason couldn't take his eyes off Paula Montgomery. Now he knew who she reminded him of —not an actual person after all, but the woman he had dreamed of marrying before he went to New York. Not her actions, more the way she looked, blonde and petite, so pretty it made him ache just to look at her.

She talked about shooting the buffalo, repeating the story of the hunt in detail. And as Jason listened, he realized his first impression of her had been right, that he didn't like Paula Montgomery, not in the least. He wanted her, though, and disliking her made not the slightest difference.

Strange, he thought. He liked and admired Vivian and yet he didn't want her while he disliked this woman and still he wanted her as much as he'd ever wanted a woman.

22

THEY CAME to the rim of the Palo Bueno on an afternoon in early May. In the canyon far below they saw the B-Bar-G cattle grazing on the new grass and, beyond the cattle on the far side of the fork of the Red River, a herd of buffalo. The bluffs on both sides of the canyon were steep yet not impassable; along the canyon floor near the walls were stands of fir; and, near the creek, groves of cottonwoods whose leaves trembled in the breeze.

"It takes my breath away," Paula said to Jason.

"Marvelous grazing country," Sir Charles said. "You say the Cheyenne once lived here?"

"The Cheyenne and others. Their camps were farther down the canyon, the valley extends sixty or seventy miles to the east. All good grazing land. Each cow shouldn't need more than ten acres of this grama grass."

Jason rode along the edge of the canyon, finally stopping and pointing down. "There's a trail of

sorts that leads to the bottom from here," he said.
He had already sent the wagons with Montgomery's tent and provisions on the long route to the
lower end of the canyon.

"We're in no great hurry, are we?" Sir Charles
asked. He had dismounted and was standing beside Jason staring down the cliff face at the rocks
on the canyon floor.

"None in particular," Jason said, "though I'm
downright curious to see if the men have started
on the ranch house. It'll be built on a rise behind
that stand of fir."

"*I'm* not afraid to ride down from here," Paula
said.

For the first time, Jason looked closely at Sir
Charles. The other man's hands were tightly
clenched on the reins of his horse, his florid face
had paled and sweat beaded his forehead. Why,
the man was plumb afraid, Jason thought. Heights
had that effect on some people, he told himself.

"After all," Paula went on, "you won't find any
Russians down in the canyon firing their cannon
at us."

Russians? Jason frowned, trying to make the
connection. Oh yes, he reminded himself, Sir
Charles had fought the Russians in the Crimea.

"That's quite enough, Paula," Sir Charles told
her. He spoke without conviction, as though knowing his words would have little effect.

"We'll ride east along the rim," Jason said.
"There's a better way to the bottom fifteen miles
farther on."

"I think we should go down here," Paula said.

"It's shorter and I'm hot and I'm tired. I haven't
taken a good bath since we left Denver."

"We'll do as Briscoe suggests," Sir Charles said.

Jason swung his horse away from the rimrock and the other two followed him. After they had ridden less than a mile, Paula galloped up beside him while Sir Charles stayed behind, making no attempt to join her.

"I would have gone down that switchback trail without giving it a second thought," Paula told Jason.

Jason said nothing. This expedition to the Palo Bueno canyon, the coming home to Texas he had looked forward to so eagerly and for so long, was turning into a disaster. And he had a half million dollars at stake.

"I know what you're thinking, Jason," Paula said. "You're worrying about your money. 'I mustn't antagonize Sir Charles or he won't advance the money,' that's what you're telling yourself."

Jason glanced over his shoulder and saw that Sir Charles still lagged some fifty feet behind them, riding heavily, seemingly lost in his own thoughts.

"You're not far off the mark," Jason said.

"Then I'm going to tell you something you evidently don't know and haven't guessed. Sir Charles has the money, that's true enough, but I'm the one with the brains. I'm the one who's willing to take risks. And because I've the brains and the initiative, I'm the one who makes the decisions. If Charles had his way he'd still be living in New York idling his life away eating and drinking and playing billiards at one of his clubs."

"Not in London?"

"London? Don't make me laugh, Jason. After what happened in the Crimea he never had the nerve to show himself in his London clubs."

"Mrs. Montgomery," Jason said, deciding the time had come to talk plain, "if I was married and felt about my wife the way you feel about your husband, I wouldn't stay married to her for more than two minutes."

"Even if she had the money? Even if she had a great deal of money?"

"I remember a few years back when I was trailing south of here, east of the Pecos. I'd sold our beeves at Fort Stanton and I had ten thousand dollars in the strongbox in my wagon, and that's an awful lot of money to me. Well, Mrs. Montgomery, we ran out of food and water and I didn't think we were going to make it out of the desert alive. Here I am, I thought, looking death in the face and me with ten thousand dollars and all that money's not going to do me one whit of good. Ever since then I haven't lusted for money like maybe I did once."

"Every day I discover new talents in you, Jason. Why, you're a homespun philosopher, a philosopher of the plains."

Jason bit back a reply, riding on in silence.

"You don't like me, do you?" Paula asked.

He glanced at her and saw a slight smile curling her lips. "No, ma'am," he said, "I can't rightly say I do."

She laughed. "At least you're an honest philosopher," she said. "You don't like me even though I like you? I do, you know, I think I could like you very much. I like men who know what they're about, are good at what they do, men who aren't afraid. Big men. Men who are hard and lean. Why, you're blushing, Jason. Did you think I was talking about you? Or is it the sun making your face so red?"

He wanted to strike out at Paula, to punish her for the way she made him feel. He had an urge to pull her from her horse, take her across his knee and paddle her. He remembered spanking another woman long ago, a woman with hair the color of gold. Tamar. He pushed the thought of Tamar from his mind. There's no point thinking of what's gone for good, he told himself.

All at once he felt an excitement rise in him, felt himself harden, and he looked across at Paula. Her eyes held his for a moment and she smiled a knowing smile.

"It *is* terribly hot," she said, undoing the top button of her shirt. "There doesn't seem to be any breeze just when you most need one."

Jason saw the flash of her white skin where the top of her shirt fell open. He spurred his horse ahead.

"I think you like me better than . . ." he heard Paula say but the rest of her words were lost to him. As he rode, he heard her laughter following him.

They reached the floor of the canyon in the early evening and rode westward in the purple dusk until they came to the camp. The men, under Luis' direction, had thrown up a temporary bunkhouse and were beginning to fell trees for the main house.

The next day Jason and Luis tramped over the site, laying out the rooms by drawing lines in the dirt with sticks.

"When the building's up," Jason told Ike, "I'd like the men to dig a tunnel from the side here into those trees across the way."

"A tunnel? What you wanting with a tunnel?"

"If the Indians leave the reservations again, they'll return to their old camping grounds. And sure as shooting, they'll head for the Palo Bueno. I don't expect trouble but I want to be ready in case it comes. We could be bottled up in this canyon just as the Indians were by the pony soldiers. A tunnel would at least give us an escape hatch if worst comes to worst."

"Makes sense," Ike said. "We'll get on it soon's we can."

"One other thing. About Sir Charles and his wife."

"I been meaning to mention that man," Ike said. "He called one of the boys 'my good man,' Randy Soames it was, and Randy says to him, 'I'm not your good man,' and Sir Charles didn't take that none too kindly. I know 'cause I saw him and he was swelled up fit to bust."

"Sir Charles means no harm. He's English. Worse still, he's rich and a city man so he's used to a different way of living, used to having servants and all."

"I keep expecting him to put his boots outside that tent of his one night," Ike said, "figuring I'll pick them up and give them a good shine."

"I wouldn't be surprised at whatever he did. Now listen, Ike, you tell the hands to be respectful to Sir Charles, just like they would to any guest, and if a storm starts to brew they're to come to me."

"That's fair."

"What I started to say," Jason went on, "was that Sir Charles and his missus want to do a bit of hunting while they're in the Palo Bueno. I'm needed here to help Luis with driving out the buffalo and settling in the herd, so I want you to pick a good man to go with them. A good tracker who'll let Sir Charles do the shooting and who'll see he doesn't get himself killed. And who'll know enough to keep his mouth shut and not answer back."

"That sounds like Silent Sam."

"Yes, I guess I was sort of thinking of Sam maybe being the one. He should be able to get downwind of a herd of antelope or two."

"Sam was saying he saw traces of bears down the canyon," Ike said. "They might take a look-see on their way to the Plain. How long a hunting trip you thinking about?"

"Oh, three or four days. We'll leave that up to Sir Charles." Jason paused. "And to his wife."

When he saw Sam and the Montgomerys ride out of camp the following morning, Jason gave a sigh of relief. He hoped the hunting would be good enough to keep them busy for a week or more.

In spite of himself, he was angry at Sir Charles. Why couldn't the man keep a better rein on that wife of his? Paula must have caused him trouble before; you'd think he'd stand up to her, lay down the law. After all, the money was his. Maybe Sir Charles figured he'd never be able to find another woman as young and as good looking as Paula. Pretty as she was, no woman was worth the aggravation. Some men, now, seemed to like a bossy wife. Maybe Sir Charles was one of that kind.

Jason spent the day with Luis and some of the other men driving the buffalo down the canyon.

"They're liable to keep coming back," Jason said to his partner as they got ready to return to camp. "If they do, we'll have to kill them."

Luis nodded. "I have given instructions to the men," he said, "to corral a bull and four or five of the better cows. To breed with the cattle."

"I can tell you're not taken with my notion."

"I think they'll breed. I'm afraid the cattalo will be sterile or too many of them will be. Yet we should try."

Jason reached down for a handful of soil, letting

it trickle through his fingers. He stared into the distance, suddenly remembering the white squaw showing him this canyon. He smiled.

"You love the land, this land of ours," Luis said.

Jason blinked, grinned at Luis and swung onto his horse and they loped toward camp.

After a few minutes they heard a galloping horse and looked behind them.

"The wife of the Englishman," Luis said, reining up. "She rides alone."

"What could have gone wrong? I can't imagine them running into Indians this near camp."

Paula reined in beside the two men.

"Now don't look at me like that, Jason," she said. "We weren't ambushed by Indians, if that's what you're thinking. Charles and I had a slight misunderstanding. Nothing serious, we have them all the time. He said if I didn't like hunting antelope with him, I could jolly well go back to camp and I told him I jolly well would and he said I jolly well should then. Of course, they rode with me to within sight of your men before they left me."

Jason saw Luis raise his eyebrows a fraction of an inch. With a sigh, Jason shook his head and they continued on in the direction of the camp.

After supper, Paula leaned over to put her hand on Jason's arm. "Will you send one of the men to my tent?" she asked him. "There's some carrying I want done."

He looked at the fair hair curling on her shoulders, the blue eyes meeting his as though in a challenge. She was wearing a checkered man's shirt with a buckskin skirt and leggings and once more he felt the excitement grow in him. Her voice, he thought, had been like a caress.

"I'll help you myself," he said.

He pushed himself to his feet and followed her to the tent that had been pitched a quarter mile away. He lifted the flap, nodding to her to go in ahead of him, but when she hesitated, he started forward just as she stepped ahead and they collided. For a moment her body was warm against his and then she laughed, looking up at him before going in.

When Jason followed her inside he saw that the tent was lit by a single lamp on a folded table near the center pole. There were two cots, one on each side of the tent, a pile of buffalo robes in a far corner and a small chest of drawers with a mirror attached to the back. The top of the chest was littered with an array of bottles and tins.

Paula went to tilt the mirror up, standing in front of it smoothing her hair. "You wanted some carrying done?" Jason asked her.

"Yes," she said, gesturing to a dark corner of the tent. "I'd like that tub moved to where I can use it. Then it'll need to be filled so I can take a bath. I'm absolutely filthy from our ill-fated hunting expedition."

Jason pulled the copper tub into the space between the cots, then left the tent without looking at Paula. He took two buckets from the chuck wagon, went to the stream and filled them, and began carrying the buckets up the hill to the tent, all the while trying to force thoughts of Paula Montgomery from his mind. He found, though, that she was all he could think of.

He pictured her sitting in the tub, naked, her bare arms and legs covered with soap, pictured her reaching over her shoulder to wash her back with a brush, causing the water to lap around her breasts. He slowed his pace, his excitement rising in spite of himself, his sex thrusting against his levis. Bending down, he filled his cupped palms with some of the cold water he'd dipped from the creek and splashed it on his face. Only then was he able to pick up the buckets and go to the tent.

He stopped outside the closed flap. The night had darkened and the lamplight shone through the canvas but he heard no sound from inside.

"I've brought the water," he said.

"Come in, Jason," Paula told him. He pushed his way inside. She was standing beside the tub wearing a white gown held together by a blue sash tied in a bow.

"In the tub, Jason," she said.

"What?" he asked.

"The tub," she said. "Pour the water into the tub."

He picked up the bucket nearest him and poured. When he'd emptied the second pail, the tub was still less than half full.

"Could you bring two more?" she asked.

Jason stared at her, only half listening as he wondered what, if anything, she wore beneath her gown. He could see half of her white breasts to either side of the deep Vee of the neckline.

"Please?" she said.

He forced his attention to what she had asked. More water, she wanted more water. He picked up a bucket in each hand and went down to the creek and returned with the water. When he'd emptied the buckets into the tub, Paula knelt beside him and leaned forward to put her hand in the water to test it. He couldn't avoid seeing her gown gape open to expose her full breasts almost to the nipples.

"Brrrr," Paula said. "It's so cold."

She stood up suddenly, so close to him that he

felt her warmth though their bodies weren't touching. The scent of her was in the air all around him, a scent he couldn't name, the heavy odor reminding him of stories of the Arabian nights, of exotic dancing girls and of deep and hidden caves where oriental potentates stored man-sized jars filled with spices.

"The water's too cold," she said. "Could you possibly heat a kettle for me?" He blinked, bringing his attention back to her words. "I know I'm a terrible bother," she said.

"I'll bring some hot water," he told her.

"I haven't thanked you yet for filling the tub." Paula stood on tiptoe and leaned to him, her lips brushing his. Jason stepped back, not wanting her to feel his hardness. "Some men," she said softly, "think I'm worth it."

He hurriedly left the tent, getting a kettle from the chuck wagon and heating the water on the rack over the dying campfire. Luis was standing nearby smoking a cigarillo and watching him. Luis still courted Vivian, he knew, though even after five years she continued to ignore him. Or at least that's the way it seemed to Jason. Now Luis said nothing and when Jason glared at him the Don turned away and stared across the canyon to the dark wall on the far side.

Holding the kettle of boiling water away from his body, Jason walked back to the tent. When he was thirty feet away, he stopped, for he could see Paula's shadow as she walked back and forth in front of the lamp. She lowered her arms as though removing her robe and appeared to throw the garment to one side. He thought he saw the outline of her bared breast against the canvas.

Jason put the kettle on the ground, strode to the

tent and, drawing aside the flap, stepped inside. Paula stood across from him in front of the mirror rubbing a cream into her face. She still wore the robe and in the mirror he could see that the gown was still tied with a bow.

"You didn't bring the hot water," she said, turning to look at him, one hand still slowly massaging her cheek.

In two steps he crossed the tent and looked down into her glistening blue eyes. Reaching out he took one end of the sash in his hand and pulled, the bow coming undone and the robe falling loose at her sides. He spread the robe apart, drawing in his breath as he saw she was completely naked beneath, her body as white and lovely as he'd imagined it.

"I was beginning to think you were afraid of me," Paula said.

"Turn around," Jason told her.

She looked at him with a question in her eyes.

"Turn around," he said again.

Obediently she turned so her back was to him. He took the robe by the collar and pulled it down over her arms until it fell free. He tossed the robe to one side. She wore pink and white slippers and nothing else. For a long moment he stared at the curve of her back and buttocks, at her white and unblemished body.

"May I turn around now?" she asked.

"No," he said. "I'll tell you when. I'm not through with this side yet."

She laughed, the laugh almost a chuckle. After a minute he said, "All right," and she turned to face him. His eyes roved down over her breasts to her legs and to the blond hair between them.

He reached to the lamp to extinguish the low-burning flame.

"No," she told him. "Leave the lamp as it is. I want you to see me. And I want to see you."

He started to undo his belt.

"No, not yet." Paula took a step forward so her bare breasts lightly touched his shirt.

Unable to hold back, he gathered her in his arms and pulled her roughly to him. She gasped but when he looked at her she was smiling and her eyes were closed. His lips found hers and she opened her mouth, her tongue probing. She bit his lip, bringing the taste of blood to his mouth. Jason forced her down to the earthen floor of the tent while reaching for a buffalo robe to put under her.

She pulled his hand back to her body. "I like to feel the ground under me," she said, leading his hands to her breasts.

He cupped her breasts, his thumbs circling her nipples as he felt her writhe on the ground beneath him.

"Hurt me," she said, "hurt my breasts."

He gripped them tighter, his lips going from her mouth to her nipples and, taking one of them into his mouth he caressed it with his tongue.

"Bite them," she whispered, and his teeth closed over the nipple until she cried out.

"Yes, yes," she murmured, her breathing quick. "Now the other one. It's jealous."

He shifted his mouth to her right breast, caressing it with his tongue before he closed his teeth over her nipple. As she twisted under him, moaning, his excitement grew and he held his desire in rein only by forcing his mind from her, trying to make it a blank.

As though he could! She enclosed him with her legs, pulling him to her. Her hands went to his waist, unbuckling his belt, pushing his pants down along his hips. Once she'd released his sex she grasped it in both of her hands and led him inside her.

"Take me," she whispered, biting his ear lobe. "Take me now."

He thrust inside her, his hips beating down against her body. His mouth covered hers and he felt her teeth nipping at him, the taste of blood in his mouth, his hands on her breasts, twisting them, punishing them as her arms wrapped around him, her legs locking above him so she rose and fell with him in a wild frenzy.

"Hurt me," she said, twisting her mouth to one side.

Paula's voice rose to a muted scream as his body slammed into hers in a last burst of passion and he felt himself release within her as her body moved with his, throbbed in unison with his, her nails raking his back. Even when he finally lay quiet, she pulsed against him.

At last she lay still. She pushed herself from beneath him and got slowly to her feet. He heard the rustle of her robe as she slipped it on.

"Get out," she said.

Jason looked up at her. Paula's back was to him and she'd folded her arms across her breasts.

"Get out," she said again, not looking at him.

He pushed himself to his feet, pulling his shirt down and buttoning and buckling his pants. His lips hurt where she'd bitten him and he wondered if anyone would notice the bruises in the morning. He picked his hat from the floor and stepped toward her.

"Don't touch me," Paula said. "I hope you're satisfied. I never wanted you, you know. I hope I never see you again."

Jason started to speak, shrugged, turned and

ducked his head to leave the tent. As he walked quickly away he remembered he'd left the kettle somewhere nearby but he couldn't see it in the dark. The hell with it, he thought.

He went down the hill to the stream where he knelt on the bank and washed his hands and face as best he could. He felt dirty, his whole body seemed wet and slimy, not just his sexual parts.

He wished he'd never seen the Montgomerys, either of them. He'd betrayed the one and made a fool of himself over the other. Paula had a right to despise him, to despise herself and what they'd done. Why, he didn't even like her.

Remembering her passion, her wildness, her need to be hurt, he shook his head. Why couldn't Sir Charles keep his wife where she belonged? he thought again. The fault was more his than Sir Charles', though, he'd acted like a bull in heat. She'd wanted him, he didn't doubt that no matter what she said, and he'd wanted her.

How long had it been since he'd last had a woman? Five years, almost six. Not since Janine. He felt a sharp pang as though he'd betrayed her. Not so much by what he'd done but rather how he'd done it and with whom. Animals. That's how they'd acted, not like a man and a woman coming together in love. No, not even in lust. They'd been animals rutting in the dirt.

23

THE NEXT MORNING Jason was saddling up when Manuel, one of the cowhands Luis had brought from Mexico, came in from the line camp down the canyon.

"*Oso,*" he told Jason. "Bear. Black bear. Maybe ten mile." He pointed.

"After you've had your chow," Jason told him, "ride out and see if you can find Sam and Sir Charles. Tell them we're after bear."

Manuel nodded and walked away to the chuck wagon. Jason swung into the saddle and was going south from the camp when he saw Paula walking down the hill from her tent. She hadn't appeared for breakfast.

"Where are you off to?" she asked. From the casualness of her voice no one would have been able to guess what had happened between them the night before.

"One of the hands saw a bear. I'm riding down to take a look."

"Have one of the men saddle my horse," she said, "and ask him to put my rifle in the scabbard. I've never hunted a bear, much less killed one."

"Your experience runs more to two-legged animals?" he asked.

"Mr. Briscoe, I haven't the faintest idea what you're referring to, "she said blandly. "I don't think I care for the tone of your voice, though."

"If you're thinking of your half million dollars, you know what you can do with it."

"Didn't you sleep well? Did you have nightmares, perhaps? I had a bath before I went to bed even though the water was rather cold. I slept wonderfully well. There's nothing like these wide open spaces to make you sleepy. Now, would you please have my horse saddled?"

"Of course," Jason said. "I'll saddle her myself."

Jason Briscoe at your service, he thought. The hell with them. She could play whatever kind of game she wanted but he'd be damned sure the Montgomerys were on their way back to Denver in the morning.

"He showed the white feather, you know," Paula said as they rode down the canyon. When Jason said nothing, she went on. "I'm talking about Charles, when he served in the Crimea. He should never have told me but I suppose he thought I'd sympathize with him, let him use my fair bosom to cry on. That was just after we were married when he didn't know me very well. I can't abide cowards."

"I don't want to hear about it, Mrs. Montgomery," Jason told her.

"You're going to whether you want to or not. He was leading a cavalry charge against some Russian batteries near Sebastapol, a very minor skirmish, I believe. They found him the next day lying amongst some boulders and thinking he'd been wounded they carried him back to hospital. It turned out he hadn't been hit at all, Charles had just turned tail and run. Do you wonder he has nothing to do with the men he served with? They can't abide him. But then no one can, no one who knows him well."

They'd been following the stream looking for the place where Manuel had sighted the bear. Now Jason knelt to study paw marks at the water's edge, two sets, one smaller than the other, perhaps a female with her cub. Following the tracks, he walked leading his horse across the grass toward a thick wood with Paula riding behind him.

"I'd leave Charles if it weren't for the money," she said softly, almost as though talking to herself. "I disgust you, don't I? You think I'm mercenary. I am, I admit it. At least I'm honest with myself, I always have that. And Charles won't live forever, he's more than twenty years older than I am. Twenty-one to be precise. His health isn't all that good. Why, when he gets angry at me I think he's going to have apoplexy."

Jason heard hoofbeats. Looking down the canyon he saw three horsemen approaching and as they drew nearer he recognized Manuel, Sam and Sir Charles.

"My lord and master has arrived," Paula said. "I didn't think he'd let me out of his sight for long."

Sir Charles reined up, looking from his wife to Jason, a frown on his face.

"Damn it, Charles," Paula said, "I'll tell you right now that whatever you're thinking might have happened, did happen. Now that I've cleared the air, can we get on with the hunt?"

"The bear's taken cover in those woods," Jason said. "By the looks of the tracks it can't be far ahead of us, no more than a mile at the most. Probably making for a cave on the side of the canyon."

"Are black bears dangerous?" Sir Charles asked Jason.

"Oh my God," Paula said, raising her eyes heavenward.

"Shut up, Paula," Sir Charles said without glancing in her direction.

"They can be if they're protecting a cub or if they're wounded or cornered. A black bear's no grizzly but they're big beasts, weigh six to eight hundred pounds. Don't ever let one get too close, they can kill you with one swipe of their paw."

"I say we have a go at the bear," Sir Charles said. "The head will make a magnificent trophy."

Jason looked narrowly at him. The Englishman seemed composed, more sure of himself than he'd been on the trip to the canyon. Did he suspect the truth about himself and Paula? Would she tell her husband just to torment him? He wouldn't put it past her.

"I'll go first," Jason said.

He led the way into the trees with Sir Charles to one side and a step back, Paula and Sam following some distance behind. The bear's trail headed, as he had suspected it would, toward the canyon wall. They passed a tree where a bear's teeth had stripped the bark at eye level and, far above Jason's head, his claws had made deep gouges in the wood.

"Marking his stomping grounds," Jason said.

They came out of the trees into an open stretch of gradually rising ground with brush and trees a hundred feet ahead of them. Past the trees they saw the north face of the canyon rising in a series of rock ledges.

Jason stopped, holding up his hand. They heard a crackling in the brush ahead and caught a glimpse of brown.

"I'll go first," Sir Charles said, stepping past Jason who hesitated a moment, then nodded.

"Shoot for the neck," Jason said.

Sir Charles gave a grunt of assent and pushed into the brush with Jason behind him. There was no sign of the bear. The animal must be making for his lair, Jason thought.

Sir Charles advanced cautiously with Jason behind and slightly to one side. Suddenly they heard a roar ahead of them and a massive shape lunged from the brush, coming from their left so that Sir Charles was between Jason and the bear. Jason couldn't shoot. He darted to his left but already the bear was rushing down on the Englishman.

Sir Charles stood his ground and fired, the shot striking the bear's shoulder, but still the huge animal came on. Sir Charles fired again, the bullet plowing into the bear's chest, staggering it, but now the bear was only a few feet from the Englishman.

Still holding his rifle in one hand, Sir Charles leaped aside, the bear swiping at him with a huge paw, striking him and sending him spinning to the ground. Jason fired, point-blank, as the bear rose on its hind legs, looking this way and that as though baffled. A damn big one, Jason thought, firing once more. The bear dropped to all fours and turned and shambled off through the brush and up the slope toward the canyon wall.

Jason sent one more bullet after the bear before

it lurched out of sight. He ran to Sir Charles. The Englishman was sitting up examining his shoulder. The bear's claws had ripped his leather jacket and torn his skin. Several streaks of blood showed red but the blow had been a glancing one and Sir Charles' wound wasn't major.

"The brute bloodied me a bit," Sir Charles said. He stood and pulled his torn jacket over the gashes. He showned no sign of fear, Jason noticed.

"You'd better wait and have that bandaged," Jason said. "If the bear's not dead, she's dying. I'll wait and then go in and finish her off."

"No." Sir Charles reloaded his rifle. "That bear's mine and I mean to kill the blighter myself. Can't claim the beast for a trophy unless I'm the one who brings it down."

"Wait," Jason told him. "I think it's a female with a cub and that's about as dangerous as you can get and now that she's wounded she'll charge any man she sees. Unless you're damned lucky she'll see you before you see her. The best thing to do is wait awhile and then—"

"Do you know, Briscoe," Sir Charles interrupted. "I'm not afraid of that bear. When she came for me all I felt was the excitement, the blood churning inside me. I thought to myself, 'This is the moment I've waited for all my life.' "

"I never saw a man face up to danger better than you did," Jason told him, meaning every word.

"Charles, you have blood on your jacket." Paula had come up to join them. "Did you fall?"

"The bear clawed him," Jason told her. "He stood firing till the beast ran him down."

"How much did he pay you, Jason," she asked, "to tell me that story?"

"That's quite enough, my dear," Sir Charles said.

Paula ignored him. "You haven't answered me, Jason," she said.

Sir Charles walked to his wife, carefully laid his rifle at his feet, and slapped her face. Paula took a step back, her hand going to her cheek. She stared at Sir Charles.

"You'll regret that, Charles," she said.

"I may, my dear, yet it's something I've been wanting to do for the last four years. And I must say I rather enjoyed it." He turned to Jason. "I'm going in and finish the bugger off."

"I'll go with you."

"No, sir, you will not. I'll go in alone." He stared at Jason. "This is my bear, not yours." He glanced from Jason to Paula. "And that, sir, is my wife. Do I make myself clear?"

"Perfectly clear, Sir Charles." By God, Jason thought, he was beginning to admire the Englishman. "I'll wait here and cover you as best I can while you go in after her. Remember, don't—"

Sir Charles held up his hand. "I appreciate your advice, Briscoe," he said, "but I've done some hunting in my time. I think I'm a match for one of your black bears."

Sir Charles retrieved his rifle from the ground and pushed ahead into the brush. From time to time Jason saw the English hunter's brown jacket as he followed the bear's spoor. After five minutes Sir Charles came out on a rise near the base of the cliff where he stood on a jumble of fallen rock with a ledge covered with brush just above his head.

For a moment there was silence. Sir Charles paused, as though undecided. Jason could hear his own breathing. The woods were still. Looking beside him, Jason saw Paula with her gaze fixed intently on her husband, her face set. He couldn't read her expression.

The bear appeared on the ledge above Sir Charles' head.

Sir Charles didn't see her. Jason called a warning, heard the enraged growl of the bear as she raised herself to attack. Jason swung his rifle to his shoulder and from the corner of his eye saw Paula raise hers. She aimed, then lowered her gun a fraction, sighting, he thought, not on the bear but on her husband.

Jason lunged at her to knock the rifle from her hands but before he could reach her she fired. Sir Charles fired at the same time and the bear plunged from the ledge, narrowly missing him. The bear lay on the rocks, unmoving, and Sir Charles turned to them, raising his rifle above his head in a gesture of triumph. Sam ran forward into the brush toward the hunter and his kill.

"You almost spoiled my shot," Paula said to Jason.

"I thought for a second you meant to kill him."

"Kill Charles? You entertain evil thoughts, Mr. Briscoe. Why would I kill him? I rather think I might enjoy fighting with my husband. I can foresee some splendid battles ahead of us."

"I suspect you're not going to win all of them."

"I don't think you understand me, Mr. Briscoe. Whatever made you think I wanted to win them all?" She smiled at him. "And you can stop worrying about the money you need to finance your ranch. This particular trophy should be worth at least a half million dollars."

"I'd say that's up to Charles," Jason told her.

She stared at him, opened her mouth, closed it again. "You know, you may be right," she said finally.

24

THE SIX MEN rode through the night, their horses' hooves pounding on the hard, dry Texas earth. A half moon slid in and out of the clouds alternately hiding and revealing their grim faces. They veered right at the river and climbed the long slope to the ranch.

The men swung down from their horses at the fence in front of the ranch house, looping their reins over the rail. Hands on the butts of their pistols, they advanced on the house.

"I wouldn't come no further." A bearded man stood on the shadowed porch with a shotgun cradled in his arms.

The men stopped. As if by signal, one of them stepped forward. "We mean to see Print Varner," he said.

"I'm not rightly sure Print wants to see you, Luke."

"We got no quarrel with you, Josh," Luke told

the man on the porch. "It's Print we got business with and we're not leaving till we see him."

"If you got a quarrel with Print," Josh told him, "then you got a quarrel with me."

"Stand aside, Josh," one of the men behind Luke said, "or you're liable to get a bellyful of lead."

"Just tell Print we're here," Luke said. "Tell him we're here representing the Association. Tell him we want words with him and we want them now."

"Josh don't have to tell me nothing."

Print Varner came from the shadows of the porch and walked down the two steps to stand face to face with Luke Rand.

Luke sensed the sudden tension in the men behind him. He glanced into the darkness at either side of the porch, wondering if Print had men hidden there. He knew Print had nerve enough to face any man alone but, on the other hand, he'd never been known as foolhardy.

"Did you want words with me?" Print asked Luke. His voice was soft and deadly.

"We've had our fill of you, Print," Luke said. "You've been swinging too wide a loop and we was sent here by the Cattleman's Association to give you fair warning. You're to clear out of Pinto County."

"Why not speak for yourself, Luke? Why hide behind the Association? Or ain't you got the guts?"

Luke stared coldly at Print. "I think you know I got the guts. I ain't backing down, I never back down. 'Cause some of the men want to follow the ins and outs of the law, don't think we ain't got guts."

"Let me get this straight once and for all. Are *you* telling me or is the Association?"

"The Association's telling you and I'm telling you. Clear out of Pinto."

"Before you get a feather-coating and a ride on a rail," a voice behind Luke said.

"You speak mighty big," Print said, "when you're standing behind Luke Rand."

"Let me handle this," Luke said to Jim. "Is the message clear, Print?" he asked.

"Real clear. And know what I say? I say you can go to hell."

"Hell's where you're going, Print, on a shutter. We're not here to gab, we're here to tell you. You got thirty days to pack it in. You know I'm not one to threaten idle, Print. Thirty days."

"Ain't the accused even allowed to hear the bill of particulars against him?" Print asked.

"Jack Beatty shot in the back and put alive in a cowhide and left to be crushed to death. Hector Torres missing, last seen heading for your place the day after he had a run-in with you about you branding his calves. I don't count the two other men who ain't been around since they tangled with you 'cause there's no proof. And there's your herd increasing at twice the rate of any other man's. You've been wearing your branding iron smooth by working it overtime."

Print smiled, then laughed without mirth. "My answer's the same," he said. "Nobody runs Print Varner off his spread. You and the rest of the Association can go straight to hell."

Luke turned and walked to the horses, the rest of the men following him. They mounted and wheeled from the ranch with Print's curses echoing behind them.

"Stay put," Print said, turning to the men hiding in the shadows. "They won't be back, I'll warrant you that, but it don't do no harm to be sure."

Print strode into the house, slamming the door behind him. Tamar, who had been standing by the open window, watched as he turned up the lamp.

"Sons of bitchin' bastards," Print said. "You heard them, didn't you?"

"I heard them. What do you care? You're planning on leaving anyway."

Print walked past her, shutting and latching the window. "I was. I was just waiting to hear you'd be traveling with me. Now I'm not so sure."

"I don't know about going with you, Print. Like I told you, I don't know."

He went to her, put his arm about her waist and drew her to him, kissing her. She returned the kiss, then broke free and walked to the window where she stood looking out into the night.

"It ain't like it once was," Print said. "You and me, I mean."

"Nothing's ever the same, as you well know. You're not the same man you were when you were a colonel fighting for the South. I'm not the same woman you found on the prairie and brought with you here to the Keechi."

"Who would of thought it, you with a good-sized herd of your own." He paced back and forth in front of the fireplace. "This country's getting crowded. They're pushing us out, them and their damn Association. And when I was down to Austin last month I saw a herd of mustangs all fenced in with this new-fangled bobbed wire. Didn't hurt them none, neither, once they found out what they were up against. Pretty soon they'll be fencing in this land. Someday there won't even be an open trail north to the railroad."

"The railroad's promised they'd come to us," Tamar said. "Pulling up stakes and going out to the Palo Bueno country only puts us farther from it. Why not leave here and go somewhere closer?"

"Land's cheaper in the Panhandle and the grazing's good in the Palo Bueno. Ain't no damn homesteaders ruining the land with their plowing. There's room for a man to breath in the west."

"Say the true reason for once, Print. Admit you're following Jason Briscoe. Admit you've never forgiven him. Vivian going with him is the reason, isn't it?"

Print stared coldly at her. "We had an understanding, Tammy," he said, "never to mention her name again."

"Your hate's blinding you, Print."

"You hate the bastard as much as I do. You ain't forgot he killed your husband, have you?"

Tamar sighed. "I haven't forgotten," she said. "If you're hankering to go west so bad, why let Luke Rand and the rest of his crowd stop you?"

"You heard them, didn't you? Ordering me off my own land, giving me a month to haul freight. I'd brand myself a coward if I was to back off now. Nobody's ever called Print Varner yellow and nobody's ever going to."

"Nobody thinks you're a coward, Print." Her shoulders slumped; all at once she looked tired. Tamar took her shawl from the back of a chair and put it over her red-gold hair.

"I'll ride back to your spread with you," Print said.

They rode in silence with a half moon rising in the now-clear sky in front of them. The night was cool, the wind sweeping in from the west, soughing through the timbers on the hillside. From across the river Tamar heard the bark of a coyote and, in the oaks nearby, the mournful hoot of an owl.

She glanced at Print riding beside her and, from the set of his jaw, knew he was pondering what he should do. If only they hadn't ordered him off, she was sure he'd have been gone in a month's time, with or without her.

Though her desire for Print had waned with the years, it had never died. His kiss could still excite her, his lean hard body send quivers through her. Her body yearned for him; she felt a craving for him whenever a few days passed without him bedding her.

Yet a sliver of doubt had entered her mind long ago, like the thorn of a cactus, and the doubt had grown and festered. Why had Eli shot Print and fled the county? She knew Eli, or at least had thought she did, and the boy, a man now, wouldn't have tried to kill Print without some good reason. Or reasons he deemed good. She remembered what Print had told her about Eli seeing him shoot the rustler and wondered if that would have been enough of a reason.

Print's laugh interrupted her thoughts and she shivered in spite of herself. The sound of Print's laughter, so without warmth, always chilled her.

"You been mighty quiet," Print said.

"I was thinking of Eli."

"You do too much thinking. And too damn much reading of books."

She felt her anger rise. "And you do too damn little of both, Print Varner."

"Simmer down," he said. "You know I bear no grudge toward the boy for shooting me. He didn't know what he was doing. I suspect he was put up to it."

"I would have thought he'd write me," Tamar said. "Not a word in all these years. Only rumors.

Someone's seen him in California. Or he's supposed to be in Arizona or New Mexico. Or he's on the dodge. Stories told around campfires by men with time on their hands."

"I suspect he's in New Mexico like Abe Green heard."

"A man they hire for his gun? That's what they told Abe he's become. Eli a gunhand? I'll never believe that. He was always a good boy, a gentle boy. The kind that goes out of his way to please you."

"And I got the scar to prove it."

Tamar shook her head, riding on in silence. Eli must have had his reasons for shooting Print, she told herself.

The entered the Swanson spread, dismounted, and Tamar began unsaddling her horse.

"I'll do that for you," Print said.

She looked at him. "Don't bother," she said. She uncinched and removed the saddle, took off the blanket and carried them into the tackroom, coming back to unbridle the horse. "I guess I need to show you I can do more than fret and read books," she told him.

He took her in his arms, kissing her, holding her, letting his hand trail down her back to cup her buttocks and press her body to his.

"I reckon there's lots more you can do," he said, his voice husky with desire. Suddenly he released her and, putting his foot in his horse's stirrup, mounted. "I'll be coming back," he said. "Give me an hour or two."

"Where you going, Print?" she asked.

"I got business that needs tending to." He spurred his horse down the hill and onto the trail leading back to his own place.

What's he up to? Tamar wondered. She went

into the tack room, took a bridle from the wall and, going to the corral, slipped it over the head of her horse. She pulled herself onto the mare's bare back, nudging the sorrel with her knees down the hill after Print.

As soon as she topped the first rise she saw him ahead of her, riding at trail lope, and she set out after him, keeping a goodly distance behind in hopes he wouldn't hear her horse's hoofbeats. Print rode on, seemingly oblivious to her. At the fork leading to his ranch he didn't hesitate but bore away from the Varner place.

I was right, he's up to something, Tamar thought as she passed the fork. The road dipped ahead of her and she lost sight of him. When she saw him again he was a quarter-mile ahead riding toward the Shinhollow road. She drew in her breath. Luke Rand's place was in Shinhollow.

Without Luke Rand, she knew, the Association would be about as dangerous as a leaking feed sack. Luke Rand *was* the Association, had organized the other cattlemen in the county and had finally goaded them into confronting Print. She was sure of that.

Tamar was less sure where the truth lay in their quarrel with Print. At first she had thought Print was the victim. After all, Vivian had left him and Eli had tried to kill him. Jason Briscoe obviously had no use for him. Her passion for Print had clouded her thinking, or so she'd decided once she began to wonder whether all of them could be wrong.

She'd never been wholly blind to what was going on. Some of Print's wholesale branding of mavericks had been a step or two beyond what was strickly legal. Maybe during the War and for a year or two after all the ranchers had cast a wide loop, had been free and easy with their hot irons, but times had changed. And Print seemed to have no intention of changing them.

She'd seen dead cows on the range with the brands of other outfits and wondered whether the calves had found their way into Print Varner's herd. She'd noticed other cows branded real shallow, as though maybe a damp cloth had been placed between the iron and the hide, and she wondered if those brands had been changed once the hair had grown out and the original brand had faded.

She didn't doubt that Print might operate close to the line between legal and illegal. But blaming him because a man drops out of sight? Cowhands were fiddle-footed, they were her today and gone tomorrow more often than not. And Jack Beatty? Print would no more kill a man by wrapping him in a cowhide than he'd back down from a fight.

Tamar reined in for she could no longer see Print ahead of her. He must be almost to the Hollow, she could see where the road dipped into the fold between the hills. Luke Rand's place was just beyond, not more than a half mile from where she was now.

She waited, unsure what to do. She could ride on and maybe overtake Print. If he didn't like her following him, he could go plumb to hell. She started to nudge her horse ahead, then hesitated. Without knowing exactly why, she guided the sorrel off the trail to the right and let him pick his own way, circling toward Luke Rand's place.

When she heard hoofbeats coming from the trail she had just left, Tamar thought at first it was Print. She saw a rider loping from the direction of the town and realized it wasn't Print after all.

It must be Luke Rand, she thought. He'd gone on to the town with the others, maybe lifted a few at the saloon, and was now returning home. Where was Print? Was he waiting for Luke? To talk to him? Print wasn't much for talk. To try to force Luke to back down? Or . . . ? Tamar shivered.

She urged her horse back toward the trail, intending to intercept Luke. As she came to the trail she saw him riding away from her a hundred yards ahead. She was about to gallop after him, to warn him, for she felt a premonition, a fear, when she heard the shot.

Tamar heard the rider's strangled cry as he fell from his horse, saw the horse dragging him, his foot caught in the stirrup. Seeing the horse stop, she was about to ride on, to go to him, when suddenly she saw another man leave the shadows ahead of her and she drew in the reins and left the trail. She slid from the sorrel's back, twisting the reins around the limb of a bush, and ran to the brush growing beside the trail.

The other man approached Luke Rand's horse and she recognized Print Varner's silhouette. He stopped beside the horse, kneeling, and she could no longer see him. Another shot rang out and Tamar gasped, covering her mouth with her hand.

She edged forward cautiously, hidden from the trail, dividing the brush with her hands and peering through to see Print lifting Rand's body onto the horse. Print led the other man's horse to his own, mounted, and headed toward Rand's ranch.

Print had she and killed Luke Rand in cold blood.

Tamar couldn't grasp the fact, let alone accept it. If he had killed Rand without compunction, without warning, what crimes had he been guilty of in the past? No, she couldn't bear to think of that, not now.

She followed Print by running along the side of the trail. When he stopped in front of the ranch house, she crouched in the darkness and watched as he lifted Luke Rand's body onto his shoulder and disappeared inside. Luke, she knew, lived alone. The night was quiet, the ranch house was dark. After a few minutes she thought she saw movement near the door. Yes, Print had come outside again. She saw the flare of a match and a moment later flames spurted inside the house.

Print sprinted to his horse and leaped into the saddle, spurred onto the trail and galloped past Tamar, looking neither right nor left. His hoofbeats faded behind her. In front of her, the flames swept higher, bursting from the windows to lick along the outer walls and onto the roof. The wind brought the tang of woodsmoke; there were no sounds other than the crackling flames.

She hurried back to her horse and mounted. Once she regained the trail she rode back the way she had come a short time before. She slowed, realizing Print would reach her place before she did and find her gone no matter how fast she went. The hell with Print, she thought. Print must have killed Jack Beatty years ago, she decided, probably shot him in the back and wrapped him alive in a hide just as tonight he'd killed Luke, bushwacking him and leaving his body in the burning house.

And Eli had seen him kill Beatty. That more than accounted for his change toward Print. But was that enough to lead Eli to shoot Print? Tamar shook her head.

Eli had waited until after George was killed. Why? A dry sob choked her. Print meant George to die, she was certain of it. Even if Jason had actually done the shooting. Because of her, because Print wanted her. She remembered the dance, Print's warning that George was suspicious, Print's telling her to play up to Jason. She should have seen through that. George thought Print was the finest man on earth—he never would have suspected him.

Somehow Print had goaded Jason into shooting George or George into challenging Jason. And so George was killed—George, who had never meant to harm anyone. Eli had found out and shot Print. Tamar knew in her heart that this was what had happened, that this was the truth.

Print's horse was hitched in front of her place and through the window she saw a light on inside. After unbridling the sorrel, Tamar turned her loose in the corral. As she walked to the house, she clenched her hands at her sides until her nails bit painfully into her palms.

By the time she pushed open the door she had made up her mind. Could she carry out her plan? By God, she thought, she'd have to. Her first impulse had been to kill Print. No, she could never do that, she could never kill a man she'd bedded with, a man she had once thought she'd loved.

Print was waiting inside, sitting in a chair with his stocking feet up on the woodbox. His face appeared pale in the lamplight, his brow damp and smudged. When he looked at Tamar, the light glinted from his brown eyes.

"Where the hell you been?" he asked her.

"I rode down along the river. I couldn't sleep, expecting you back any minute."

He nodded. Taking a last drag on his cigarette, he threw the butt into the fireplace. "Get your clothes off," he told her.

She sat on a chair and pulled off her boots. Standing, she unbuttoned her shirt, teasing him, seeing his eyes on her as she slowly undid the buttons. She slipped the shirt off, holding it in front of her for a moment before she turned her back to him and tossed the shirt to one side.

Tamar cupped her breasts in her hands and faced him. "Like them?" she asked him.

He stared at her. "What's got into you tonight, Tammy?" he asked.

"Nothing," she said, undoing and sliding her pants down over her legs. She stopped with her hands on her inner thighs. "Yet," she added.

When she was naked, she stood staring at him. "You're smiling," he said, eyeing her suspiciously.

"You smile, Print, I can smile too. No, wait," she said as he came to his feet and tried to take her in his arms. She held him off. "I want to undress you," she said. Her fingers undid the buttons of his shirt, then moved down to his pants. When he was naked he walked to the bed and lay on her back on the blanket with her legs spread.

"Is this the way you want me, Print?" she asked.

She turned over so she was lying on her stomach. "Or like this?"

She raised herself to her hands and knees, glancing at him over her shoulder. "Like this? As though I was a bitch in heat?"

She sat on the edge of the bed. "Or some other way, Print?" she asked. "Just tell me, I'll do whatever you want."

She dropped to her knees on the floor and looked up at him. "You used to like it when I knelt in front of you and did it to you," she said. "Is that what you want tonight?"

"Do you know what you're acting like?" Print asked her. "A two-bit whore."

"I am? And how would a Georgia gentleman like yourself know what a two-bit whore acts like? Don't scowl at me, Print. I'm only trying to please you. Why don't you tell me? I'll do whatever you want me to do."

"Just shut up and get into bed."

Tamar stood and pulled the blankets back, sliding beneath them. Print immediately yanked the blankets off and threw them aside. She smiled when she saw he wasn't aroused. He worked over her, clutching her to him, bringing her hands to him until he was hard and then he spread her legs and entered her, finishing quickly. As soon as he was done he rolled over and lay beside her, drawing in deep breaths.

Tamar had felt nothing. She had wanted to punish herself, to debase herself, and she had. But what now? Print meant to go off to the Palo Bueno bent on revenge. Jason Briscoe was as good as dead.

If Jason had taken us with him, me and Eli, that day I asked him, she thought, then Print and I wouldn't be lovers. And Eli wouldn't've gone wrong. She sighed and shook her head. No use to blame Jason. The fault was Print's Yes, Print's, but hers too. She hadn't meant to be the cause of George's death and Eli's trouble—still, she was. Now Print aimed to kill Jason. And he'd concoct some scheme so Jason wouldn't have a chance.

Could she stop that from happening? She rose on one elbow and stared down at Print.

"I've made up my mind," she said. "I'm going west with you. As long as you leave right away."

He sat up and stared at her. "You're a strange one, Tammy," he said. "I don't reckon I'll ever understand you."

"I don't reckon you ever will," she told him.

25

Print Varner walked down the dark street of the town to Knox's Feed and Grain store. He stopped, took the makings of a cigarette from his pocket, rolled and lit it, leaned back against the rail in front of the store to smoke. The street was quiet, the town asleep.

"Print Varner?" a voice from the shadows beside the store asked.

Print turned and got a quick impression of a man dressed in black. He couldn't see his face.

"I'm Varner," he said.

"Turn the other way," the man told him.

Print shrugged and turned.

After a moment's silence, the man said, "I ain't got all night."

"I need some help," Print said. "For a job that needs doing."

"From what I hear you're pretty good at doing your own jobs. Least Luke Rand might think so if he was around."

Print smiled to himself. "You referring to the accident Luke had, burning his ranch down and himself with it? I don't know nothing about that."

"I'm not suggesting you do," the man in black said. "I was just speculating what a man the likes of you might want with me."

"Just between me and you and this post here," Print said, "I'm fixing to leave Pinto and head west soon's I can. Taking the herd and a few of the better hands and heading out Palo Bueno way."

"Ain't that where your friend Briscoe's located? The one your wife run off with four, five years back."

"That's neither here nor there. What I need is some men. I'm leaving a few of my hands behind, they don't fit in, aren't handy enough with their artillery for the frontier. I hear tell it's not just punching cows in the Panhandle what with the Indians and the claim jumpers and the rustlers. I need a different breed of help."

"I heard a few of your boys packed their gear and left you, Print. Some say even Ed's been talking like he might up and quit one of these days."

"Ed's with me all the way," Print said flatly. "What I need are more men handy with their guns and not afraid to use them."

"Why come to me?"

"I've heard tell you might know some hands like that." Print took a last puff on his cigarette and ground it under his boot. "I've heard you've ridden with the best of them and might know where to locate them now. Men the likes of Wes Hardin. I'd be obliged if you sort of let the word get around in the right places about the kind of men I'm looking for."

"To go to the Palo Bueno? When might you be arriving there?"

"September. I'll most likely not need them for more than a month."

"Good men cost money. A top ranch hand gets, say, thirty dollars a month and found. That's a dollar a day. I'd say hands like you're talking about would come at ten times that. Three hundred dollars a month and found."

"I'd be willing to pay that if the men were worth it."

"They'd be worth every penny. Any man I sent you, you'd be owing me thirty dollars. And I'll be needing a hundred to undertake the deal. Cash on the barrelhead."

"You drive a hard bargain. I ain't got that kind of money with me."

"Didn't expect you to have, knowing you're not a fool. If you're wanting to do business, meet me here same time tomorrow with the hundred."

Print hesitated.

"Don't trust me, Print?" the man in black asked. "Tell you what. I'll ride by your place after sundown tomorrow night. Have the money ready."

"Sounds fair," Print said. "When do you reckon . . . ?" he began. Hearing a whisper of sound behind him, he whirled and found the man in black gone.

The kid swaggered into Tidwell's Saloon in Globe, a pistol stuck in his pocket. It was ten in the morning and the bar was deserted except for one man sitting off to the side, his feet propped on a chair and a Stetson pushed down over his eyes. The kid walked up to the bar and ordered whiskey.

The bartender pushed a bottle and glass across the bar top. "Two bits a throw," he said.

The kid winked at him as he poured. "Here's looking at you," he said, smiling. When he smiled you didn't notice the buck teeth so much; when he smiled his blue eyes sort of twinkled. The bartender leaned across to him.

"Still on the dodge, Hank?" he asked in a low voice.

"They still got the warrant out on me for stealing the Celestial's laundry, if that's what you mean," Hank said. "I didn't even steal the damn laundry; fact is, Sombrero Jack did and left it with me to sell and they caught him and put him in the hoosegow and then come for me. And all for stealing a damn Celestial's laundry."

The bartender nodded sympathetically. He'd listened to the story many times before. "I hear you're mighty handy with that," he said, nodding at the pistol in Hank's pocket. The boy smiled broadly, winking again.

"Ever shoot a man?" the bartender asked.

Hank jerked his head questioningly toward the man sitting at the end of the bar.

"He's all right," the bartender said.

"Never did," Hank said. "Wanted to a couple of times but I never did. Wouldn't bother me none, though."

"That's what I figured," the bartender said. "When I saw you in that fracas we had in here last week I said to myself, 'That Hank Antrim's mighty handy with his fists and I'll bet he's handy with his gun too.' That's the way I had you figured right from the first."

"You ain't still pissed at me about that fight, are you?"

"The fight's over and done with." He swiped at the bar with a towel. "Clean over and done with.

Now, as I was saying. There was a fellow in here yesterday, had a proposition to make. Asked me if I knew a man who might want to make three hundred for a month's work. Had to be handy with a gun. I thought of you right off, Hank."

Hank eyed him closely. "You're not pulling my leg, now, are you? I ain't a greenhorn, you know. I don't like it when a man tries to make a fool of me."

"I wouldn't do that, Hank. This fellow I'm telling you about, he put up at the hotel. Goes by the name of Smith. Talk to him, might be worth your while."

"Three hundred, you say?"

"That's right. A man could buy a lot of rotgut for three hundred dollars."

Hank drank down the last of the whiskey and slapped a coin on the bar. "I just might mosey down to the hotel and do me some listening," he said. He swaggered to the door where he stopped and turned, lifting his hat and smiling his engaging smile. "I'm much obliged to you," he said.

The man at the end of the bar unwound himself from his chair and shifted his hat back on his head. He couldn't have been more than nineteen or twenty but looked older.

"What the gospel?" he asked. "What you told the kid?"

"Swear to God," the bartender said, putting his hand to his chest. "I thought you must have heard of the proposition before this or I would of mentioned it when you came in. I told the kid to get rid of him, to get him out of town. He's a mean bastard when he's crossed. One of these days he's going to kill a man and I don't want it to be me."

"Who's making this offer?"

"The man what told me goes by the name of Smith like I said. The one doing the hiring is a Texan named Print Varney or Varner at the Palo Bueno over on the Staked Plain."

"Print Varner!" The young man came suddenly alert.

"You sound like you've heard of him."

"I might have. What else do you know? Isn't the Palo Bueno where a man called Briscoe has his spread? The one who's supposed to have English money behind him?"

The bartender shrugged. "I don't pay much heed to Texas talk," he said. "I told the kid all I knowed. Honest to God."

The young man nodded and left the saloon. The bartender watched him go out and muttered, "And good riddance to you, too." A couple of men on the board walk outside glanced at the youth coming out and then gave him a wide berth as he walked to the livery stable.

Print Varner, Eli thought. He knew he hadn't killed him, had known that for a long time. So now Print was on the prowl again, heading for the Palo Bueno, heading for Briscoe country.

Eli wondered how Tamar was, where she was. He should have written to his sister, yet he'd been too ashamed at first and afraid as well, not knowing if they were after him for shooting Print, and then with one thing and another he'd never set pen to paper. He'd sure like to see Tamar again. And Print. The next time he met up with Print Varner, he wouldn't miss.

Eli rode north out of Globe into the barren Arizona hills. He'd always sort of wanted to take a look-see at the Staked Plain country, he told himself.

* * *

The driver saw the barricade and rose in his seat, pulling the horses to a stop in front of the felled trees.

"Throw down your hardware," one of the three masked men called out to the driver and the guard riding shotgun. The guns thudded to the ground.

The youngest of the three Jerome brothers vaulted into the back of the wagon and began throwing aside the piled buffalo robes. Underneath he found the strongbox. He placed the muzzle of his pistol to the lock.

"No need to go to all that bother," the driver said, a smile on his face. "It's open."

The youngest Jerome twisted the lock and removed it. He lifted the hasp and then the lid of the strongbox and looked inside.

"Shit," he said in disgust. He glanced down from the wagon at his two brothers. "There ain't nothing here. Not a fucking thing."

The oldest brother, Mike, scrambled into the back of the wagon and stood staring into the strongbox. "A damn decoy," he said.

"The gold's safe at Fort Dodge by now," the driver said. He'd turned in the seat, keeping his hands over his head. "I guess you boys had all this trouble for naught," he said.

Mike Jerome pulled his kerchief down from his face to his neck. "Not all for naught," he said.

The driver stared at him, eyes widening in alarm. "What . . . ?" he began, then stopped as the other two Jeromes also removed their kerchiefs.

"That's mighty careless of you boys," Mike Jerome said to his brothers. "Now these gentlemen know who was meaning to make off with this here shipment of gold."

"We won't breathe a word, so help . . ."

The first shot caught the driver in the chest and spun him around. A fusillade of shots followed and the driver and guard crumpled onto the high seat of the wagon. Mike Jerome walked forward in the wagon bed and examined the bodies, grunting in satisfaction.

"See," he said to the two dead men, "it's not for naught. We had us a bit of target practice."

"But we didn't get no gold," his brother complained. "You said there'd be gold for sure."

Mike shrugged. "Means we'll have to head south and spend some time in the Palo Bueno country. I hear they're offering right good wages down there. Three hundred a month, wasn't that the figure?"

"That's what I heard."

"Then we're wasting our time here."

The two men in the wagon leaped to the ground. Without another glance at the two dead men, they mounted and rode south.

26

PRINT VARNER trailed his herd up the Prairie Dog Fork to the mouth of the Palo Bueno Canyon. His ranks had been increased by eight men, the three Jerome brothers, Hank Antrim from Arizona, and four other gun hands, two Texans and two Kansans. Print hoped they knew more about using their guns than they did about handling cows.

Ike McLeod, riding from the home ranch to the line camp near the mouth of the canyon, was the first to sight Print's herd. He reined his horse toward them and galloped up to Print who was riding point. As Print stopped, two of the Jeromes and Ed and Josh rode up behind him and sat their horses looking Ike over, their faces impassive.

"You boys got any Texas cows there?" Ike asked.

"Who wants to know?" Print folded his hands on top of his saddlehorn.

"I'm Ike McLeod from the Briscoe outfit." Out of sheer cussedness Ike always called it that even though he knew full well the right handle was the

Briscoe-Grandez-Montgomery ranch, the BGM.

"Why would you be wanting to know if these are Texas cows?" Print asked.

"Texas cows got ticks and we don't want the fever here in the Palo Bueno."

"I'll be damned." Print snorted. "Jason Briscoe's sure become high and mighty. He don't want ticks when a couple of years back his cows were the biggest tick carriers in Texas. Now don't you find that kind of funny, Ike?"

"Who's laughing?" Ike said. "This is Briscoe land and if I was you I'd drive my herd around to the Canadian."

"Now ain't that something?" Print turned to the men behind him. "This uppity nigger is making out to tell me what to do. Telling me where to take my cows." Print smiled at Ike.

"Listen, nigger," he said, "I know about this land in the Palo Bueno 'cause I made it my business to find out. Briscoe and his halfbreed outfit owns some and he don't own some, he bought the land in a crazy patchwork way meaning to keep others out. You just ride along home to Massa Jason and tell him Print Varner intends to graze his cattle wherever he damn well pleases. Do you hear me?"

Ike looked from Print to the men backing him up. "I hears you, white man," he said in a slow slave-drawl. He turned his horse and rode slowly up the canyon.

Print took his Colt from his holster and fired into the air. "Run, nigger, run," he shouted. Ike glanced behind him without hurrying his pace.

"What do you intend to do?" Josh asked Print as soon as Ike was gone.

"I plan to make camp down here on the Fork, graze the herd, and bide my time," Print said. "I plan to be patient and let Briscoe make the first wrong move. I'll goad him till he makes a mistake so when questions are asked later, when it's us ranching in the canyon where Briscoe is now, we'll have all the right answers and there won't be a damn thing nobody down in Austin can do about it."

Print turned to Ed. "I got a little job for you, Ed," he said. "Now here's what I want you to do . . ."

"It's me he wants," Vivian said. She walked to the window and looked down the valley past a stand of firs to the grazing BGM cattle. "Print's been waiting and letting the hate fester in him and now he's come to bring me back. He never gives up what he thinks is his, never. I should know, I lived with him long enough. Too long. Well, I won't go back."

"*Señora,*" Luis said, "this Varner will never have you as long as I am alive."

"He wants more than you," Jason said. "He hates me, has since I met him. There's been bad blood between us right from the first."

"He told me that something about you reminds him of the Yankee who took his land after the War. Print tried to stop him and Print's wife was killed in the shooting. He killed the man later. Hanged him in a hotel room back in Atlanta."

"Now here I am with his next wife," Jason said. He walked to stand beside Vivian. "You don't have to go with him," he said, putting his hand on her arm. "I owe you a great deal. I don't know how I could have raised Jan without you."

"I couldn't love the boy more if he were my own," Vivian said.

Jason turned to Luis and Ike. "I want more

loopholes put in the walls of the ranch house," he told his foreman. "I want the men to know that if there's any trouble at all with Varner or any of his men they're to ride back here to the main house. Pronto."

"Do you expect this will lead to fighting?" Luis asked.

"Yes, knowing Print. And those men Ike saw down-canyon sound like gunslingers, not cowhands. Print's come meaning to pick a fight or else make me pick one. I don't plan to accommodate him if I can help it but I don't mean to back down either."

"Did you see Tamar?" Vivian asked Ike. "Tamar Swanson?"

Ike shook his head. "I know the lady but I didn't see no women."

Jason pictured Tamar as he'd last seen her in the cabin after George Swanson's death, remembered her bitterness, her silent hatred. Once he'd thought that there'd be something between him and Tamar one day, he'd felt a bond, a kinship with her. He shook his head. Nothing would ever come of it now, he thought. Funny how he never could get her completely out of his mind.

"Vivian," Jason said, "I'm going to ask Sam to take you and Jan back to the Colorado ranch until this blows over. I want you to leave first thing in the morning. Before sunup."

Vivian glanced fleetingly at Luis. "I don't want to go, Jason. My place is here with you, with all of you."

"No, I want Jan away from any fighting. I'd never forgive myself if I kept him here and something happened to him. And you're the only one to take him. You have to go, I can't afford giving up another man, we've got few enough as it is."

Vivian sighed, started to protest and then fell silent. With another look at Luis she turned to leave the room. "I'll start packing," she said.

"It's that bad, is it, *compadre?*" Luis asked after Vivian was gone.

"Yes, and it's going to get worse before it gets better. I'll have Sam get word to Montgomery in Denver, have him send reinforcements from the other ranch. That'll take time. Until help arrives, we're on our own."

The next morning Jason and Luis watched as two horses were saddled and a pack horse was loaded for the journey to Colorado. Jason drew Sam aside.

"Last night," he told him, "Manuel was riding along the rim and he came on one of their men camped on the creek above the falls. From what he tells me it's a man named Ed, a cowhand I used to know. I'm telling you because I want you to steer clear of him when you ride out of here."

"There's just the one?"

"That's all Manuel spotted. I'm having Ike go with you till you're well clear of the Palo Bueno canyon. Once you're clear, ride straight north to Dodge and telegraph Sir Charles from there."

Sam nodded.

Vivian came from the house with Jan behind her, the boy dressed in boots and cut-down levis and a brown buckskin shirt. Tall for his age, he was dark like Jason. You could see his mother, though, Jason thought, in the curve of his mouth and the tilt of his snub nose. Jason drew in his breath and sighed, wishing Janine could be here to see her son.

Jason picked Jan up and hugged him. The boy squirmed in his father's arms until Jason put him on the ground.

"Men shake hands," Jan told him, "they don't hug each other."

"You're right," Jason said, holding out his hand to his son. "Shake."

Jan shook hands with his father and then walked to where Vivian, already mounted, was waiting. Jason lifted the boy and sat him in front if Vivian. All at once Jan reached down and hugged his father, kissing him.

"Remember," Jason told him, "Sam's the boss of this here expedition."

Jan nodded, trying to smile, but Jason saw the glint of tears in his eyes.

Jan released his father and turned to Vivian. "Sometimes men hug each other," he told her.

"Of course they do," she said, smiling at him.

Luis stepped forward and took Vivian's hand in his and raised it to his lips. "My heart of hearts," he said. "My thoughts ride with you always. *Vaya con Dios.*"

Vivian leaned down and kissed him quickly on the cheek. She nudged her horse ahead and, with Sam riding beside her and the pack horse following, they left the ranch and headed for the trail leading up to the canyon's rim. Ike rode from the corral to join them and the party left the Briscoe spread in the pale white light of early dawn.

The sun was up by the time they'd climbed the switchback trail to the cap rock. The stream rushed by on their right so Ike led the way left, taking a circuitous route around the wooded area where Manuel had seen the Varner man camped.

Ike reined in his horse after riding ten miles with them; in all that distance they'd seen nothing out of the ordinary. Ike waited until the three horses were out of sight before he turned and headed back toward the Palo Bueno. He'd covered half the distance when he saw puffs of dust off to the south heading, as he was, for the canyon. He hesitated, then rode on, the other riders—he saw there were two of them—drawing closer as they converged on the cap rock.

Ike reached the rim first. None of the Briscoe hands were in sight in the canyon below but he saw smoke curling from the chimneys of the ranch house beyond the firs. He debated whether to fire a signal shot but decided against it. He was probably looking for trouble where there was none, he told himself.

The two men came on and as they neared him Ike saw the riders and their horses were coated with the dust of the Staked Plain, like they'd been riding long and hard. Not more of Print Varner's men as he'd feared. Or were they gunhands riding here to join Print?

Ike waited, beginning to hum to himself, not a cow song but a spiritual he'd often heard his mother sing years before, the familiar melody easing the tense wait. The two riders halted twenty feet from him and Ike stopped humming as he waited for them to make the first move.

"We're looking for the Briscoe ranch," the lead rider said. They were both young, Ike saw, no more than twenty. Of course most hands were that age or maybe a tad older. Most men, as they got older, started hankering to marry and settle down.

"That's it down there," Ike said, nodding toward the canyon.

"I'm Eli," the rider said, "and this is Matt who come along from Tucumcari with me. I knowed Jason Briscoe down in Pinto County and I remember you. You're Ike, ain't you? Still work for Briscoe?"

"I'm his foreman," Ike said. The word still made him swell with pride.

"I come to warn him," Eli said, "and hire on if he'll have me. Print Varner's been hiring gunfighters, paying them three hundred a month."

"We already seen some when Varner trailed his herd in yesterday."

"We'll ride along with you to the ranch," Eli said, "if it's all the same to you."

Ike hesitated. He could have offered Eli a job with the outfit right off, but something about the boy bothered him. It was his hands, Ike decided. They weren't the hard calloused hands of a cowboy, they were soft hands.

Ike wheeled his horse to one side and gestured to the two men. "I'll lead the way," he said, "the trail heads down along the creek to the canyon."

The three men rode from the cap rock into the Palo Bueno along the switchback trail, past the falls and along the Fork to the ranch. They found Jason sitting astride his horse outside the corral. He looked at the two strangers, then looked a second time at Eli. He knew the boy from someplace, he told himself, but he couldn't rightly place him.

"I'm Eli, Mr. Briscoe," the boy said, "and this is Matt. He came along for the ride."

"Eli," Jason said. Tamar's kid brother. He smiled at him. "Too bad your aim wasn't better that time you winged Print."

"I heard back in Arizona he was headed this way. It Tamar with him?"

"I don't know, Eli, nobody's seen her."

Eli turned to Matt. "Jason Briscoe here saved my life once," he said. "Brought me home after I run off. I'm beholden to him." Again he looked at Jason. "We'd like to hire on with you if you'll have us."

"Like I told you once years back, there's always room for your gear in my bunkhouse." He turned to Ike. "The Varner bunch's acting mighty peculiar," he said. "They've taken their cows from the Fork and they're watering them on one of the other creeks, not letting them back to the Fork at all. I don't know what they're up to."

"I've heard a lot about Print Varner," Eli said. "Whenever his name's mentioned, I listen real close. They tell of him killing men, poisoning wells with strychnine, rustling cattle."

"Poisoning wells," Ike repeated.

"Ed's up there camping along the Fork at the head of the canyon," Jason said. "Do you reckon Print would stoop to trying to poison the creek? Is that why he's watering his cattle where he is?"

"I wouldn't put nothing past the bastard," Eli said.

"Ike," Jason ordered, "you ride up there and have a look. Don't go alone. Take . . ." He looked around him, trying to decide who to send.

"Let me go," Eli said.

Could the boy—Jason still thought of him as a boy—handle himself? Likely he could with a gun but mightn't he be too rash? Ike will keep him in tow, he reasoned.

"I've had some experience along these lines," Eli said.

"As I remember," Jason said, "you always wanted to be a scout. Or was it a lawman?"

"Both." Eli stared at Jason, wanting to tell him what had happened these last five years, hiring his gun out, sometimes on one side of the law, sometimes the other. A man paid to kill with no questions asked and no quarter granted. Jason might understand, if anyone would. But Eli said nothing more. You were safe only if you kept your mouth shut.

Jason looked at Eli's young-old face and his stomach tightened. The boy had seen too much, done things he couldn't call back. Bad had happened to Eli, not good. And all because of Print Varner.

"All right," Jason said, "you go with Ike. Take a fresh horse from the corral."

As Eli began unsaddling his mount and Matt made his way to the bunkhouse to stow his gear, Jason left to give orders to keep the cows from the creek and above all not to use the water for drinking.

Fifteen minutes later Ike and Eli were riding up the switchback trail. After they topped the rim rock, they headed west along the creek until they came to a grove of cottonwoods.

"Manuel saw Print's man in there," Ike said, motioning Eli to circle to the left while he approached the trees from the other side.

Ed heard the hoofbeats of Ike's horse nearing his camp. Following Print's orders, he doused his fire and mounted, crossed the creek and began riding south. Ike spotted him as he left the trees, hailed him, shouting to him to stop.

Ed ignored the warning shouts, spurring his horse. Looking back over his shoulder, he saw Ike galloping in pursuit. He dug his spurs into his horse's flanks, sure he could outrun the black man. All at once he heard another horse ahead and to his left. The second rider came charging toward him, angling to cut him off.

Damn! Ed thought. He swung away from the second man, veering right with the other rider following, bearing down on him. Ed's hand went to his holster. Print had said not to start any gunplay but Print wasn't here with two of them riding hell-for-leather at him. He heard a shot and the zing of a bullet above his head. The rider to his left had fired.

Damn, but he wasn't going to be no sitting duck. Ed jerked out his pistol and pumped off a shot, wild he was sure, and he saw the second rider, no more than a hundred feet away now, leap from his horse, a rifle in his hand. The man braced himself, feet apart, taking aim.

Ed hunched low, firing again. Again his shot went wide. He started to swing his body to one side to use his horse as a shield, Indian-fashion, but he was too late. A bullet struck him in the left side. He felt a shock of pain and he lurched from the saddle, falling free. Ed was dead before his body struck the ground.

Eli walked to Ed and turned his body over with his boot. When Ike came riding up, halted, and looked down at the dead man, Eli said, "Wish it'd been Print instead of Ed. I used to like Ed."

Ike shook his head, not happy with the way it had gone, but knowing it was too late now. Talking wouldn't change anything.

"Want me to bring him back with us?" Eli asked.

"No," Ike said, "we'll leave him for now and see what Jason wants done. First let's have a look at his horse."

Ike chased down Ed's gelding, roping him. When he searched the saddlebags, he found nothing out of the ordinary. "Let's have a look at his camp. If there's any poison, he'll have it there."

When Ike was through inspecting the camp, he looked at Eli. "Clean as a whistle," he said. "Seems like he wasn't poisoning the creek after all."

"I'll be damned," Eli said.

27

Josh KEPT his horse at a lope as he rode along the canyon rim to take Ed's place in the camp on the upper creek. His fingers felt the scar on his left cheek, his souvenir of the fight at Bull Run. I've been with the Colonel a long time, he thought, more than fifteen years.

Sometimes Print was a mean son-of-a-bitch but if you got to him in time you could stop him from turning crazy mean. Like that business with Jack Beatty. If I'd of been with him when he caught Beatty rustling, Print wouldn't have used that hide.

When Print acted that way, Josh wondered why he stayed with him. Well, it would pay off, for one thing. Not that he followed the Colonel just for what he'd get out of it. Colonel Varner needed him, trusted him; he'd told Josh many times he couldn't get along without him. Josh wasn't like Ed, Print said, who talked too much and asked too many questions.

Josh shook his head. Ed had been getting mighty restless lately; he wondered how long the Colonel would keep him.

All at once Josh stopped and swung to the ground, kneeling and examining the tracks he'd seen in the soft earth along the creek. He wasn't much at cutting sign but he could tell that three horses had passed this way. He frowned, for the horses had come up the trail from Briscoe's and were heading away from the canyon. What was Briscoe up to? he wondered. Could he be sending for help?

Josh remounted and followed the tracks for a time, saw them circle the cottonwoods that concealed Ed's camp and then head north. He'd have Ed tell Print and ask what the Colonel wanted done. They couldn't be taking chances, not with the Palo Bueno almost within their grasp.

Josh made for the cottonwoods but he hadn't gone more than a half mile when he spotted a dark form on the ground off to his right. Swinging that way, he raised puffs of dust as he crossed the table-land.

God damn, he muttered to himself as he looked down at Ed's body. He knelt beside Ed, feeling for signs of life and finding none. The bastards, he thought, they killed him in cold blood and left him for the buzzards. Josh picked up Ed's hat and placed it over the dead man's face, then walked around the body looking down at the confusion of prints of men and horses. They seemed to lead to and from the cottonwoods.

Josh rode into the woods and poked around Ed's camp, finding little but able to tell someone had searched the camp ahead of him. He'd ridden with Ed a long time, ten years and more, and he felt a sense of loss along with his anger. Ed might have his faults, and what man didn't, but Ed didn't deserve to be gunned down without a chance.

Josh remembered the tracks he'd found leading north. That trail, as best he could tell, was fresh and whoever it was that rode from the Briscoe spread couldn't be many miles away. Had they killed Ed? He doubted it but couldn't be sure.

Josh pondered his choices—to follow the tracks to the north or to return to Varner's camp in the Palo Bueno with Ed's body. What would the Colonel do in his place? he asked himself as he often did when in doubt. He nodded, for he knew what the Colonel would do. Leaving Ed's body, he swung his horse to the north, following the tracks of the three horses.

He made good time. Whoever was ahead of him had made no effort to cloud their trail and their course was as unswerving as that of a buffalo in flight. They were headed due north toward Dodge. By nightfall, though, he hadn't overtaken them, so, instead of stopping to rest, Josh rode on. He'd almost decided to make camp when he saw a fire imperfectly concealed in the lee of a rock shelf ahead of him.

Dismounting, Josh led his horse back the way he'd come, tethered it, then crawled forward to the top of a rise where he could look down on the camp. There were two of them at the fire, a man and a woman. He didn't know the man but he recognized the woman right away. Vivian Varner, Print's wife. Josh felt a surge of elation—he'd done the right thing, following them.

He took his Colt from his holster and stealthily approached the camp, staying hidden behind the outcropping of rock. When he was near enough to hear their murmured words, he paused, then stepped into the firelight.

"On your feet," he ordered the cowhand. Sam looked into the dark bore of the muzzle and stood up. "Drop your belt to the ground," Josh said. Sam unhooked the gunbelt and let it fall.

Josh heard a cry of surprise from the darkness to his left and whirled in that direction. A small boy ran at him, beating at his legs with his fists. Josh kicked the boy's feet from under him and the boy fell. Vivian cried out, pushed herself to her feet, and came for him. Josh sprang to one side, eluding her, and saw Sam kneeling and tugging a pistol from the gunbelt.

Josh fired and missed, fired again and Sam grunted, dropping the gun he'd finally freed from its holster. Josh fired a third time and Sam jolted onto his back. Vivian, the boy clutching her skirts, stood staring at Josh.

"Josh, oh Josh," she said. "You don't know what you've done."

The boy, crying, tore himself away from Vivian's restraining hand and flung himself at Josh, trying to bear him to the ground. Holding the boy off with one hand, Josh glanced at Sam who lay unmoving on the ground. He holstered his gun and picked up the boy, putting him under his arm. He turned to Vivian.

She was gone. He heard the sound of steps in the darkness and ran toward them. Stopping to listen, he heard a scrambling ahead of him and ran forward again, the boy still under his arm. Again Josh stopped to listen. This time he heard nothing. Returning to the campfire he kicked among the buffalo chips looking for a stick to use as a torch but found none.

"Miz Varner," he called. The boy under his arm was squirming and sobbing. "Hush up," Josh told him and the boy screamed. Maybe that's the way to bring her back, he thought. He pinched the boy so he screamed again.

"Miz Varner," Josh called. He heard the barking of a coyote, nothing more.

Vivian stumbled, her foot caught in a hole and she fell. She lay on the hard ground listening to Josh call her name, hearing Jan's cries. She brought her clenchd fist to her mouth, biting her knuckles as she fought off the impulse to return and comfort the boy.

Josh won't hurt him, she told herself. She knew Josh. He might kill a man if he thought he had to, as he'd killed Sam, but he wouldn't hurt the child. Print had sent Josh after *her*, not Jan, she was sure. To bring her back. She'd never return to Print, never. She'd seek help, make her way to the Palo Bueno and tell Luis and Jason what had happened.

How far was she from the ranch? Though they'd ridden all day they hadn't made good time for Sam had deliberately paced them because of the boy. So she was perhaps twenty-five miles from the Palo Bueno. All she had to do was walk to the south. Josh would never find her in the dark and if she could walk all night she'd be so far away by daybreak he'd never find her then, either.

Putting her back to the North Star, she set out to the south.

When neither Ed nor Josh had returned to camp by the following morning, Print sent two of the Jerome brothers to the creek above the canyon to find out what had happened to them. The Jeromes came to the cottonwoods shortly before noon and quickly discovered Ed's body. The hat had blown off his face and was snagged to a mesquite some distance away.

After searching in the woods and up and down the creek without seeing a sign of Josh, they put Ed's body across one of their horses and headed back toward their camp.

Vivian, crouching amidst brush farther up the creek, saw the two riders searching, saw them put the body on the horse, and watched them ride off. She waited until they were out of sight before she grasped a limb and pulled herself wearily to her feet. Her body ached, her feet were sore, and she had to fight back the lethargy that threatened to overwhelm her.

It's not much farther, she told herself. She staggered along the creek bank, frequently looking behind her, for she was fearful of seeing Josh riding toward her from the north. The Plain stretched away around her, empty and limitless.

She came to the rim of the canyon and saw the new-green of the meadowland below her and, beyond the firs, the ranch house. Looking as though nothing had changed. She found the switchback trail a short way from the creek and began making her way down into the canyon. As she trudged along she couldn't help remembering their departure the day before with Sam riding ahead and Jan turning to wave to the men standing in front of the ranch.

At the bottom of the trail, she started to run. She saw a horseman riding toward her and she waved to him, calling out, her eyes leaving the ground so she stumbled and fell headlong. She lay unable to get up, hearing the approaching horse, and then she felt hands grasping her beneath her shoulders and lifting her.

"Jan," she gasped and fainted.

When Vivian recovered consciousness she was lying on her own bed. Jason, seeing her eyes open, strode across the room and knelt beside her.

"What happened?" he demanded. "Where's Jan? Is he all right? Where's Sam?"

Vivian drew in her breath, covered her eyes with her hands and began to sob. She felt Jason's hand gripping her shoulder, shaking her. She tried to answer him but no words came.

"No, stand away." Luis' voice. She felt a cold damp cloth on her forehead and when she took her hands from her eyes she saw Luis looking down at her, concern and tenderness in his dark brown eyes.

"I did what I could," she said. "Josh means the boy no harm. It was me he was after. Print sent him to find me and bring me back."

"Just tell us what happened," Luis said. She saw Jason behind him, his face drawn and anxious.

"Start from the time you left the ranch," Luis said.

Vivian drew in a deep breath and told them, Luis encouraging her from time to time with a nod or a smile. When she finished, Luis put his hand to her cheek and said, "You were very brave. You were right, you did all you could and more. We'll soon have Jan back."

"He won't harm the boy, will he?" she asked. "I know Josh and he'd never harm a child. He won't will he?"

"No, of course he won't," Luis said. He pulled the blankets up around her. "Now sleep. By the time you waken he'll have returned the boy."

"I couldn't have fought him," Vivian said. "It was either run away or have him make prisoners of us both. I'll never go back to Print."

"You did what was best," Luis said again. "You came here and told us what happened and now we can do what is necessary. Sleep, you must sleep."

Luis bent over the bed and kissed her softly on the forehead. Vivian smiled up at him. He was such a gentle man, she thought. Isn't that what being a gentleman means, after all? she asked herself as she closed her eyes. She was so very tired. I did what was best, she repeated to herself as she drifted into sleep.

Luis left the bedroom, shutting the door quietly behind him. He found Jason pacing back and forth in front of the fireplace, his hands clasped behind his back. He looked at Luis, shaking his head.

"She should have stayed with the boy," Jason said.

Luis shrugged. "Perhaps *si*, perhaps no," he said. "Who is to say? That is now in the past. She did not, she is here and she accuses herself because she left Jan. We must ease her guilt as best we can."

Jason slammed his fist on the table, making the lamp jump. "You wouldn't be so damn calm if it were your son instead of mine."

Luis came to Jason and put his hand on his arm. "We must get him back," Luis said. "That is the important thing."

Jason sighed. "You're right, Luis," he said. "Finding fault won't help the boy. Do you think Print sent Josh after them?"

"One man when he has so many to spare? No, my idea is that this Josh stumbled across their trail on the Plain and tried to return Vivian to her husband. The question is, what will he do now? Where will he take the boy?"

"I should never have sent them north," Jason said. "I should've kept them here."

"Jason!" Luis faced the bigger man. "I've never

before seen you like this," he said. ""What's done is done."

"You're right. Let's go get the bastards."

"Listen. We may not have to." They turned to face the door, hearing hoofbeats pounding toward the ranch. "They may be coming to us," Luis said.

"No, that's just one horse." Jason opened the door in time to see Manuel dismount and run toward them.

Seeing Jason and Luis, Manuel burst into a torrent of excited Spanish.

"They're coming? Print Varner's coming?" Jason asked Luis. "Is that what he's saying?"

Luis nodded. "*Cuantos,* Manuel?" he asked.

"*Diez,* ten," the cowhand said.

"Get every man inside the main ranch house," Jason ordered. When Manuel hesitated, Jason shouted at him—"*Pronto!*" Manuel bobbed his head and ran toward the back of the ranch. Jason stepped outside and fired three evenly spaced shots into the air.

Before the sound of the gunfire died away they heard the horsemen and in a few minutes the riders came from behind the stand of firs. Print was in the lead, the others riding behind him two-abreast like a column of cavalry.

"Go inside," Luis told Jason. "I will speak to them."

"Damn it, Grandez, this is my ranch."

"No," Luis said, "it is our ranch." He turned to Jason. "Listen to me," he said. "You have told me much of this Print Varner. I believe he meant his man to be killed on the creek just as he was killed. He meant to goad us into violence and he has succeeded. Now he means to goad you because he knows you will never back down."

"You're damn right I won't," Jason said.

"And so you will be doing what he wants you to do. He will taunt you, make you fight him here in the open and he and his gunfighters will kill you."

"Not before I take a few of them with me."

The horsemen had left the firs in the lower canyon and were beginning their climb up the gentle slope leading to the ranch.

"Yes," Luis said, "but they will kill you. Without three or four of their men, if we could kill that many, they are still powerful. Without you, *amigo,* we are nothing."

"You can look after yourself, Luis," Jason said.

"*Si,* I can handle myself, that is true. Your men, though, *our* men, will follow you wherever you lead. Without question. As you know, they will not follow me in the same way."

Because he's a Mexican, Jason thought, that's what Luis means. Jason knew it was true. He looked at the approaching horsemen again, then back at Luis.

"I can't stand aside and let you take all the risk," he said.

"*Madre de Dios!*" Luis shouted. "If you insist on confronting Print Varner now we may all die because of your stubbornness and he will still have you son. Listen to me, *amigo,* I know you are brave, but this is a time for a cool head and that is what you do not have. I do. Allow me to speak to *Senor* Varner, it is our only hope."

Jason started to shake his head, hesitated, and finally gave in. "I know you're right, Luis, but it's a damned hard thing for me to do. Me and the boys'll cover you from inside."

"No matter what Print Varner says, do not let him goad you into showing yourself."

Jason grunted and went into the house, leaving the door ajar.

The horsemen wheeled up to the ranch, Print stopping in front of the porch with his men ranging themselves behind him.

"I'm here to see Jason Briscoe," he said. Luis saw Print's gaze flicking over the house, taking in the newly cut loopholes between the logs.

"I speak for *Señor* Briscoe," Luis told him.

"And who the devil are you?"

"I am Don Luis Grandez." Luis stood on the edge of the porch with his hand on his hips. He was unarmed.

"Tell Briscoe I want him," Print said. "I ain't speaking to no Mex."

"I have the honor of being a citizen of the United States of America," Luis said quietly.

"Damn it, get Briscoe out here and be quick about it," Print demanded. "One of my men's dead and I want to hear what Briscoe has to say for himself."

"*Señor* Briscoe says you are to speak to me." Luis swept his arm to take in the ranch, the woods, the grazing land, the entire canyon. "This is our land," he said. "You are on our land, your man was on our land when he was killed."

"You had no cause to kill him. He wasn't in the canyon. He was camping on the upper creek minding his own business when he was gunned down."

"We are even then," Luis said. "One of your men is dead as is one of ours."

"I don't know what you're talking about."

"Sam Claiburn was riding to Dodge City when one of your men killed him."

Print looked genuinely puzzled. "Who the hell's Sam Claiburn?"

"Who *was* Sam Claiburn you mean," Luis said. Print was becoming confused, Luis saw, this wasn't going the way he'd planned. The men behind Print shifted uneasily as though unsure what Print intended now that they faced Luis instead of Jason Briscoe.

Print made one more attempt. "Briscoe!" he shouted. "I know you can hear me. You're a yellow-bellied coward, hiding behind this Mex. I figured you'd be man enough to fight your own battles."

Luis smiled at Print, though he was tempted to look over his shoulder. Would Jason rise to the bait? Long minutes passed and then with an oath Print rode forward and Luis thought he meant to gallop onto the porch. At the last moment Print turned aside and led his men back along the trail down the canyon.

Jason came to stand beside Luis on the porch. "I damn near let him goad me into going for him," Jason said.

"He seems to know nothing about Josh and your boy," Luis said. "Not yet."

"Maybe I can get to Josh before he joins up with them," Jason said.

Luis pointed to two men riding toward the switchback trail. "They wouldn't let you. Besides, Josh must have the boy back at Print's camp by now."

Jason grunted in reluctant agreement. "Print'll be back," he said. "I'll put more sentries out."

"We should rig tripwires in case he waits until night."

"Good idea," Jason said. "When Print comes, we'll be ready for him."

As Print and his men rode down the canyon they met Josh coming the other way.

"Where the hell you been?" Print snarled. "Give you a simple job to do and you're gone two days."

"Wait till you see what I brought you," Josh said.

"You were supposed to bring back Ed. I had to send the Jerome boys for his body."

So the bastard reckoned Ed was more likely to get killed, Josh thought. Print meant him to be shot up there on the creek. I should have known, should have stopped him somehow. Josh mumbled as though in apology. Best not let Print see I'm on to him, he thought.

"Speak up!" Print shouted.

Wouldn't anything go right today? he wondered. He'd tried to force Briscoe into making a move so he could kill him and all he'd got was a God-damned Mex talking riddles. It didn't suit him to gun down an unarmed man, even if he was a greaser, not in front of the men he'd hired. And now here was Josh with more riddles.

"I had to kill one of Briscoe's men," Josh said. "The boy told me his name was Sam."

So that's what the Mex was yapping about. "What boy?" Print asked as they rode into their camp.

"That there boy."

Josh pointed toward Tamar who was holding Jan on her lap. The boy was playing with a string of Indian beads.

"Who is he, damn it?" Print asked.

"That's Briscoe's boy," Josh said.

Print dismounted and walked to stand over Tamar. "He says his name's Jan," she told him.

Print tousled the boy's black hair. "Where's my father?" Jan asked him.

"Your father's at his ranch," Print said. "He's been having a pack of trouble so he asked me to look after you until he gets everything under control. Tamar here will see to you till then."

"What have you got in mind, Print?" Tamar asked, frowning at him.

"I gotta think," Print told her. "You take charge of the boy. Make sure you keep your eyes on him."

"No harm's to come to the boy, Print," Tamar said. "I'm telling you that here and now. Are you listening to me, Print?" Her green eyes flashed.

"Nobody's about to hurt the boy," Print said. "Just you take him and keep him out of harm's way."

Tamar shot a last look at Print before she took Jan by the hand and led him into the tent. He meant to use the boy to hurt Jason, she was certain of that.

"Just what are you meaning to do?" Josh asked Print.

"I'll do the asking," Print said. "And the first thing I want to know is how that Mex found out about you killing their man."

Josh lifted his hat and held it in one hand, fingering his scalp. "I reckon the woman told him."

"What woman is that, Josh?" Print's voice was very quiet.

"Miz Varner. She run off into the dark when I shot this Sam and what with the kid and all I couldn't catch her. She must of got back to the ranch this morning."

Print drew in a long breath, then smiled at Josh.

"I did the best I could, Print," Josh said.

Still smiling, Print clapped him on the shoulder. "You did good, Josh," he said. "Whether I get Vivian back today or tomorrow don't make much difference, not after all this time. But get her back I will."

Josh relaxed. "How you meaning to do that, Print?" he asked. "From what I seen of it when I come to meet you, that ranch is built mighty like a fort with those log walls and all. It'll take some doing to rout Briscoe and the rest of them out of there."

"There's more than one way to skin a cat," Print said. "And if skinning don't work, I've got an ace in the hole now." He gestured in the direction of the tent. "Thanks to you, Josh, thanks to you."

28

THE HANDS ate quietly in the large kitchen of the Briscoe ranch, Jason and Luis, Eli, Ike, Manuel and the others. Vivian carried plates of pork, beans and sourdough bread from the stove to the table.

There had been no sign of Print Varner after he had ridden away that morning. The hands said little as they drank their coffee and smoked their cigarettes or pipes. Waiting. Vivian cleared the table and began to wash the tin plates, the knives and forks.

"Sam's got no family," Jason said at last, "excepting a brother. When I get the chance I'll see to it the money owed Sam goes to him. Right now we got too much trouble. I'll miss old Sam."

"We all will," Luis said.

The men nodded, muttering agreement.

"Ought to lynch the bastard what shot him," Chicago Luke growled.

One of the men came into the kitchen after his four hour turn at standing picket duty.

"Any sign?" Jason asked, seeing it was Matt, the boy who'd come with Eli.

"Nope," Matt said as he speared a slab of pork onto his plate. He looked at Jason. "This ain't no good time to be asking, but when this is over I'd like to work for you if you'll have me, Mr. Briscoe."

Jason looked at him, seeing the boy's earnestness. "We pay new hands twenty-five dollars a month and food," he said.

"The money don't matter," Matt said. "I've been on the prod ever since I ran away from home when I was thirteen and I'm tired of drifting."

Jason touched his shoulder. "You've got yourself a job," he said.

Jason walked from the kitchen into the ranch's main room with Luis behind him. The canyon outside was already deep in shadow but the sky above was a bright blue. Opening the door, Jason stepped onto the porch and listened to the evening songs of the birds.

"I used to think this was the best time of all," he said to Luis.

Luis said nothing, going to the porch rail and looking down the canyon into the gathering dusk.

"They're coming," Jason said. "I can feel it."

"*Si*, tonight. They are waiting for the dark and then they'll make their move. What do you expect them to do?"

Jason shrugged. "Print Varner tries real hard to be clever. Some day he's going to be so clever he'll outsmart himself."

"As long as it happens this time," Luis said, "not the next time or the one after."

"That's for damn sure."

Luis noticed that Jason hadn't mentioned Jan since morning, when Print rode up to the ranch.

He was keeping his fear inside where, Luis thought, it was stretching him tight as a singed hide.

The sky over the canyon darkened and soon they saw the first stars. There There was no moon. The two men went inside, Jason going to each of the hands, assigning them their posts for the night and their hours of guard duty. When he returned to the main room he found Luis running a swab up and down the barrel of his Spencer repeating rifle.

A shot sounded and echoed in the distance behind the house. Luis laid the rifle down and buckled on his holster belt. He loaded the Spencer and followed Jason outside in time to see a man slip from the darkness and approach the house.

"Eli," Jason said, recognizing him. "Was that your shot?"

"It was. They tripped the wire on the hill behind the corral. Or something did. I chanced a shot. Nothing there at all, far as I can tell. Thought I'd best let you know before I went ramming around in the dark."

"I'll go with you," Jason said.

Luis followed them around the house to the corral where the horses were nervously pawing the ground. Eli led them through the darkness to the far side of the corral where he pointed up the slope behind the house. Jason knew that the rise was gentle for maybe forty feet and then steepened for another forty before coming to the sheer cliff-face of the canyon.

The three men stiffened as they heard a hoot in the darkness above them, the sound echoing from the cliff.

"Just an owl," Luis said.

"No," Jason whispered, "that's not an owl, it's

a man. There's too much of an echo for an owl."

"I'll go take a look-see," Eli said, moving off into the dark.

"Look!" Luis gripped Jason's arm.

Above them a lighted flare and another and another. Fire sprang up into the night and in its light they saw men hurling brands on top of hay piled in a wagon. A shot came from above and to their left and one of the men by the wagon staggered and pitched to the ground.

"Eli got him," Jason muttered, raising his rifle.

The wagon began to lumber forward and they could see that its tongue was tied into place to keep the wheels from turning. Jason squeezed off a shot and Luis fired too, but now the smoke billowed back over the men behind the wagon and they couldn't see if any of their shots hit home. There was another shot from Eli followed by an answering volley from the hillside. Jason heard a man cry out in pain.

The wagon was rolling now, gathering speed, the fire blazing high, the smoke trailing behind like a thick black cloud. The flaming wagon would strike the rear of the ranch, Jason saw, sending firebrands cascading over the entire back of the building. He looked toward Luis but the Spaniard had disappeared. His rifle in one hand, Jason ran toward the wagon, stumbling on the uneven ground.

He'd covered less than half the distance when he realized he'd be too late. Already the fiery wagon was almost even with him and would soon be beyond. He swore and turned back to go to the ranch to organize the men to fight the flames, knowing they faced a well-nigh impossible task since they'd be working under Varner's rifle fire from the hillside behind the house.

As though to underline his fears, a fusillade of shots came from above him. Looking back, he saw the black outlines of two men beside the wagon. One of the men climbed to the wagon seat, the flames leaping around him as he slashed at the ropes holding the wagon tongue in place.

For a long moment nothing changed—the wagon hurtled at the ranch, one man clinging to the seat slashing at the ropes, the other man running alongside; shots echoed from the hill above. Then the second man stumbled and fell just as the wagon swerved and tilted from side to side as it careened downhill, bouncing higher and higher until it lifted into the air and spewed buning hay skyward, the tongues of flame falling harmlessly to the bare ground near the corral. Horses whinnied in fright. There was another volley of shots, from the ranch this time, the flashes punctuating the darkness below the fire. Shots answered from the hillside.

Jason plunged down the slope. The burning wagon lay on its side with two wheels turning slowly. A dark form sprawled nearby with the firelight glinting from the silver ornaments on his jacket. Luis. Someone ran from the house, a woman, and Jason realized it must be Vivian. She gripped Luis beneath the shoulders and began trying to drag him away from the flames.

Jason came up beside Luis and grasped his legs to hurry him into the house. A shot zinged past his head. The door swung open ahead of them and they hauled Luis inside. Vivian knelt beside the Don, whispering to him, pleading with him.

"Don't die, Luis," Jason heard her say. "Oh, my darling, don't die. I love you, Luis, don't leave me."

Jason hastily ran his hands over Luis' body. He'll be all right," he said. "He's breathing okay and I can't find any bullet wounds. The burns ought to heal."

"Thank God," Vivian said. "We've wasted so much time, Luis and I. What a fool I've been."

Hearing shots from the front of the house, Jason strode into the main room just as Ike shouted, "Hold fire," to the men stationed at the loopholes in the log walls.

Jason looked through one of the slots. The night was dark and the air clouded by gunsmoke but after a few minutes he made out two forms on the ground twenty feet in front of the porch.

"When they saw the fire in the back they charged," Ike said. "Must have thought we'd all be busy in the rear. They got something of a surprise."

"Two of them?" Jason asked.

"And at least one more wounded. I don't figure they'll try that again."

Eli, Jason thought. He'd forgotten about Eli what with the burning wagon and Luis getting hurt. Jason hurried through the kitchen to the rear of the ranch and, tagged by Matt, rounded the corral. The hay still smouldered on the ground and Jason could hear the crackle of flames from the burning wagon. Though there were no sounds from the hillside, they cautiously made their way to where Jason had last seen Eli firing. They found no one there.

As they started back to the house, Matt spoke in a whisper "You reckon Eli's dead?"

"Can't be sure," Jason said.

"I got a feeling he is."

"You been friends long?"

"Eli don't make friends. But he brung me here, Mr. Briscoe. It weren't no matter of me just coming along like he said. Eli brung me. Got me out of a peck of trouble, Eli did."

Jason nodded in the darkness, feeling easier about Eli. The boy still had good in him. "Call me Jason," he said to Matt.

One of the Jeromes brought Eli down the slope behind the house on the back of a horse.

"He's hurt bad," Jerome told Print.

Print glanced at Eli, not recognizing him. "Take him back to the camp," he said and the gunfighter rode off leading the other horse. When Tamar heard the sound of hoofbeats coming into camp she ran out of the tent.

Jerome dismounted and walked back to the second horse, putting his hand to Eli's chest.

"Dead," he said, pulling the body from the horse and letting it sprawl on the ground. He remounted and rode back to join Print Varner.

Tamar ran to the man lying face up beside the fire and stared down at him.

"Oh, my God," she whispered. She knelt and took his head in her hands, lifting it onto her lap, cradling it. "Oh my God," she said again. "Oh my God, oh my God." And then she began murmuring his name, "Eli, Eli, Eli," her voice becoming a chant as she poured out her grief.

"Is he killed dead like Sam?"

Tamar didn't hear the words at first. When they were repeated, louder, she looked over her shoulder to find Jan standing behind her.

"He's my brother," she said, tenderly laying Eli's head on the ground. She went into the tent and returned with a blanket, covering Eli's body.

Then she lifted Jan into her arms and held him to her.

29

"WHAT'RE THEY DOING?" Ike asked.

Jason, crouching beside his foreman, frowned. "Looks like they're building a bonfire. I don't know what Print Varner's got in mind."

Luis came up behind them. When Jason turned he saw that the Spaniard's face was pale except where the red and blistered skin discolored the left side of his cheek.

"I am, as you say, fit to fiddle," Luis told him.

"They're waving a white flag," Ike said. Jason looked through a loophole and saw a cloth being swung back and forth on the barrel of a rifle.

"Hold your fire," Jason ordered. He went to the door and opened it a few inches. "We're listening," he shouted.

"I want to talk to you." Jason recognized Print's voice.

Jason felt a hand on his shoulder. "I will go," Luis said.

Jason shook his head. "Not this time."

He stepped onto the porch and saw Print Varner come from the darkness toward him, the flames of the bonfire throwing half of his face in shadow. Jason stood at the edge of the porch and waited as Print came slowly to him, stopping when he was an arm's length away.

"I got something for you," Print said.

Print held out his hand and Jason saw he had a brown cloth. He didn't say anything as Print held up the cloth in both hands so Jason could see it was a small buckskin shirt.

"This here belongs to your son," Print said.

Jason said nothing; he'd recognized the shirt as soon as he'd seen it. "Speak your piece," Jason said after a pause.

"We happened on the boy on the Plain," Print said, "and we're keeping him safe for you." Print's face clouded. "You stole my wife," he said. "You know what I did to the bastard that killed my first wife? I hung him."

"I didn't steal your wife," Jason said. "She came to me of her own free will. Because of you and Tamar. And she told me the truth of what happened to that other wife of yours."

"The God-damned carpetbagger killed her."

"I heard *you* killed her, Print, in the fight when he ran you off your land."

Print shook his head slowly from side to side like a steer bothered by gnats. "He killed Lucy and I hung him," he said stubbornly.

Jason didn't answer, watching the other man. He's like a tree that's got bent when it was young, he thought, and if you let it go too long without straightening it there's nothing you can do.

Print smacked his fist into his palm. "I want my wife," he told Jason, "and the canyon."

"Your wife doesn't want you," Jason said. "And

the canyon's not mine, it's mine and Montgomery's and Luis'."

"That Mex?" Print snarled. "Greasers don't own nothing in Texas. It's your land. If you don't give it to me along with my wife, you'll never see your son alive again."

Jason stepped forward as though to strike him and Print edged back, tossing the shirt to Jason. "You have till sun-up to make up your mind," Print said. He turned on his heel and walked back to the men waiting in the shadows near the bonfire.

Jason entered the house and, motioning to Luis, went with him into the room they used for their office. Jason sat behind the desk, opened one of the drawers and brought out a bottle and two glasses. Luis stared in surprise at the liquor but took the filled glass when Jason offered it.

Jason told him what Print had said.

"Ahhh." Luis sighed. He stood and walked to the bookcase and idly fingered the leather bindings.

"I know how you feel about giving this up," Jason said. "I know the choice isn't mine to make."

Luis turned to him. "The choice *is* yours," he said. I've never had a son, yet I know what one means to a man. Whatever you decide about the land, I will concur. Vivian is another matter."

Jason finished off his drink and put the glass on the desk in front of him, twirling it between his palms. "We could take the bastards," he said. "I've been watching and they've made a semi-circle around the ranch with their flanks to the canyon wall. The tunnel goes beyond their lines."

"Ah, yes, the tunnel. The tunnel to fight the Comanches."

"We could get men behind them and they'd be as helpless as a coyote with his paw in a trap."

Jason shook his head. "Print is loco. I can't trust him not to harm the boy. I don't rightly know what to do."

Luis pulled a silver watch from his pocket. "We have . . ." He stopped and shook the watch, holding it to his ear. "I fear it is in need of repair," he said, putting the watch away. "There must be five hours yet until the sun rises."

Jason swung his chair around and stared at the wall. Luis got quietly to his feet and left the room.

Jason sat without moving, his eyes open but unseeing. The ranch was nothing. Jan meant more to him than the cattle, the land, the buildings. Jan was all he had left of Janine. The future belonged to the boy. If he had to spend the rest of his life working to repay Luis and Sir Charles, he would.

Jason made two vows—to do nothing to risk Jan's life and to kill Print Varner.

The first light of dawn was showing through the ranch's windows when Jason strode into the main room. "Luis," he said, "Ike, I want to talk. I've decided to give up the ranch but Vivian is free to stay with us. I won't turn her over to her husband."

"There's someone coming," Matt said, turning from his post at a loophole to Jason.

Jason peered out into the dim light of early morning and saw a man walking with short quick steps toward the ranch, not from the direction of the now-dead bonfire but from Jason's right. No, not a man, he thought, seeing her long hair. Long red-gold hair. His heart began to race.

Tamar! And in her arms she carried Jan.

Print saw her at the same time. The men nearby looked to him for direction, their rifles ready. Print took a step forward. No, he told himself, I can't reach her before she's to the house. The only way to stop her is to shoot her. He raised his hand and the men waited for his signal to fire.

Tamar, he was losing Tamar. Print suddenly realized what she had meant to him and for a brief moment he wished. . . What? He didn't know, not for sure. He only knew that what was happening was all wrong, that somewhere along the way he had missed a turning and now it was too late to go back.

Or almost too late.

"Don't fire," he shouted, letting his hand fall to his side. He saw the door to the Briscoe ranch swing open and saw Tamar disappear inside.

Without speaking Tamar handed Jan to his father. Jason hugged him, his eyes looking over the boy's head at Tamar. Jan struggled to get down and Jason set him on the floor and he ran to Vivian who knelt to embrace him.

"She brought me back, that pretty lady," Jan said to Vivian. "Her name's Tamar." He turned to his father. "Can she stay with us? 'Cause those other men killed Sam and they killed Tamar's brother and I don't like them. But I like her. Can she stay here?"

Vivian rose and took a step toward Tamar, felt Luis' hand on her shoulder and stopped.

Tamar and Jason stared at one another.

"Do you want to stay?" Jason asked.

"Do you want me to?" she countered, the corners of her mouth lifting slightly.

"Later, *compadre*," Luis said in warning. Jason turned from Tamar to his men.

"What are you aiming to do?" Print saw it was the kid from Arizona, Hank Antrim.

"We'll starve them out," Print said. The boy looked at him, then shrugged.

Print strode from man to man, positioning them. They'd have to dig in, he told himself, and lay siege to the ranch. The first try at burning Briscoe out had failed; they'd have to try again. They could drive cattle ahead of them, even, and charge the ranch. They could . . .

Firing came from the house and Print looked that way, puzzled. More shots, flashes of yellow thrusting from the loopholes. What was Briscoe up to? Print wondered. A diversion, that must be it, but a diversion to hide what?

Shots rang out from behind him and to his right. Print whirled and saw men running toward him from the rear, kneeling and firing as they came, taking cover behind shrubs and trees. He saw Mike Jerome fall, bleeding from the mouth. Gun in hand, Print called to his men, trying to rally them, but he saw it was too late. They were caught in a crossfire. How in the hell . . . ?

He ran to his horse and leaped into the saddle, saw Antrim riding off ahead of him. Print spurred his horse, heading for the trail up the side of the canyon to the cap rock. As he rode he heard the firing diminish behind him and glanced back to see Josh with his hands raised in surrender, saw another horse following him and recognized the rider. Jason Briscoe.

Print was on the switchback now with Antrim still ahead of him. Below, Jason swung to the ground and stood with his rifle to his shoulder. Antrim was cresting the top as Jason fired. Print saw Antrim's horse stumble and go down, Antrim leaping clear and running ahead and over the canyon's rim. He heard another shot behind him and then he was at the top and Jason was lost to sight.

Antrim stood on the ground facing him, his

rifle aimed at Print's forehead. "Get off that there horse or I'll kill you," the kid said.

Print slid to the ground, waiting his chance. "Drop the gunbelt," Antrim told him. Print let the belt fall. "Step away," Antrim said. Print stepped back from the belt. Antrim, gun held steady on Print, picked up the belt and tossed it far to one side. From behind him Print heard the hoofbeats of Jason's horse climbing the switchback.

"You'll get us both killed," Print said.

"Not me, not on your life."

Antrim mounted and spurred Print's horse. Print ran to his gunbelt and grabbed a pistol from its holster, firing at the cloud of dust raised by Antrim's horse, knowing he didn't have a chance in hell of hitting him . . .

Hank Antrim smiled to himself as he looked back at Print's receding figure. He owed nothing to Print Varner, he thought. He'd done what he'd been paid for, the money didn't cover getting killed.

I better get a new handle, he thought as he rode west. Bill, he'd always sort of liked that name. Remembering his mother calling him a bonny lad years ago, he tried that on for size. Bill Bonney. They'd probably still call him kid, though. Billy the kid. He grinned, liking the sound of it . . .

Gun in hand, Print turned just as Jason topped the rise. Print raised his gun to fire and at that moment the sun pushed above the Plain. Print, blinking in the red-gold light of the sun, shot and missed.

Jason was off his horse, firing. Print felt a jolt and suddenly he seemed to be standing off to one side, watching himself stagger back, watching as he dropped his Colt. The pain in his chest was greater than any he'd ever known Then the pain was gone and Print was on his back on the ground. He opened his eyes, seeing the great red ball of the sun and then as the sun seemed to explode inside him he said the last word he was ever to speak.

"Tamar," he said.

EPILOGUE

SHE TIPTOED into the ranch office and stood behind the chair where he sat, completely caught up in something he was reading in the paper that had just come in by stage from New York. For the first time she noticed a glint of gray in his hair, and she reflected on the good years they'd had—calm, fruitful years, with the farm prospering and the two bright-eyed children, Jason and Janine—after all the pain and struggle that had ended with the death of Prentice Varner.

"Jason," she said, wrapping her arms around him and putting her red-gold cloud of hair next to his cheek, "that news is two weeks old. What's so exciting about it."

"Big gold strike up in Alaska," he said, turning to smile at Tamar. "Everything's wide open up there, and men are making fortunes."

"Shucks, Jason, who needs any more fortune than we've got?"

"It's not that, darlin'. It's just that everything's

pretty well settled down here. Up yonder—that's a whole damn new challenge, a new frontier."

Tamar shook her head and smiled secretly to herself. She started figuring up in her mind how long she'd have to pack and get everything ready for the long trek.

TENTH IN
THE MAKING OF AMERICA SERIES

THE ALASKANS

America's purchase of Alaska from Russia, called "Seward's Folly" after the Secretary of State who masterminded the deal, drew a rag-tag horde of speculators, thieves, dreamers, prostitutes and gamblers, when word came of a gold strike in the Klondike. Among them was a tall muscular young man who gave his name as Bryan Mathews, whom the Eskimo women called "the Man-God."

Baroness Irina Feodorovna and her equally spectacular daughter, Milla, wanted Mathews for entirely different reasons. Milla saw him as the one great love of her life. Irina saw him as a key—not only to unlock the pent-up passions of her magnificent body, but as a key through which she could conquer and rule the secret riches of this frozen kingdom.

DON'T MISS

THE WILD AND THE WAYWARD

Here is the breathtaking saga of the latter days of the wild, wild West. Here is the story of one of the last frontiers, where the mavericks, dark trail riders and gunfighters made their last stand against the oncoming forces of civilization, represented by relentless men such as Marshal Bill Tilghman, who broke the outlaw power and drove gangs such as the Doolins— along with the mysterious Rose of the Cimarron— far out into the Western badlands where they made their last stand.

THE WILD AND THE WAYWARD is the eighth novel in the new series—

THE MAKING OF AMERICA

**A DELL/BRYANS BOOK
ON SALE NOW**

THE GOLDEN STATERS

The new land of the wild California territory was as rich and diverse as the people who came there seeking a new life. It was also fraught with every peril known to man. To this vast territory on the shores of the Pacific—soon to be known as the Golden State, came Robert Sanderson, a man of iron will, determined to build a dynasty that would grow and endure as long as the land.

Robert and his son Reb strove mightily, until they stood among the great tycoons of California—Huntington, Stanford, Crocker. But within the clan was a hidden seed of destruction that drew father and son to two irresistible women: Pilar, in whose veins flowed the fiery blood of the *conquistadors*, and Lida, the beautiful actress who was the toast of San Francisco—and a dark omen of the Sanderson destiny.